Lock Down Publications and Ca$h
Presents

SOULLESS GOON

Black Magic

Written By

PRINCE

First Edition 2025

Printed in the United States of America

This is a work of fiction. Names, characters, places, and incidents either
are products of the author's imagination or are used fictitiously. Any
similarity to actual events or locales or persons, living or dead, is
entirely coincidental.

Lock Down Publications
P.O. Box 944
Stockbridge, GA 30281
www.lockdownpublications.com

Like our page on Facebook: Lock Down Publications
www.facebook.com/lockdownpublications.ldp

Stay Connected with Us!

Text **LOCKDOWN** to 22828 to stay up-to-date with new releases, sneak peaks, contests and more…

Like our page on Facebook:
Lock Down Publications

Join Lock Down Publications/The New Era Reading Group

Visit our website:
www.lockdownpublications.com

Follow us on Instagram:
Lock Down Publications

Email Us: We want to hear from you!

"The thought became an inspiration. Then that inspiration became a relentless energy which compelled action. From that action came about the desire to put up and compete. And within this healthy form of competition, some very profound gritty, gutter, grimy, and straight gangsta' material was produced for the readers of interest. No matter what, stay true to the craft and committed to being successful as you pursue the finer things that life has to offer with your writing talent and skills."

Black Magic:

"Has traditionally referred to the use of supernatural powers or magic for evil and selfish purposes."

"The life that I live or have lived, sir, is the one that I chose. And I have no regrets. I have no remorse. Nor do I make any qualms about anything. I am perfectly content with every single decision that I have made in my life, because I took a blood oath with the devil! He initiated me into his order. And I keep my word no matter what. And I believe in Black Magic! I'm Ifá. So, emphatically speaking, I'm not seeking forgiveness! On no accord. Period! For nothing!"

—Michael Antonio Gentry aka "Nightmare"

Dedication

PUBLIC SERVICE ANNOUNCEMENT! THIS BOOK IS DEDICATED TO ALL OF THE URBAN FICTION AND STREET LIT AUTHORS (Mainstream writers) WHO WRITE STORIES THAT ACTUALLY DEPICT THE STREETS AND HOODS AS THEY TRULY ARE ("Realistic fiction") AND NOT PUTTING OUT THAT WATERED DOWN OVER EXAGGERATED TRASH THAT HAS SATURATED THE GAME WE ACTIVELY ARE IN. CONTINUE TO KEEP IT GUTTER, GANGSTA, GULLY, GRIMY, GRIPPING, AND RAW. THE SAME AS THE PIONEERS OF THIS GENRE HAD. PEACE AND LOVE TO CHESTER HIMES, ICEBERG SLIM, AND DONALD GOINES ... THE "BIG THREE" OF THIS LEAGUE. PEACE!

"I Am Alpha and Omega...."
—Michael "Nightmare" Gentry

Prologue

Several Years Earlier...

Eager as ever to be accepted and down with the clique, Michael Antonio Gentry took a blood oath on this day and was initiated into the Vice Lords organization, three months shy of his nineteenth birthday. Ricky Lee Isaacs, the close friend of his, was the one responsible for referring Michael to his brother, Teddy Allen Isaacs, the official OG and supreme "Chief" of their unit. He—Teddy—was responsible for 'bringing Michael home.' Teddy was the undisputed leader and shot-caller of the group. And in a silent but effective way, Michael gained the upper hand over Ricky in the eyes of Teddy and in the objectives Teddy was looking to carry out.

The Chief took a liking to the boy. He placed certain values and emphasis towards the organization on the skills and abilities Michael possessed. In particular, with the youngster being able to blend in and out of both the black and the white circles, due to the mixed background of his. Michael was also a firebrand and a live-wire at best. There existed a calculated ruthlessness to him, and a maliciousness that no other near twenty-year-old of the gang had.

Disciplined and loyal to the core, he knew how to follow orders to the letter. His days in Boys Scouts instilled this. He and Ricky were there together years earlier. And unlike Ricky, who felt he could "get passes" on the way up the ladder, due to their leader being his brother, Michael earned his respect. Teddy detested at all cost extending favoritism towards Ricky, but Ricky never really seemed to understand it. He didn't get it.

Teddy made it his business to test Michael on personal missions, and also, on a hit or another. Being that Michael's attitude displayed he held the tendency to lash out at others upon any form of disrespect towards the leader or the gang, Teddy wanted to know if or not it was the real deal, or, a front the little nigga was putting on. So, Teddy sent him for the first killing mission of his, to go take care of a slime-ass nigga that had run off with a brick of heroin, and had also committed treason against the gang family, the way Teddy put it.

He'd spilled information on some of the inner workings and the business of the Vice Lords—for pay and territory— to one of the rivals of the Four Corner Hustlers, the 'GD's,' as the apostate had a cousin who was a part of this particular organization.

This specific hit in the making turned out not to be the first killing Michael had committed. When he was fifteen, he'd gotten into a really bad argument that led to a fist fight with another teenager. This was over a twenty-dollar bet and a thirty-five cent bag of chili cheese Frito-Lays corn chips. The gamble was on the pool table at one of the game-rooms Michael visited upon him first taking trips by train to the inner city of Chicago from the suburbs.

The other teenager, named Omar, sucker-punched Michael, once he'd realized that Michael was on the verge of winning the game that they were playing, with the eight ball being the last to go in the right corner pocket, leaving Michael talking shit and bragging about it to Omar's face in front of a lot of females present. His actions infuriated Omar greatly, and he took things serious.

Omar couldn't take it. "Bitch-ass nigga, who you poppin' shit to?" he spat.

When he punched Michael, his brother and cousins joined in. They'd jumped the poor boy. Michael took the beating to heart. It was personal now. He'd plotted two weeks in advance on how to best get revenge on Omar. He then returned to the same game-room to take care of his ass, in a way he saw fit to.

As the game-room closed this night, Michael laid low behind a dumpster he noticed was situated along the alley way Omar would use on his way home, as Omar visited the game-room nearly every day. Michael scoped out the surroundings of the location two to three days in advance before he made his move.

Armed with one of the pistols he'd stolen from his step-dad, Michael caught Omar coming out the game-room. It was him and his girlfriend. He was determined to prove to his attacker that he was about that action, the same as they were when they'd jumped him.

Michael jumped out from behind the dumpster with a ski-mask on and fired nine shots from the .22 Ruger, hitting Omar in the chest four times and in the head twice before he took off running, leaving the girlfriend of Omar in a state of panic and screaming at the top of her lungs, with both her hands clutched on the sides of her head, and bullets whizzing past. She narrowly escaped death herself, as one lead missile grazed her skull.

However, the girlfriend recognized Michael as the shooter, by the height of his physique, his bodily movement, and the glints of his eyes. Those eyes of his were magnificent and a set of alluring jewels. She could never forget them. But it was no secret who had shot Omar. The problem was that, none of the other teenagers who was from the neighborhood, nor Omar's people, knew who Michael was, and had no knowledge on where he lived. Michael basically disappeared, not to return to Chicago for another two years, but this time on a different side of the city.

SECTION ONE

Chapter 1

Four Years Later...

Cutting Teeth and Making Bones...

The traitor in the crew who Teddy wanted killed was a vicious snake-ass nigga, according to Teddy. A slime who had also been suspected of being a confidential informant for the CPD and the Feds. Teddy let Michael know who the dude was, and also where he had lived. Michael had a little knowledge of who the mark was himself, as he'd seen him in the company of Teddy on a few occasions, and also around the other gang members. The guy was a few years older than Michael and held more experience in gang life on how to smell a hit. But Teddy felt confident in sending Michael anyway, to handle the business anyway, as he held high belief in the potential future leader of the group. He believed in him. Michael's ambition was unmatched.

Teddy had long been the type of leader who had a kind heart and a peaceful nature about himself. And the dude that took advantage of him thought Teddy to be a 'free pick' of some sort because of this, and he felt Teddy "wasn't really built like that." Like he wasn't as gangsta as he made himself out to be.

Teddy had a female he was involved with who was employed as a probation officer. He had her to run a check on Dennis Ford, the name of the apostate, so as to retrieve the address and any other whereabouts that buddy could potentially be located at. She dug him up with ease, as he had long been placed on probation, due to a domestic violence charge and an assault on a female he'd once had dealings with—a classless stripper to say the least.

Teddy tipped Michael with the intel, then turned him loose. "Listen, lil bro. I'm ready for you to cut your teeth and make your bones, okay. It's a slime-ass nigga who's violated me in a major way. He owes me a lot of money. Anyway, here is the information on where to track down this clown-ass nigga, to make him pay for his fuck up. And I want you to be the worst problem for this nigga that he's ever had to deal with in life! I want you to be a terrible nightmare, by all means! Do him bad! And as a matter of fact, this is your new nickname now. One I personally gave to you ... 'Nightmare.' Wear it with honor and pride from this day forward. Only you and I know who gave it to you and how you got it. We ain't got to tell nobody about it neither. But check, go handle this for me, bro, and you already know, I got you," Teddy said emphatically to him as he held his hand on the boy's shoulder and gave 'Nightmare' the nod to take care of business. These instructions and gesture by Teddy had truly emboldened Nightmare in a tremendous way from that day forward. This became wired in his DNA.

Alone and not in need of any help to take Dennis out, Nightmare made his way to the South Side of the Chi to track down his prey. For a few nights, Nightmare studied the movement and patterns of Dennis. He had to be extra careful too, because the intended target had a reputation of his own as a gunner, and was known to clap back. He was called 'Dennis the Menace' in the streets for a reason.

Nightmare spotted Dennis's car one Saturday night at a strip club. He already knew where he lived, as Dennis shared a house with his pregnant girlfriend. She was seven months with child. They lived in a place that had a second-level upstairs area to it. For the days leading up to the Saturday he was to ambush him, Nightmare knew the time to expect dude home, so he crept on over to lay low and wait for him to show up.

It was three 3:30— *"The Devil's Hour"*—of the morning. Armed with a Glock .40 pistol, another metal pistol as back-up, and a 'Rambo' style ten-inch knife, Nightmare ducked low behind the bushes that lined the short driveway of the house. Dennis pulled up to meet the 'cousin to death' who appeared in the form of *Nightmare*.

He awaited Dennis to exit the car before he was to start shooting. But then, he quickly abandoned the thought, as he'd remembered he was given the green light by Teddy to keep any and everything that the nigga had that was worth keeping.

Dennis turned on the light inside the car and continued to talk on the phone. Shortly thereafter, the girlfriend of Dennis came down the stairs and unlocked the front door, leaving it slightly cracked before heading back up the staircase to return to bed. Dennis got out of the car and took two steps forward before Nightmare was on him at gun point, with the barrel pinned to the back of his head, ready to blow his brains out if he made the wrong move.

"Ah yeah, you bitch-ass muthafucka,' you!" Nightmare growled at his now hostage. "You thought shit was sweet, didn't you? Like you had gotten away or something, huh? Not hardly, buddy! And I ain't gonna ask you but one time, nigga. Where the fuck is the money and the work, nigga?" Nightmare demanded to know.

"I ain't got no money on me, my nigga. It's in the house, man. Just please, don't shoot me. Just don't shoot. I got kids, man, and a baby on the way," Dennis responded.

"Well then, if you know like I know, and you wanna still be alive to see them again, I suggest you begin walking. Let's go get that!" Nightmare snarled and hissed his words from behind the mask that concealed his face. "Yeah, let's go get that, and then, I'll leave you alone," Nightmare added.

He forced Dennis through the front door and then up the stairs, as Dennis led in his way of walking. Nightmare remained aggressive and kept the gun pressed hard against the back of Dennis's head. "If you scream or try anything, you dead, nigga!" Nightmare warned him.

Once they'd reached the top of the stairs, Dennis led them to the bedroom and eased the door open. Nightmare noticed the pregnant girlfriend lying atop the bed and ordered Dennis: "Keep that bitch of yours quiet, too!"

Dennis did as ordered. "Regina, listen to me, baby, and listen to me good, okay." She had not opened her eyes to look in his direction nor had she lifted her head to be made aware of the dreadful situation.

"Baby, please, I beg you, do not scream once you see what's really going on, okay? This is for real. Turn on the lamp," he said to her.

At those words, she swiftly lifted her head and was in absolute shock at all she saw. Her eyes bucked wide as she strained to make out the tall figure draped in all black standing behind her man with him in a choke-hold type maneuver, and a pistol pinned to his skull. The TV was on and provided flashes of light for them to see one another in the hostile room. She switched on the mini lamp as told, and knew that something was terribly wrong, judging by the tone of Dennis's voice.

Nightmare pulled out a pair of flex cuff zip ties he'd brought along for the occasion, and locked Dennis's hands behind his back. By Dennis being subdued and no longer posing a potential threat, this really gave Nightmare the power and the will to do all he saw fit.

"Now, where is the safe? Where you got the money stashed at, nigga?" Nightmare demanded to know.

"It's in the closet, man. Take it. Have it. And then leave us alone. She knows the combination. Regina! Open the safe, sweetie, so this nigga can get that money in it and then get the fuck up outta here!"

At the slick remark Dennis made, Nightmare smacked him hard against the back of the head with the additional .357 Magnum he'd retrieved from the ankle holster, once he'd placed the Glock inside his waistband.

Whop!

He smacked him twice more for good measure—along the side of the face—splitting him badly in the process, and leaving a deep gash in the aftermath that oozed thick blood.

Whop ... Whop!

Dennis fell over onto the bed with blood streaming into his eyes and mouth.

"Hold up, man. Hold it! Wait! I got you, man. We got what you came for," Dennis pleaded.

"Well then, get right, nigga! And tell this bitch of yours to hurry the fuck up and come off the cash!" Nightmare barked. "I ain't got time to listen to you talk shit!" Nightmare added.

The flurry of blows he'd put on Dennis startled Regina. It scared her into a nervous wreck. She leaped from the bed to the floor then entered into the closet. Through panic, she snatched the hanging clothes out the way to expose the mini safe that rested within.

***

As Regina fumbled terribly, trying combinations of numbers to open the safe, Nightmare viciously smacked Dennis across the back of the head furthermore:

Pap-Pap-Pap-Pap-Pap ... Pap ... Pap!

"Now, Nigga! Tell this bitch to get that muthafuckin' safe open! And fast! Before you die, and I kill her too!" Nightmare declared. He was very aggressive, as he smacked Dennis again so to send a clear message, that he wasn't bullshitting on no level.

Dennis started to cry, as the threat on the life of him and his pregnant girlfriend were real and hung in the balance.

"Baby, please don't bullshit around. Go ahead and open it. Don't worry about 'plan B' anymore. Forget about that. Put the real number in and let him get that shit. Hurry and open it, baby. Hurry," Dennis instructed.

Before the day, Dennis had coached her on what to do if they had ever gotten taken at gun point. The original plan was for her to not open the main safe, the one in the master bedroom. But instead, to go to the smaller safe in the opposite room, the one that kept $10,000 in it for a decoy, to appease any robber, in the hopes that they would leave once they got something, and not take off with the whole nest egg.

"Bitch, hurry the fuck up! What taking you so muthafuckin' long to get that safe open?" Nightmare barked, and then kicked Regina hard in the back, to make her move faster.

"Regina, get it open, baby," Dennis said to her.

"I'm trying, sweetie. I'm trying my best to get it open," she responded.

Without warning, Nightmare smacked her too across the side of the face with his pistol, in order to get her to move at the tune of his beat. He then turned and smacked Dennis yet again on the head, and then again as hard as he could, along the right eye, busting it instantly on impact.

With a damaged puffed eye, blood in his mouth, and blood pouring over onto his face, Dennis pleaded for dear life. "Please, man. Please. Take it easy, homeboy. You about to get that money."

Nightmare took the blanket from the bed and tossed it atop the head of Dennis, covering his eye sight so he couldn't see anything else.

"Now, shut the fuck up, nigga!" Nightmare demanded. "Don't you know it ain't never safe to jump sides or to play with another nigga's money?" Nightmare questioned, as he leered at Dennis through the ski concealing his identity.

Dennis managed to catch onto the voice of the jack-boy and knew who he was ... Little Mike ... his former Vice Lord Brother.

"Yo, bruh, why you got to do all this to us, Mike? I was gonna get that paper to Teddy. I had a family emergency to deal with that required my attention," Dennis said in an attempt to reach a compromise.

"Shut the fuck up, nigga! You done turned ghost and gotten out of sight for the past three months. So how you had plans to take care of business on what you owed?" Nightmare spat. "Nigga, you had changed ya phone number and all, and couldn't be found. So don't give me that bullshit! But now ... Now ... I got your ass, nigga! And ain't nowhere to run no more," he further added.

The latch on the safe was turned and Regina finally open the door, wide enough so the robber could see it was indeed loaded with what he wanted.

Nightmare threw a black net bag at Regina. "Here, bitch! Now put everything in the bag," he ordered.

There had been more than expected in the stash spot. Not long before that day, Dennis had gone on a lick by himself and took $70k and two kilos of cocaine. He'd also come up on a nice piece of jewelry. In the safe, there was $90k, the kilos of cocaine, and, a diamond-encrusted solid gold chain with an oversized medallion that was worth $40,000 itself.

Dennis was unable to see what was going on, with the bed cover that had been placed on his head. However, he did manage to ease his cellphone out of his pocket and palmed it in his hand behind his back. He fumbled with the buttons in an effort to try and dial the last number he'd called, to his brother, so to have the robbery situation made known to someone over the phone.

"Aye yo, man, why you doing all of this to us? It ain't got to be like this, Little Mike. It don't have to be like this, little homie. I thought you—"

"If you say one more muthafuckin' word, nigga, I promise you, it'll be your last, pussy-boy!" Nightmare abruptly cut him off and spat with the threat of death attached.

As the brief exchange of words went on between the two, Regina finished putting all of the contents from the safe into the bag. She remained crouched low with half her body in the door entrance of the closet and the other half out in the room portion. Her head was down and her eyes were fixed on the carpet.

Nightmare stepped over her and went to the nightstand to switch off the lamp. He unplugged the TV as well leaving the room pitch-black with only a flicker of light that came through the window of the rest haven.

Nightmare held gripped in the bag all of the extras that he'd come for, plus a little more to cover the violation for the delay of payment by the perpetrator, Dennis. He then rummaged around in his mind minutely over what he wanted to do so as to complete the task and orders of his leader. *Be a nightmare,* he thought.

The pregnant girlfriend had nothing to do with the issue that caused her boyfriend to have a death wish out on him. But Dennis made the terrible mistake of saying a name around her, and Nightmare feared prison time, if she were to be let free to run to the police.

Anxiety ran rampant in the mind of the young wannabe serial killer, as he brainstormed on how to bring an end to the situation at hand. *Damn, what do I do now? I can't just walk away and let her live. She's now a witness who could come back to hurt me later down the line one way or another,* Nightmare had thought.

It was Dennis, the fool who played the key role in helping Nightmare make the horrific decision to bring an end to the problems he caused Teddy. Dennis made the fatal mistake, yet again, by opening that mouth of his.

"Say, Little Mike. Why you got to rob us like this, man? Why you putting Regina through all this bullshit, bro, when you clearly see she pregnant? You ain't got to take all we got. Just take the money, my nigga, and leave everything else."

The stupid nigga continued to try and talk Nightmare into only taking the money 'he owed Teddy,' and had completely disregarded the cardinal rule to a robbery situation like he was in; you should never talk, and one should definitely never let the perpetrator know you are aware of who they are. This will surely get you popped, right there on the spot.

The situation for Dennis, Regina, and their unborn, turned out to be no different than any other scenario that ended in bloody fashion.

Nightmare dropped the bag in his hand down to the floor, as he stood over Regina from behind. He whisked out the sharp knife, the one he'd held tucked in his waistband, and put both pistols in their holsters, one on the opposite side of his waist and the other—the .357—back in the ankle-holster.

***

A surge of relentless rage shot through his body, and a rush of psychopathic madness overtook his desire to control himself. He instantly transformed into a crazy man, the one that he'd always wanted to take on being: a cold-blooded killer.

Nightmare grimaced behind the mask and swiveled his head back and forth from Dennis to Regina. She still remained low in a crouching position and took no notice of the blade that was gripped tightly in the hand of Nightmare. He grabbed a fist full of her hair and twirled it around his wrist, wrapping tightly and yanking her head back violently in the process. He reached under her neck around her throat with his right hand that held the knife, and met her jugular vein. Nightmare dug into her throat deep with the sharp blade. Ridges were on the other end. He sliced easily through the esophagus, making a groove in the neck bone.

With brute force, he brought the blade from one end of her throat to the other, separating all that existed in between. The knife was so sharp that it cut halfway through the bone, due to the amount of strength put into him slitting her throat. Her head almost gave way to decapitation.

Regina gagged morbidly when cut. Her eyes rolled to the back of her lifeless head, leaving the torso of her pregnant body tilting forward, only holding by a thin layer of meat and tendon to the head. He loosened the fist full of hair and let her body drop to the floor, causing a thud, leaving blood running like a river onto the carpet.

The horrific gag she let out caught the attention of Dennis and forced him to call out for her. "Regina? Regina! Baby, what's wrong? Baby! Baby! You there? Why you not answering? Yo Michael, what the fuck did you do to my lady, nigga?" Dennis cried out as he was unable to see, due to his vision being blocked. "Baby? Baby! Will you please answer me? You there?" He began to get louder with each and every cry for Regina.

Nightmare wiped the blade clean of the blood and then put it away. He then pulled one of his pistols back out—the Glock .40—so to deal with Dennis and put an end to his ass. As Dennis continued to cry out for Regina, Nightmare leaped atop him to a straddled position on his back, and then pressed one of the pillows over his head. He popped dude in the back of the skull twice in rapid fashion, using the pillow as a muffler.

Bang-Bang!

For safe keeping, he pulled the pillow off and drag the blanket back past Dennis's chin to reveal his face. Another shot was due to ring out, as he pressed the pistol to the temple of the already dead guy and pulled the trigger, leaving a lingering flash from the fire that lit up the room, with a deafening burst of noise which came from the murder weapon

Bang!

Then a final shot was let off.

Bang!

He put the gun away, reached down to get his bag of goodies he'd licked for, sprinted down the stairs and out the back door, dashing away from the crime scene like a murderous thief in the night, leaving the 'triple murder' for investigation by the Chicago Police Department.

Nightmare had gotten away scot-free. This really motivated him to want to murder more, as the malicious thoughts constantly tap-danced around and teemed in his head. *Once a killer, always a killer. If I did it once, I could do it twice, or maybe a third time more. That could be nicer,* he thought. He'd become madly in love—or obsessed, even—with the act of murdering. The rest, as they say, *is history.* The birth of Nightmare became a reality this night.

***

Later The Same Day...

The lead homicide detective finally arrived on the scene. A Lieutenant Detective Hector Lopez had been a part of the Chicago Police Force for several years and commanded the particular homicide division for the last five of those years. He was called to the scene of a crime that occurred on the south side of the city, one which was located in one of the very few quiet neighborhoods on this side of town. The time was about 5:20 in the afternoon when he was required to report to the scene of a double homicide by his colleagues. A gruesome discovery was made. One by the responding officer.

Detective Lopez stood six-foot three, a lanky Chicano American with a crew-cut hairstyle and a clean-shaven face. This was based on his military experience. He had big, clumsy feet that stood out due to his thin frame and sometimes pistol-leg pants he liked to wear. Lopez also loved to keep a wooden toothpick hanging out of his mouth, or he would pinch it between his right index finger and thumb when speaking, then place the instrument back in, clutching it between his teeth. Most often, it was after he'd finished off a Styrofoam plate dinner from one of the many black churches that sold meals. He loved to eat from these particular kitchens.

Lopez stepped from his government-issued patrol car and walked towards the scene. He ducked under the caution tape and into the presence of the lead crime scene investigator present, a guy he was very familiar with, as they both had done the same many times prior. He needed to be briefed on the situation. Kerry Witton was himself a veteran on the force.

"Kerry, what we got inside?" Lopez asked.

"An ugly scene, to say the least. It's not the worst we've had to encounter. But, it's running close," Witton replied, and then began to flip the pages of his notepad to give Lopez the facts.

"The department had gotten a call from a woman by the name of Shantell Langston, the apparent sister of one of the victims inside, a female by the name of Regina Langston. From what we now know, Shantell made repeated calls over the course of six hours, to the sister, Regina—the victim within—to no avail. Shantell reported that it's not like her sister to ignore her phone—let alone not make contact with family—due to the fact that she was seven months pregnant."

"Who's seven months pregnant?" Lopez asked.

"One of the two victims inside. There's a male and a female—African-American," responded Witton.

"Gotcha. Continue," Lopez advised.

"So, anyways, Shantell stated that she made it her business to no longer continue and call, because for some strange reason, her sister just wasn't answering. And instead, she mentioned she would come by her house to make a visual check and leave nothing to question. She says that when she got here, she noticed that her sister's boyfriend's car was in the driveway as it still is. This suggested to her that the couple were indeed inside."

"So we got a 'murder-suicide' scenario, I assume?" Lopez cut in to ask.

"Not hardly. Appears to be more of a home invasion that resulted in a double homicide," Witton replied and corrected.

"Uh-huh. I'm listening," Lopez then urged him to continue on.

"So, the Shantell lady says she also noticed that no lights were on in the home, which prompted her to then go to the door and knock on it as hard as she could. She tried the knob and the door was unlocked, oddly. She said once inside, the TV from upstairs could be heard. She then says that she began to call out her sister's name, but got no response. Shantell then says she went up the stairs to the bedroom where the TV was going, which happen to be her sister and her boyfriend's bedroom, pushed the door open, and that's when she saw what the reality of the situation really was. The couple lay dead, one atop the bed, and the sister, laid out on the floor in a pool of blood. Shantell says that she ran back down the stairs, got in her car and then called nine one-one. She was a hysterical mess too, when we got here. The first responding officer arrived, then us," Witton reported to Lopez.

"And what else exactly did CSI find inside?" Lopez now wanted specifics.

"One of the victims, whose name is familiar to CPD, and the other, not so. The male victim—Dennis Lamont Ford, aka 'Dennis the Menace'—shot three times, pointblank range, by a high caliber pistol. Two to the back of the head and one to the left temple. And the female, throat slit terribly bad, near decapitation. Severed the neck-bone and all along the path," Witton related to Lopez.

"Awe, God! It does sound pretty gruesome in there. Let's take a look together, shall we?" Lopez stated and they both began to walk towards the entrance of the home.

They entered the bedroom where the bodies still lay. Lopez cringed a bit as he observed and then stuck his toothpick back in his mouth. He began to brainstorm while looking on at the bloody crime scene. The true impulse of a serious detective kicked in.

"I told you it was a gruesome mess in here, didn't I?" Witton put out there again for Lopez.

"Yeah, you did, Kerry. This place really is a mess. A bloody, nasty, cold-hearted mess at that. It took a real demon—or a group of demons—to do such a thing like this, especially to a pregnant woman," Lopez said as he leaned down to get a closer look at the face and wounds of the butchered female.

He stood tall again and rubbed his head as he scanned the crime scene, chewing on his toothpick. He cringed his face once more, as he could hardly stomach the fact that the department now had an additional serial killer on the loose, one that needed to be caught, and long before he was to strike again.

He continued to rotate his head and look on in disgust. "This scene has all the hallmarks, all the features, and all the characteristics, of a place where you would only witness such a thing go on. In the pit of hell! And this is terrible ... and saddening. Because what we're looking at right now is a situation from someplace where we can't even imagine in real life what the families are gonna have to go through. Something unfathomable. This is a nightmare for the families of these victims. A nightmare, by all means, I tell you. Nothing but a fucking nightmare!"

SOULLESS GOON | PRINCE

Chapter 2

Years Later...

Luckily For Him...

As he sat and reflected deeply over all that had transpired from the beginning of his legal battle, the man known throughout the Chicago underworld only as "Nightmare" couldn't find himself anything else other than happy and anxious as ever at being on the cusps of getting set free once more, and living the good life all over again. It had been a long, fought-out journey for Michael Antonio Gentry. Nothing short of a blessing, though. However, he deemed it a manifest destiny.

After being found guilty in Federal court for crimes ranging from murder, Continuance of a Criminal Enterprise, and RICO Statute violations, luckily for him, things nonetheless seemed bright.

Gentry and eight others from his crew were hit with heavy penalties to serve. Michael, obviously, received life plus an additional forty years, while the maximum the cohorts were handed down was thirty-five years, with the lesser of them all being fifteen years. Also, there were four co-indictees of Michael's who were acquitted and/or had a "hung jury" in the separate trials they opted to have. The most notable of the four was the second-in-command, a Ricky Lee Isaacs. He walked on the greater offenses, and the jury was undecided on the lesser. So was the same for a female associate of the organization.

Throughout his prison bid, Gentry kept written notes—mental ones—on laid plans to all he held objectives to do. With the passing of each day, reality began to truly dawn on him on exactly how fortunate and lucky he'd turned out to be. He'd met an extraordinary figure of a woman. One who possessed a profound legal talent, intelligence, and a charismatic appeal as he'd not been exposed to in years. It was these qualities that helped set things right for Gentry, to establish proper judicial precedence in the Federal Circuit where the legal showdown occurred. Over time, the female mentioned ended becoming the full-time attorney and companion of the once-infamous street kingpin. This was Jettica Renee Jackson, but she was affectionately known as "ReeRee" to those who knew her like that.

The acquaintance between the two was forged mostly by another female that Michael actually knew. This was in addition to his research of the lawyer on his contraband cellphone, and in the law library of the prison. It didn't take him long to figure out she was the truth. And the firm she worked for was a reputable force to be reckoned with. Gentry eventually retained the fierce attorney, and his 2255 Federal Habeas Corpus petition was filed to begin the process.

***

Michael's female friend, someone he grew up with, attended college with ReeRee. It was she—Tomeka Lashay Whitmore—who referred him to the lawyer. The two ladies recently reconnected through the years, upon ReeRee completing law school and landing a position at a top law firm. The bond between ReeRee and Tomeka was established while they were enrolled in the University of

Miami. The two shared a level of intimacy to the union as well. This was typical.

Tomeka stated to him, "Michael, I know you're in need of a bona fide lawyer, and I got somebody special in mind I wanna refer you to, if you're interested?"

His response was, "'Meka, you already know that I'm interested in any type of help I can get. Especially from the predicament I'm in. And, I can definitely use a good lawyer to fight for me and potentially get me out this muthafucka, you know."

"I know that's right, bro. And this is a female who I use to roll with daily. We did almost everything together in college. At least while we were there temporary. But, we partied together, hosted private dances together, and also, shook our asses together in the many strip clubs and other social settings as a team, to earn money to pay rent, tuition, and to cover other living expenses throughout our stay in the Sunshine state. We were a sexy duo, I tell you," Tomeka related. "And of course, this was long before I went on to graduate with a degree in business and account management, and moved to Midwest America—'The Lone Star State'—Texas."

"That's right, you do got family there, don't you?"

"Yep. And, eventually, I met this Hispanic nigga, and we got married. I gave this nigga him three kids, bro, before he started to fuck around on me. With a *white bitch* at that!"

"Damn! That's cold."

"Who you telling! But, the marriage ... that shit didn't last long. We divorced a few years afterwards. I had to move on about life and utilized my learning and degree, to start what eventually became a successful business of my own You know I own and operate a carpet cleaning service, and I also got a bakery that specialize in gift baskets of sweets and things of this nature."

"That's good to know. But ... this lawyer chick and friend of yours ... tell me more about her."

"Her name is Jettica, or 'ReeRee,' as she prefers outside of work. She wasn't as fortunate as me, bro."

"What you mean by this?"

"It wasn't ReeRee's calling like mine, to meet a nice guy, and go on to tie the knot. She was not as blessed. ReeRee had to bear the brunt of emotional pain and turmoil early in life, over a break up in high school with an ex-boyfriend. She miscarried, and never fully recovered psychologically before college. Atop this, ReeRee got seduced and snatched up by a now ex-pimp nigga while we was fresh in college. This nigga held a reputation for being brutal in his gorilla style of dealing with his women. He was a so-called player in the pussy game by the government name of Nathaniel Wiggins, but on the streets, he was called 'Cadillac Nate.'"

"Say whaaat!"

"Hell yeah. The nigga had the name pinned on him by his pimp buddies, because of the assortment of colors and the different types of Cadillac cars his short, black, bald-headed, and arrogant ass drove in his glory days in the game. This history of him was told to me by ReeRee, personally. She loved and hated the nigga all at the same time. But ... the point I'm trying to make is ... it was the nigga Nate who actually turned ReeRee out to the pimping and whoring shit she learned to love and appreciate so much. That shit became addictive to her. She was the main girl, and the fast stepping, star-studded, top girl in a stable of four that Nate maintained at any given time. And this muthafucka made sure to keep his prized possession ReeRee literally knee-deep in the strip clubs, and out handling business for long hours of the day. He also kept her away from those isolated whorehouses, out of fear he would lose her to another female, because they are the ones who mainly operated these spots, and Nate was all too familiar with the sexual appetite and lesbian desires ReeRee had. So, before you ask, yeah, she likes to go both ways," Tomeka uttered with a grin about her face and gazing intensely into the screen of the cellphone camera lens.

"Her past is interesting. Wow! And I assume that 'Nate' ensured he kept her logged in on social media too, and looking to catch someone to get busy with and draw money from? But, from my short-lived level of experience in this area, I already know that he also had contacts to prominent top-paying high profile members of society. Muthafuckas' he was connected to. The majority of these are well-to-do rich white guys who Nate played golf with, probably. But from how this sounds, that nigga had absolute power and control over ReeRee's very soul, and he managed to maintain this dominance over her by the definite threat of death, or the fear of being physically harmed in a serious way, so to shock the psyche of her, to make her really believe that his crazy money-worshiping ass just may actually 'kill' her one day if she disobeyed him in the least."

"That's about right. I didn't know all of this until years later. But, ReeRee did confess that it was these very thoughts of the crazy bastard doing this that had seeped from her mind down to her heart, and eventually translated into her falling in love with being paid for what she'd learned to do so well ... catering to men and always seeking to please them or see them through any serious situations. ReeRee loved the game itself, bro. Her spirit was transformed by it, and she relied on these 'pay-to-play' meetings to support her livelihood. The same way as she do now as a lawyer," stated Tomeka.

***

Nightmare wanted to respond to this and share his analysis, "So ... if I may say this to you about what I take of her history ... the answers to how she came to perform so well in the courtroom just may lay in the reality of her former profession in the pussy game? Is this what you really tryna say, 'Meka?"

"Basically. Because ReeRee made it her business to perform exceptionally well for any and all of her 'top paying customers' when she was selling pussy and blow jobs. And likewise, in her later years as a legal talent, she utilized these same skills to perform well for 'top paying clients' and defending them in trials or otherwise. The same concept, only a different arena and playing field. Trust me on this. I was there to witness them both."

The truth was, ReeRee was Nate's girl from the tender age of eighteen to twenty-three. He never once took his foot out of her red ass at any time she violated the order of business or the rules he'd put down. When he did lash out and beat her, he'd regret it later on when ReeRee was unable to go out and work, and he was the one to blame for damaging the goods. ReeRee vowed to make payback a motherfucker against Nate at the first opportunity that she were to get. She really wanted to kill him. But on the flip side, she appreciated him for exposing her to the real world, and on how to navigate her way through it.

Tomeka continued, "But real talk, Mike, if any nigga that I know of resembled the qualities and characteristics of Cadillac Nate, in personality and charisma—the shit ReeRee loved and adored in a man—it would be you, Michael, in this regard. And the reason I say this is because of my knowledge of your brief history as a pimp yourself. And, like Nate, Michael, you stayed down, dirty, and hardcore on a bitch's ass without slack when it came to the issue of getting your bread. And really didn't make a difference which hole your hoes chose to get your money out of, whether it be the pussy, mouth, or their asshole. I know you meant business; that you was serious; that you was focused as a pimp. And a bitch had better have your money, or else. This was the simple and plain message to your girls, and there was nothing to be misunderstood about it. The same applied to Nate."

"So you done seen him before and knew him yourself, I assume?" he asked.

"Oh yeah. But Nate damn near pushing sixty years old now, and long retired from the pimp-game. He elevated in a legit way and landed a job with the Georgia Department of Corrections as a prison guard. The nigga worked his way through the ranks to become a security warden at a prison or something like that. It's close to his hometown of Camilla, Georgia. But anyway, he ended up marrying his last standing hoe, his 'bottom bitch,' some woman named Julia. He helped her get hired at the same prison too."

The notion Tomeka made was that, had it not been for Nate exposing ReeRee to the game in the way he had, she probably wouldn't have taken a liking to the wicked bravado and the intriguing charisma she'd highly admired in Michael himself, once she reviewed his case and profile when she was contacted by him and Tomeka about representation. And add his "gift of gab" he often put on display, related by Tomeka, the lawyer was drawn in more and more. While at the same time, in knowing that Nightmare was the complete opposite of a player than little Nate was, ReeRee knew that he'd turned out to be a different type of animal altogether. However, one she felt could indeed be tamed.

The potential bond to develop between Michael and ReeRee was made possible years beforehand, when the ties of Nate and her were cut. And the story goes. She craved what Nate had to offer, in a new version of a nigga, someone like Nightmare. A certified street thug was what she desired to have business with, and a personal dealing with. Nightmare came with both advantages.

"So what actually happened to break up what ReeRee and Nate had going on?" Nightmare asked.

"Shid ... the nigga tripped out one night! ReeRee was able to break free from his ass while he held her pinned to the ground and was slapping her silly out of his mind! She'd gotten to her feet, pulled a gun she had in her purse, and shot that brutal bastard twice, directly in the gut, and in his inner left thigh. A bullet ripped through the main artery and nearly caused him to bleed to death. But the nigga had his pimp buddy who was there with him to rush him to the hospital."

"Oh! So he basically ran her away from him, because he couldn't control his anger and emotions, huh?"

"Yep! What kinda pimp nigga was he who couldn't get that shit in check? But anyways, after the incident, ReeRee came to Texas to lay low with me. She then ran to Memphis, Tennessee, to be with family there, in the event a warrant may had been issued for her arrest behind the shooting. No charges were ever filed though, because that nigga Nate simply respected the game and didn't press the issue of seeing to it she got locked up. He told the police at the hospital that he'd gotten robbed and was shot in the process. The typical outcome of many armed robberies in the Overtown section of the city."

"Oh yeah! I done heard a lot about Overtown. That's almost as rough a place to live as is Chicago," Nightmare came back with.

***

A year and a half later, ReeRee finally re-enrolled into college to complete her learning and get her degree. Constitutional Law and Criminal Justice were her subjects. She transferred from the University of Miami to UCLA. Only two years out of law school, she made a name for herself and a mark in the federal courts. Her biggest case by far became that of Nightmare's.

"But look, 'Meka, tell me more about her background, shit like this. How she grew up and shit. I wanna know personal things about her, so I'll have the advantage when it comes time for me to make my move to catch her, and make mine. Because you already knowing, I can have any women in the world that I want. And that's a fact," he stated

Tomeka said, "ReeRee mixed, like you, nigga!" She let out with a laugh. "Her daddy a West Philly roughneck nigga that was rugged and street-tough; yet, a supreme gentleman at heart in regards to manners and his grooming regimen. An

African American man, that is. He and ReeRee's momma met in the Spanish Harlem neighborhood of New York City while he was on one of his cocaine re'up runs to the Big Apple, from what she's told me. He went to be supplied from one of her kingpin uncles at his café on 149th Street and Broadway. The uncle, a cool ass nigga named Pomme Ortiz, introduced his sister, Rosa Ortiz, to one of the most trusted and valued customers of his Fish Scale product. He was the one and only *Lyndale Cornelius Jackson*, aka 'Lenny J.' This ReeRee's dad. The introduction was a compliment and a genuine gesture to the partner Lenny J, for the hundreds of thousands of dollars he'd spent with him through the years of doing business. But, long story short about the daddy, Lenny J had fucked up and gotten pulled over early one morning by state troopers on the New Jersey Turnpike, just out of Newark. ReeRee say he had five kilos of powder cocaine and $12,000 cash, as he was on his way back to Philly. He ended up doing 141 months in the Feds. And when he got out, he relocated to Memphis, Tennessee, where he has family roots and they own land and property. Throughout his career though as a dope boy, he would always send money to his family to pay property taxes, to buy additional land, buy houses, and to renovate the family's existing properties. ReeRee was fifteen when her daddy stepped out of prison. He took her and her momma Rosa with him down south."

"So they still together?"

"Nope. Lenny J and Rosa separated three years after he got out, and she relocated back to New York, leaving ReeRee to live with her daddy, because she was in her senior year of high school and hated the thought of leaving her friends and cheerleader team. She would spend summers with her momma though. And it wasn't too long before she was to graduate and would be on her way to college down in Miami anyway. That's when we met. So, her momma never tried to force her to go back to New York," Tomeka made Nightmare aware.

***

ReeRee was a promising and ambitious female who held the potential to be a big-name litigator upon graduation from law school. She experienced a midlife scare and had fallen victim while weak at an early age. Not to mention, something more that would later come out about her life. Through sheer courage and the willpower to survive and make it in a career field, she made it through the abusive traps of the deceitful and cutthroat tactics of Cadillac Nate, and through the early death throes of pimping and street life. She had surpassed the multitude of temptations her body and other physical attributes wrongfully suggested she should utilize, in order to take advantage of the numerous men from all shades and races that she'd had the luxury and pleasure to encounter. She managed to shake it all off.

It was the strength that ReeRee exhibited, along with the other unshakable features she possessed, that Michael greatly admired—at least from everything that his homegirl Tomeka related to him about her. But of all, it was the quality of her spirit he instantly took notice of on social media posts and videos. And he felt her energy resonate through his own soul. It turned him on in the initial attorney-client visit, and at the very sight of her—she was such a gorgeous female— he felt in his heart, he had to get acquainted. This was the natural impulse of a man—him specifically—to become aroused by a sexy woman. If she's intelligent, then that's even better for the type of man he'd professed himself to be.

Chapter 3

Rewind Then Press Play...

When the female lawyer Jettica, first came to see Nightmare for an attorney-client visit, she strongly advised him that he should undergo a series of psychiatric examinations. This was so, to disprove the prosecution's theory to the Judge who would review the legal documents she were to file on his behalf, that Michael, wasn't some psychopath, drug-dealing, sadistic serial killer that the U.S. Attorney's Office made him out to be in trial. That he, in fact, was a very intelligent man, someone who had morals, and had nothing to do with the multiple murder counts that he was wrongly convicted of based only on circumstantial evidence, and not something more direct.

Michael's original trial lawyer attempted the same strategy, but he refused. On three separate occasions. Due to the sway this legal counsel held over him, for more than one reason, he would not do so a fourth time. He accepted the offer to speak with a revered psychiatrist of lawyer Jettica's choosing.

"Hello, Michael! I'm Doctor Cecil Britt. And I was hired to examine you by your attorney, a miss Jettica Jackson. Are you aware of this?"

"Yes! I am. Nice to meet you, Doctor Britt. And if possible, let's make this short, simple, and sweet. Let's get straight to the point of this whole thing, shall we."

"I wouldn't have it no other way, Michael. It makes my job so much more easier," said doctor Britt. He talked slow and dragged out his words, similar to the TV celebrity Ph.D., Doctor Phil. He was tall, bulky in a way, and resembled Doctor Phil as well, with his bird's nest balding head and pale skin complexion.

"I can understand that. So ... let's get going, shall we," Nightmare stated.

"Absolutely. The way I like to begin is by asking a very direct question, and I look for you to give me a very direct answer. And mind you, you're protected by attorney-client privilege, so nothing you say cannot and will not be used against you in no type of way, okay."

"I respect this."

"Great! So, is there anything you'd like to say to kinda sorta get something off your chest or that you want to emphatically say to me? Anything?"

"Actually, there is," Michael uttered, then exhaled, and proceeded to say what was on his mind. "The life that I live or have lived, sir, is the one that I chose. And I have no regrets. I have no remorse. Nor do I make any qualms about anything. I am perfectly content with every single decision that I have made in my life, because I took a blood oath with the devil! He initiated me into his order. And I keep my word no matter what. And I believe in Black Magic! So, emphatically speaking, I am not seeking forgiveness! On no accord. Period! For nothing!" he declared.

The doctor took a long, stern look at his patient. He didn't readily respond as he thought maybe there was more. There wasn't. Michael merely locked eyes with him and awaited his response to what he'd said.

"Is that it?" asked Doctor Britt.

"Yep!"

"Very well. Now that the first portion of phase one is taken care of, let's move on to the second portion. This is where I like to have my patients hit 'rewind' on their life, then press 'play' for me by relating everything they want to tell me."

"I can do that."

"Okay. Go!"

"Well, for starters, might I have you to know that I was born and raised in the suburban city of Chicago, Park Ridge, Illinois, on July 2, 1974. My father, Thomas James Gentry, was a hulking, oil-black giant of an individual, who stood at six-foot-ten inches and weighed two hundred seventy pounds. He was a very muscular and husky type man with a full body frame. If you recall from images of the sports legend, my dad fit the description and was a taller version of the late, great former heavyweight boxing champion, Jack Johnson. My father passed away at the age of forty-three. I was only fourteen at the time that he suffered a massive heart attack."

"I'm sorry to hear this. My belated condolences."

"Thank you."

"And your mother?"

"Oh, my mother, on the other hand. She was from a totally different background and culture than the man she married and had a son by. Her name is Catherine Diane Tolbert, who later became Catherine Gentry, then Catherine Mobley. She hails from Springfield, Illinois, and was raised by a family that heavily valued far right-wing Republican style of politics. When my mother graduated high school, she'd moved out of her parents' home for the inner city of Chicago, to attend a small college and obtain a degree to become a social service worker."

"That's a very good profession to work."

"I agree. But, my mother ... in my own words, is a lily-white woman with crimson-reddish hair that flowed down her back, and she had a petite frame she loved to cover with sundresses or dark blue denim jeans. This was so to signify the political party she favored and always voted for (The Democratic Party). Totally the opposite of what her parents and family adhered to. And through her work and services in predominantly Black communities in Chicago, she developed a strong love and thirst for only the dark and brute type Black guys who held an interest in the 'Jungle Fever' thing. Then, along came Thomas, a guy she'd met at a convention, and within six months, they'd married and she was pregnant with child—me, her one and only. At the death of my father, my mother remarried, to a man by the name of Wallace. He had very similar features and characteristics as did my father. And Wallace, my stepfather, took great care of his wife and step-son, me. But, if I may, the point is this. My black ass is a mixed seed. I'm a 'Mulatto' nigga—pardon my language—just as the 44th president of the U.S., Barack Hussein Obama."

"You have a good way of providing perspective, Mister Gentry," the doctor stated.

"I appreciate that. But, I stand at six-foot-seven and I weigh two hundred and thirty pounds. As evident, I own a lean and chiseled physique, due to the intense calisthenic workout regimen I religiously devote myself to and have kept up for the past nineteen years or so. I also practice being a Vegan. Therefore, I don't ingest any flesh whatsoever. And because of such practice, it helps to keep my body fat low and eliminate cholesterol to prevent me from tapping out in my early forties possibly, as did my old man from cardiac arrest. Any food items with a face on it, I DO NOT EAT!"

"Honestly, Mister Gentry, I wish that I had the type of discipline to do that as you have. Because I believe I'd die without a piece of meat to eat," Mr. Britt let out with a chuckle.

The casual conversation continued between the two.

As for Michael and his personal style, he always kept his hair well-groomed and nicely lined up. He had a superb pattern of waves which held capabilities to make a person "sea-sick" if in exposure for a prolonged period of time. His eyes were a mixture of brown, teal, and emerald in color, and had an intense whiteness about them at the outer areas, around the pupils. He took after his mother with the structure of his nose, as their "European" genetics showed well regarding that particular feature; slightly pointed and narrow as the beak of a sparrow hawk.

Throughout Michael's reign in the streets of Chicago and elsewhere, the street legend known as Nightmare, donned and styled himself in the best threads and attire his street money and dope money could buy. He was a natty dresser and loved high-end designer labels, as anything less wouldn't do. The product of choice for him and his crew was heroin, and the riches from their operations kept them relevant in the Chicago underworld.

Michael went on to relate his life to the doctor:

"Shit, doc, honestly, life was good for me and my comrades, as we lived in an upscale way and dined in the finest restaurants in the Chicago and Detroit areas. This lavish lifestyle though, came crashing down on us when the muthafuckin' DEA rushed in on us, so-calling themselves executing 'No Knock' search warrants and indictments for arrest. They caught us down bad too. But no pity. Again, I am not seeking forgiveness for nothing I've done," he muttered in a serious tone.

They continued the session.

***

The first and only plea offered to Michael was a nine-hundred-month sentence (75 years). At no time did Michael ever contemplate taking such a plea. He'd reasoned that, by going to trial, he would retain full rights to appeal the legal errors and technicalities that were bound to occur.

There were a total of eighteen constitutional errors that came about, some related to Brady violations and Substantial Due Process Defaults. These were absolute grounds for reversal on Habeas, the particular phase of the case he was now at.

His prison bid began in Leavenworth Federal Prison in the state of Kansas, and he'd begun to catch wind of ReeRee then, as he and Tomeka got back in contact with each other. She'd reached out to him and they talked on the phone and exchanged letters. Tomeka mentioned ReeRee by name with a brief reference. This was before the lengthy discussions about her took place. It wasn't until he'd gotten transferred to the Fed pen in Terre Haute, Indiana, that he began to really research her and take it more serious about retaining her.

Nightmare began a solid friendship with a guy by the name of Ernest Williamson, aka "Slick." This particular dude—Slick—had previously been represented by a guy who worked for the same law firm as did Jettica, a Brett Preston, and Jettica was the only one, a helpful assistant to attorney Preston. They both—Brett and Jettica—were what the legal world would refer to as "Philadelphia Lawyers," working cases, and eventually, they ended up winning a favorable ruling in Slick's behalf, after he'd been wrongly accused and charged with conspiracy offenses, firearms charges, drug trafficking, and lesser related offenses.

Slick had gotten jammed up in Camden, New Jersey, after Federal agents amassed a list of Federal crimes they alleged had stemmed from the cities of Hudson, New York; Philly; Mount Vernon, New York; Clearwater, Florida; and a few down in his hometown of Moultrie, Georgia. The original sentence was "Life" for Slick, but in the end, his time got cut to fifteen years.

Without needing to be convinced any more than he already had, Nightmare contacted the law firm ReeRee worked for and held a consultation phone call. He then had his parents get in contact with the firm to establish an escrow account for the retainer fee to be deposited. They wanted $350,000 to represent Michael, and he specifically asked if "Jettica" could be the lead attorney on the petition prior to his money being paid. ReeRee was, and her boss gave her the option to pick who she wanted to assist in representing the Kingpin. She returned the favor to Brett Preston, and the legal duo began work trying to destroy the convictions of the government.

On the flip side of things, the relationship between Michael and his friend/under-boss/co-indictee, Ricky, had gotten shaky through the years that Michael was locked away in prison, as Ricky was dealt a good hand in being acquitted in trial and avoiding a prison cell. The two had ties and contact with one another nonetheless, but not anywhere near as expected. It was more of a power struggle between the two and a battle for the throne. This caused a rift between them.

Nightmare didn't want to relinquish the top spot of their crew, but was virtually ineffective in governing from prison. And Ricky wanted to hold total leadership and sought to move the team towards a different direction.

Ricky also refused to do as ordered by Nightmare, in having the four people that Nightmare wanted whacked to be finally killed. They had testified for the government and helped put Nightmare and the others away. But Ricky felt it unnecessary to bring unwanted and aggressive attention back their way by the Feds. Especially not the attention that had to do with four people being murdered, who "so happened" to have testified on those they'd been arrested and indicted with.

***

The understanding between Nightmare and Ricky got more complicated by the day, as Ricky had not checked in the amounts of money Michael wanted him to hand over from the continuation of the heroin operation that was restarted two years after Ricky's acquittal. Over a four-year span, Ricky and the team had amassed somewhere between twenty-five to thirty-five million dollars from illicit profits.

There was a split with the team due to differences of opinions, ways of running things, and the wayward philosophies which Michael attempted to keep in use. Ricky drew the majority of the group, as they simply "followed the money" and had a visible leader, while the rest, the hardcore and die-hard band of the crew, believed strongly in Nightmare. They felt confident in their hearts that he would someday be resurrected from prison and return to the streets. They always held belief that he'd find means to get free from any predicament or situation, no matter how bad it may have seemed to be at the time. He had always spoken of his "Black Magic" and spiritual protection aiding and assisting him. But exactly when would it be put to use, they questioned?

Not only that, although he was locked away in Federal prison, Nightmare still had eyes, ears, arms, and reach that extended to every segment of the underworld and ghetto that he once controlled as the high-ranking and prominent figure in the vicious Vice Lord set of the "Four Corner Hustlers" organization, headquartered in Chicago. He was a double O.G. (second-generation original gangsta), and he'd earned these stains the hard way. However, while inside, he had "rolled" from the Four Corner Hustlers set and became an "Undertaker Vice Lord." An elder member made it possible. Ricky knew nothing of this.

Although long removed from the streets, Nightmare still called the shots, ordered whackings, and controlled the operation, unchallenged by any—until Ricky was acquitted, got out of jail, and rebuilt the operation how he saw fit, by tying in with the Italians and getting supplied by them. It got even deeper as it went on.

***

At the point of being retained by Nightmare, ReeRee immediately initiated an attorney-client visit and flew out to Terre Haute, Indiana to meet with her new client. This was the second of many. Upon arrival this time, and being escorted to the designated area within the prison, she patiently awaited with laptop open, case file properly arranged and tab-oriented, and pen at the ready to document any necessary material which was subject to arise within the meeting.

Her attire for the occasion was a light gray to off-white short-sleeved, button-down top, with a tight, form-fitting, dark gray colored cotton and soft wool skirt, which went down below her knees. She also wore a thick black patent-leather belt around her waist to accentuate her outfit, and a pair of black patent-leather pumps to complete the look. On her left wrist, ReeRee had on a thick black bangle bracelet, a black opal gemstone ring with a rose gold casing on her left ring finger, a rose gold band on her left thumb, a rose gold band on her right thumb, and a leather band Cartier watch on her right wrist. ReeRee was left-handed.

She remained very calm and serene while she awaited her client to be brought from the back of the facility. Thirty minutes after getting to the prison and passing through all the security protocol, he was walking through the door of the attorney room where ReeRee stood to her feet and greeted her client with a handshake in formal fashion.

"Hello, Mister Gentry. How are you, sir? Nice to meet you again," she said to him.

"I'm good, Miss Jackson. Nice to meet you again as well. And I'm just happy to have this process finally going," Michael replied.

"It's good to know you're in positive spirits," she said and briefly paused. "I've filed two documents on your behalf thus far. I did send you a copy of each. Have you received them?" she asked.

"Yes, I did, along with your letter," he responded.

"Good. They were the 'Entry of Appearance' Motion, and the actual standard form for your Habeas Corpus Twenty-Two Fifty-Five petition—a 'Bivens' filing. The first, letting the court and the government know that I am now your attorney of record. And the second, to initiate the legal course of action to have your issues heard in the court," she related. "And the psychiatric examination I had you perform helped to reinforce the Habeas petition."

"Understood, Miss Lady. That's very much understood. And if anything, Miss Jackson, what legal technicalities were there that you might've discovered, that occurred in my trial? Anything that may constitute reversal?" he wanted to know.

"Well, Mister Gentry, the key thing I took notice of was that the main evidence the government relied upon to convict you, so happened to be the main issue to have gotten your co-indictees acquitted in their separate trials. There is also what is called a 'Brady Violation' in your case—"

"'Brady Violation'?" he cut in and repeated, so as to have an explanation provided, due to him being without knowledge of legal terminology or of the law itself.

"Yes ... a 'Brady Violation.' What this essentially means is that the U.S. Attorney's Office withheld evidence that you could have benefited from in your trial. Exculpatory Material is the legal term for this," she related.

Michael jotted down all she mentioned to him for later research in the law library. He wanted to fill his notepad as much as he could with legal material to keep him busy and active on his own case.

ReeRee continued, "We have a lot going good for us with that one ... the Brady thing."

"Oh, you think so?" he responded in question.

"Absolutely. And I definitely believe strongly it would have served you best to have had a change of venue out of Chicago as your co-indictees had done. The testimony of government witnesses, in combination with your street nickname in the record, made matters terrible for you at trial, Mister Gentry," she stated.

"I knew I should've had my trial moved someplace else! But the trial lawyer I had was against it. His claim was that he'd done quite a few trials in Chicago, and felt comfortable on home base. But I can't continue to dwell on that. We've moved on, and I now must approach this from the perspective of how you want to attack any errors which occurred," Michael responded to his legal counsel, but never addressing her comment about his street name.

"Also, Mister Gentry, the government's main objective was to use the 'RICO Statute' to convict you. They really had no concern for the others. But they took the extras that came their way. As I've stated, there appears to be a violation of 'Brady,' and if we are successful in being granted a ruling on these grounds, then that will technically destroy the entire case. You'll be allowed to plea to a far lesser charge and have the sentence reduced, possibly time served," attorney Jackson articulated.

"That's music to my ears, Miss Jackson. Music to my goddamn ears!" he let out with a huge smile.

"So, anyway, the Habeas process, this could take anywhere from one year to three, maybe longer, depending on the caseloads of the judge that the case would be assigned to, and so on and so forth. Yours? Definitely longer rather than sooner," she continued in explaining the particulars to her client and some of the things he could expect. She also made mention to him of the possibility in her getting him transferred to Lewisburg, Pennsylvania, a more easier drive for her to and from New York City, as she would visit him there and her family on the same trip in the future.

Chapter 4

The visit lasted for the better part of four hours. Upon leaving from the prison, ReeRee flew to New York City, rented a vehicle, and drove the rental she had to Harlem, so she could visit with her mother and family there. Next, she made the ride to Philly and visited her dad and family in the city of Brotherly Love. It was a four-day visit to the East Coast for ReeRee, and then, she was headed back to her home in LA, by flight from Philly.

All throughout the visit, Nightmare made it a priority to thoroughly size up ReeRee, and contemplated what type of angle he could go at her with on a personal level. He never was the one to be in the presence of a woman who had it going on like ReeRee and not attempt to get to know them. He strongly felt as though he could have any woman he so pleased, if he'd gotten the vibe from them that they may admire his handsome appearance. And besides, he already had an advantage over ReeRee. She was friends with his friend.

Nightmare found an attraction to ReeRee and was able to see straight through her and all her ways of being a woman with extraordinary sex appeal by the end of the visit. She certainly gave him a lot to think about in regards to his case, and, on a personal level even.

True indeed, he held the qualifications to have played the role of someone who could 'fake it till he make it' and really put on for ReeRee, had he so chose to. But this would've been completely foolish on his behalf as a man, 'the boss' type nigga and street commander who he presented himself as, to have fronted by posing to be someone he's not. And in all actuality, he was simply a guy with a life sentence in prison and had hired the best legal help one could ever be in need of. It just so happened that he had become attracted to the attorney he'd hired. She turned him on in a major way. He felt really good about his $350,000 investment, but even more so in the prospect that he could catch her and have her as his lady.

Nightmare observed all the signs and detailing of an arousal in her as they talked and made heavy eye contact. They marveled at each other, as he also took notice of her jugular vein becoming inflated and pulsating in an appealing way as her heart rate increased, and she toyed around with parts of her bangs that dangled, and with her ink pen. Her reactions to Michael's handsome face, fit body, and articulation was the natural thing that any woman would be subjected to if placed in such an encounter. But time would be the determining factor of this for her and him, as they were certain to meet on many more occasions in the same fashion.

***

Meanwhile...

Back in Los Angeles, ReeRee was now in the comfort of the home she shared with her lover, Jackie. They had found themselves relaxing, enjoying wine, and in the company of each other in the newly built sauna bath-house that they had long wanted constructed in their backyard. They had a wood-paneled fence erected as well, to ensure more privacy, as they soaked and lavished in the Jacuzzi for a bubble bath. It was situated inside the mini structure.

The surround sound system played at a modest level. They listen to neo-soul music and watch videos from the 80-

inch smart TV that complemented the haven. The two sponge-bathed one another, as ReeRee situated herself between the legs of Jackie to be washed and massaged.

Jackie initiated conversation about Jettica's trip. "So tell me about this new client of yours, sweetheart?" Jackie asked, wanting to be informed of the attorney-client visit.

ReeRee sighed with pleasure she felt at being slowly washed and caressed about the breasts by her dark chocolate boo thang with her right hand, and being penetrated and tickled at the clit with the left.

"Yes, Jackie. His name is Michael ... Michael Gentry. He's from Chicago. And is known on the streets as 'Nightmare.'"

"'Nightmare!' You don't say!" Jackie retorted.

"Yes ... Nightmare. And from the looks of things, some of the material the government found him guilty of illustrates only what may go on in such a thing," ReeRee responded.

"Huh!" Jackie sighed. "How many murders?" she asked.

ReeRee responded, "Accused of nine, but only found guilty of one."

"Kingpin ... CCE ... RICO?" Jackie continued.

"You got it, suga. All of the above," ReeRee came back with. Her tone then momentarily turned from talking about a client to a more sensual and intimate exchange. "Ooh yeah, Jackie, keep going, just like that," she let out at the sensation she'd felt from Jackie's finger pulling at her G-spot. The talk continued about Nightmare. "He and the majority of his people got nabbed. It was him, though, who turned out to be the main man they wanted. But eight others were convicted alongside Mister Gentry. There were also four that got lucky... acquitted. Their lawyers moved to have a change of venue. Smart thinking by them. Michael got life plus. But ... he has a ray of light at the end of the tunnel," ReeRee related.

"How so?" Jackie now felt she absolutely had to know.

"A Brady violation, it appears. If I can prove it properly."

"And if so, he walks?" Jackie asked.

"That's correct, indeed," ReeRee replied to her lover's question.

"But the better question is ... how did you become a part of this case to begin with? My reason for asking is that, morally, my conscience would be affected to know that I'd helped a demon get free, after the government had worked so hard to get him and his crew?" Jackie uttered.

"Well, for three hundred and fifty thousand dollars ... and ... a specific request for my legal services ... that's how I got involved," ReeRee replied without relating the specific details, being she didn't want Jackie offended.

"Well, as a criminal defense lawyer, you continue to work hard for the money, baby. And me, as a prosecutor, I'll continue to send them to prison without mercy. Or to meet their maker—'Satan'—if the death penalty is called for. But enough of that," Jackie said, then kissed ReeRee on the nape of her neck. She repeated and then began to caress ReeRee's melon-sized breasts with both hands. They were covered in bubbles, and she ran her tongue in and around her ear, sending shock waves of sensation through ReeRee's body.

"I can't wait until we're finally married, baby," Jackie stated, so as to bring ReeRee back to the thought of a same-sex union they'd tentatively agreed to have.

"I can't wait myself," ReeRee reluctantly acknowledged, basically telling Jackie all she'd wanted to hear, so to make her feel good. Truthfully, her mind wasn't quite made up just yet.

There existed a big difference between the two. On one end, Jackie was a full-fledged, one-hundred-percent gay and lesbian woman, who didn't hide it and wore her sexuality with pride. While on the other, ReeRee was only bisexual, and still loved the masculine conquest of a man over her very being every so often. Her disposition and preference made her question whether or not she actually wanted to tie the knot and be stuck in a marriage with another woman. While at the same time, she did want more kids to fully raise of her own and not rely on someone else—as opposed to "adopting from Africa," as Jackie suggested they'd do someday.

ReeRee rose from between Jackie's legs and sat on the edge of the tub in the seat section. She awaited Jackie to ease up on her like a hungry crocodile moment before ambushing its prey. ReeRee then bust her legs as wide as she could, tilted her head to the rear, and leaned back. Jackie went in headfirst, resting on her knees in the tub, her arms underneath ReeRee's hind legs, and bracing her hands on ReeRee's hips. She kissed ReeRee's inner thighs tenderly— first the right, then the left. She then took a swipe upward with her tongue between the pussy lips of ReeRee's, slurping at the clit, then tickling with her tongue before slurping yet again.

The heat from Jackie's mouth, in combination with that of the Jacuzzi water and the sensation she'd felt, sent tingles shooting up the spine of ReeRee. She palmed Jackie by the head with both hands and pulled her in closer, burying Jackie's face in her love haven. Jackie's entire mouth covered ReeRee's juice box as she put additional passion and pleasure into the art of pleasing her lover in satisfying fashion.

Jackie then palmed ReeRee's breasts and massaged them delicately. She pinched both nipples hard while she still ate the pussy and caused ReeRee's body to lock up.

"Ah. Ooh, Jackie!" she exclaimed. "This feels so good, baby. You are the best," ReeRee panted and let out.

Jackie hummed hard and responded to ReeRee's pleas. "You say it's good to you, baby? And I'm the best?"

"Yes baby! God, yes! Those are my words. You know how to bring out the best in me. Keep going. I'm about to cum, my love. And cum hard, is what I wanna do," ReeRee moaned out, as Jackie intensified the pleasure she gave, then penetrated her right middle finger deep into ReeRee's anus.

"Ooh," ReeRee sighed, then inhaled deeply and held her breath as she reached her climax. "Ah! I'm cummin', Jackie.

I'm cummin,' suga," she bellowed, then creamed all in the mouth and on the face of Jackie.

Once she'd drained all of her juices and could flow no more, Jackie lifted her head, dotted both nipples with love potion, and then locked lips with ReeRee, mouth-to-mouth, as they tongue-kissed like there wasn't no tomorrow.

"I love you, ReeRee. And don't you ever forget that, okay?" she professed, and they continued to kiss passionately.

***

ReeRee and Jackie had been in a relationship dating back to their days at UCLA. Jackie was the first born of five—three females and two males—to West African parents who immigrated to America when Jackie was Thirteen. Their native country was the French Ivory Coast (Côte d'Ivoire), as this is to explain the origin of her full name, Jacquelyn Francois-Claudel.

Jackie's family and native background had a bit of a notorious element to it, which, luckily, she no longer had to worry about. At least not in the United States. The women folk of her family and country were victims themselves, and had also seen other female victims of severe abuse, rapes, killings, mutinies, maiming, kidnappings, and acts of extreme violence back in Africa.

The lesbian duo started out dating in the beginning, to somewhat get a feel for each other, and then they fell in love with this particular taboo. Jackie had never been involved with a male companion on any level in her life, and would cringe in disgust at the very thought of a dick being penetrated inside her. She'd had too many experiences of being repeatedly molested, sexually assaulted, and sodomized at the hands of men—**African Black men**—upon her village being, almost always, raided and terrorized in wars over blood diamonds and/or any political unrest. But most often, just for the hell of it by local gangs.

She was literally raised and taught by her grandmother, her mother, aunts, and elder womenfolk about the brutal and atrocious acts of violence that almost always seemed to occur against women in her country, in addition to eventually becoming a victim herself at age seven. In her mind, after having suffered and endured such "nightmares," so to speak, it became "natural" for her to develop a bond and have love and affection for another female—sexually or otherwise—as opposed to being in love with an untrustworthy, abusive, ravenous, dirty, low-down dog that men were to her.

Lesbianism became her preferred lifestyle in its pure and rawest form. She would remain this way indefinitely.

Chapter 5

Choosy Lover...

The understanding and relationship between the attorney and her client—Jettica and Michael—gained strength, both on a business level and a personal one. With each visit she made to the prison, things got more interesting. She was successful with his transfer, and he'd asked her to make one to two appearances a month, if possible. She obliged, being that his case was the most complex and toughest one she'd ever accepted in her career.

Their friend, Tomeka, did play a critical role in the acquaintance between the two. Michael slyly used Tomeka as the middle person to forward emails and personal handwritten letters and gifts to ReeRee in his efforts to woo her to the best of his abilities. ReeRee had not known that it was Tomeka who told Michael her entire life story, including the parts of the two of them being intimate, and that of her being involved with Cadillac Nate.

After the initial two attorney-client visits, he made it a priority to keep in contact with Tomeka through the contraband cellphone he always seemed to get his hands on. He allowed Tomeka ample opportunity to chat away about ReeRee.

"'Meka, you referred me to the right lawyer, my girl. I can't thank you enough," he said.

"I told you, bro. She got it going on, don't she? And in two good ways ... as an attorney ... and as a desirable. Didn't

I tell you?" Tomeka responded, smiling like crazy on her end of the phone.

"Girl ... what you talkin' about?" Michael let out ecstatically. "Shorty is the truth," he replied with excitement at the thought of ReeRee.

"She has always been a beautiful and sexy female. You should have seen her though, back when we first got to college together. She woulda sho-nuff blew your muthafuckin' mind, bro. But she ain't lost too much nothing, if anything at all. Not having babies helped her out too. At least I don't know of her having any."

"So she don't have any kids?" he asked.

"Nope. Not to my knowledge. And she not lookin' to have any no time soon. She about to get married too, at some point soon," Tomeka revealed.

"She about to get married at some point soon?" Michael retorted.

"Calm down, my nigga! Damn! She ain't got no other nigga in her life. It's another female. Jackie is her name. Some black-ass African bitch that moved here as a teenager. She proposed about a year ago," Tomeka mentioned.

"Oh okay. So it's really no threat?" he sought to know.

"Nope. Not to a nigga like you, no way. And to be honest, I really don't think Jettica's interested in being married. Not to another woman at least. As good as I know her. She only enjoys the pleasure she gets in being with a woman intimately, and the freedom by not being attached to a nigga, and from being dominated and controlled by a man. But I'm sure she still gets dick down too. The both of us one and the same," Tomeka related on the sexual orientation of her longtime friend and previous lover, ReeRee.

"I got you on that. Because if anybody, you would be qualified to speak on her like that," he responded.

"Exactly, bro."

"Little known fact too, Mike," Tomeka began to relate more.

"What's that?" Michael asked.

"Keep in mind what I told you before, about her history in the pussy-game."

"Oh, yeah, that's right," his interest really perked now.

"Yep. In fact, the both of us do, I now confess. I didn't tell on myself before."

"Down in college, you say, right? In the strip clubs and shit?" he figured.

"You guessed it," she replied.

"Shit, y'all had to do what y'all had to do. That's understandable," he acknowledged.

"I just knew it was best to let you know everything. But without a doubt, we were real professional, and real particular in how we did our thing. In a safe and decent way," Tomeka said for the record.

"'Meka, you know I ain't the type of nigga to cast no judgment on nobody. That's not my position. I just need to know what's the best way you believe I can get her to go for me on a personal level?" he asked and wanted to know.

"Well, there's two things my girl is so fucked up about when it comes to a man—"

"And those are what?" Michael anxiously cut in.

"Any nigga that knows how to speak real well for himself. And also, a well-kept nigga—sharply dressed, clean, well-groomed—you get my drift?"

"Shit, that's second nature for me," he responded.

"You took the words right out of my mouth, bro. I was just about to say that. She picked up this admiration from the pimp nigga Nate when he had her down in Miami," Tomeka related more accurate history.

"Oh, so not only was she involved with a pimp nigga, she's infatuated with the pimp and suave-type niggaz in general, huh?" he inquired.

"Really, bro, she's infatuated with the game itself, bro. It don't hurt that you're already familiar with that type of world yourself. But my total suggestion to you is, just pop flavor to her and spit linen in her ear on the next visit, and pay attention to her reaction and body language. Trust me, if you good at it, you'll get the results you lookin' for," Tomeka stated and smiled into the screen of her laptop to encourage Michael.

"Shit! I've already done that so far. But I'll be sure to do just that again," he responded.

"I definitely suggest you do just that. ReeRee is an exceptional conversationalist, and she's one hell of a socialite, bro. She's a divine diva at heart and personality-wise. She's also an angelic princess in spirit," Tomeka shared the inner qualities of ReeRee that she knew personally. Those that she knew would arouse excitement in the nature of her homeboy, as he looked on with a smile.

He licked his lips while contemplating what all he intended to say in his next phone call to his lawyer, and in their next visit. Their conversation went on, as Tomeka equipped him with more quality information on her girlfriend—that which she knew firsthand.

The reality of it all about ReeRee was that she held great desire to be truly wanted and loved in an affectionate way, much like many normal women. She despised men who were of the voluptuary mindset, as she hated the thought of being looked at only as "a piece of meat." She didn't want anything to do with the liking nor the "love" she'd received purely based on her looks and the sexual appearance she possessed. ReeRee almost always attracted such unwanted attention.

She hadn't met a man yet who caught her off guard and appealed to her as Michael had. Not in quite some time. The thing was that he was in prison, and also a client of hers—someone that she had to assist and stay professional with. But the personal yearnings and feminine nature of hers had gotten invited, and curiosity overtook ReeRee in many regards. And even if it kills the cat—curiosity, that is—she knew it became important for her to get a grip on herself before it actually does. Or else, fall prey to the whims and sensuality that Michael was capable of putting into effect.

***

Having It Both Ways...

Aside from the relationship ReeRee was involved in with Jackie, she'd met and dated a guy by the name of Andrew Proctor, a producer in the music industry from College Park, Atlanta, Georgia. He was in L.A. on business frequently, which was also the times he would often spend with ReeRee. They had done it this way anytime he'd come through. They shared a long-distance relationship, as this had best suited them both—being he didn't want her knowing everything about his personal life so soon, and she the same.

Andrew knew a little about Jackie but not much, as he really didn't care what ReeRee had going on outside of what they had, so long as he got his time and respect whenever he visited. They were to spend the weekend together at one of the upscale hotels Los Angeles had to offer. ReeRee had lied to Jackie by telling her she was flying to New York to be with family.

Jackie had begun to get suspicious of ReeRee already, being that she stayed gone on trips too often for her liking and had all of a sudden begun to be showered with gifts— the kind that had value to them. Jewelry, designer bags, and designer brand label clothes were some of the items that Michael bought for her and presented through Tomeka. Jackie had knowledge of ReeRee receiving gifts from clients, but not to the proportion or price tag that Michael was sending, along with those that Andrew was known to send as well. It was becoming a bit too much for Jackie, as she went through fits and bouts of jealousy when left at the house alone.

She brainstormed on many occasions, trying to figure out what her beloved ReeRee had going on, and if or not she was losing her. But she was to know more than she could handle in due time. Much more.

Andrew and ReeRee returned to the hotel suite after a night out at the Sayers Lounge and enjoying a few rounds of cocktails. She put her phone on Airplane Mode so as not to be disturbed and played music from her playlist. *No Ordinary Love* by Sade was the song to set the mood and create the erotic feel to things, as the delightful tone of the vocalist brought about a calming and relaxing effect.

ReeRee took her heels off and slipped out of her dress, leaving only her bra and matching lavender G-string on for cover. She walked over to the bed and lay across it to rest her feet momentarily, as Andrew removed his shoes and clothes. He left on a pair of solid white boxer-briefs by Joe Boxer. He was shirtless, and his skin glistened from the light of the lamp. Andrew was in possession of a lean physique, and his almond-hue complexion complimented the tones and chiseled muscles he tightened for show as ReeRee looked on.

In this instance, she said to him, "I see your gym membership still valid," she shot out in compliment.

"Oh yeah, you got to know that, honey," he responded with a smile, revealing his recently cleansed white teeth.

"I also see you ain't pissed off one of your 'ATL shawties' so much so to the point that they would have to use a knife ... a razor ... or some other sharp object to straighten you out with," she said, referring to the bulge in his underwear. His well-built python rested, coiled up and threatening to bust free from the garment.

"You got that right too," he replied with another smile, nothing short from a sinister background, it appeared. He licked his lips and stepped closer to the side of the bed where she lay.

ReeRee stood to her feet in front of him and then looked up into those hazel-colored eyes of his. Andrew stood at six-foot-three and weighed about two hundred ten pounds. She wrapped her arms around him and they tongue-kissed intensely for the better part of two minutes, nonstop, before pausing to catch their breath. She gently palmed his manhood as it now bulged further, due to him being aroused from the kissing and the hugging. She then reached into his boxers and pulled his dick from its hiding place and eased his drawers down to his knees. This was the first time ReeRee had physically laid eyes on his manhood. The most they'd ever done was have video phone sex. Nothing more. A kiss or so here and there.

"Mm uh, Andrew! My God! That's a lot of dick you got on you, boo," she said and tapped the head with four fingers, causing it to spring up and down. He was fully erect. She did it again, then held it with her right hand, squeezed it tight, and stroked twice—drawing the blood to pool at the head so it would inflate to a monster size, along with the veins. "And if you must know, I'm the type of girl who likes to have it both ways. But of course, you know this already about me."

"That, I do. And ... all eleven inches of this here dick of mine is yours to keep. So long as you continue to take good care of it, and bless me when I see fit for pleasure," he teased, waggling his manhood with one hand from side to side.

"No need to worry about that. I will," she emphatically assured. "And had I known you were holdin' like this ... nigga ... I'd been claimed it as mine by now," she responded with a pleasing look about her face and an excited smile.

"It's definitely the right time to do so," he said, and poked her in the belly with his erection.

"Ooh-ooh!" she cooed like she were the "Pillsbury dough girl" and then playfully pushed Andrew onto the bed and fully removed his boxer-briefs. She popped her bra loose and untied her G-string, then stood in the nude, with her large, 36 D-cup breasts sitting high, firm, and pretty. Her belly button was pierced and she had a gold hoop attached. She went into a belly dance routine for Andrew as the strip club banger *Money* by Cardi B played on her phone.

Andrew backed up to the headboard of the bed, flush up against it, and stretched his legs out. He licked his lips as he looked on at the performance ReeRee provided him and the seduction dance moves on display.

ReeRee could easily go for being one of those voluptuous models that grace the pages of smut and street-based magazines, with the thick booty and proportioned body she had. But an accurate description of exactly who she favored in many ways proved to be a lighter version of Megan Thee Stallion. She and ReeRee were identical to each other—height, weight, ass, hair, legs, and stance.

ReeRee danced for Andrew maybe ten minutes before she sauntered over to the bed, cat-crawled to the top, eased up his legs until she reached his dick, and then took him into her mouth—all in the same motion. She began to passionately bob up and down on his dick with those full-sized glossy lips of hers, coating it with her saliva and stroking him to peak erection. She gripped his manhood with both hands and continued to stroke and suck, then stroke and pull with her lips at the same time.

"This feel good to you?" she asked seductively.

"Hell yeah, it do, sweetie. Hell yeah, it do," he responded with a contorted face caused by the pleasing sensation he felt behind getting his dick sucked.

"That's all that matters—that you're satisfied, baby," she said, then hummed on his balls before getting up to go and grab what she had on the table. She retrieved the condom she'd brought along for the occasion, tore the wrapper loose with her hands, and re-assumed the position she had between Andrew's legs prior to getting up.

He was still standing tall, erection-wise, awaiting her to put the protection onto him. She rolled the condom down his manhood and pinched the tip for him to properly unload into. He was then ready to roll, and so was she.

"Now, let's really get it crackin', playboy," she said, and then straddled atop of him, laid her breasts on his chest, and began situating his dick into her love hole.

There were maybe two inches inserted when she began to gently slide up and down, working him into her tight hole, one stroke and one inch at a time. Finally, she'd worked all of him into her world, and she rode up and down, up and down, and up and down—allowing her juices to drain from her love box and flow down the condom-coated dick like the fruity liquid from a melting popsicle.

ReeRee straightened her back, sat upright, and began to bounce hard on the dick, as she rubbed on her breasts and pinched on her own nipples.

"Ah yeah. Ooh, this dick is nice and fulfilling inside of me, Andrew," she said, as she felt her pussy lips gripping and pulling on his manhood each time she tightened and lifted up. She moaned and panted at the pleasure she felt from the nice, fat dick she worked. ReeRee then spun around and began to ride reverse cowgirl so as to give Andrew an eyeful of all the action from behind. ReeRee worked it good maybe fifteen minutes—going up and down, back and forth, then up and down—repeating her motions to perfection.

Andrew then urged her to get up, as he stood to his feet at the end of the bed. He pulled her to the edge of the mattress by her legs and then pinned them down to her sides. He penetrated deeply once more and began to bang her hard in the 'Buck' position for a few good minutes. He had reached his climax and began to stand to his feet, pulling out of her and yanking the condom off. He spilled himself all over her belly, breasts, and neck area, as she sat up and took him into her mouth to drain the rest of what he had left to give.

He was done for the time being and collapsed onto the bed. She went to the bathroom to spit out the contents that rested in her mouth, and to also get herself situated once more. A job well done for their first time together. Singer Phyllis Hyman would totally agree to this, as her song played from the phone—titled *First Time Together*.

Chapter 6

Meanwhile...

Back on the Chicago home front, one of Nightmare's main men from the neighborhood and his crew reached out to him and provided the protégé with information he'd long awaited to hear—almost five years, to be exact. His main girlfriend—the one he was with before the indictment and arrest; the one Federal agents had gotten ahold of prior to the indictments being unsealed; and the one who they'd whisked away to a safe location so they could flip her into becoming a government witness.

This bitch sang against Nightmare on everything she knew. It was like she was a member of the Mississippi Mass Choir on the stand against him. She was the one Nightmare had long wanted killed. Baby girl was spotted and kept track of as she made a return visit home to attend the funeral of her grandmother. Nicole Beverly was granted immunity from prosecution following her assistance in securing a conviction against her longtime lover, Nightmare.

The former bodyguard, hitman, and loyalist to Nightmare—Minister Fareed Akbar—had come out of retirement and was back in the murder game. He was looking to do more work. He wanted to complete contracts and make lots of dough. Here was a man who was eight years the senior to the guy he took orders from, who had run into an old girlfriend of his—the mother of Nicole—and was informed that her mother, Nicole's grandma, had passed away. He consoled and comforted his fling, Pauline, in her time of grief.

Minister Akbar was at one point a staunch advocate and student of the Nation of Islam and had been so for all his life. He often visited Chicago's Muhammad Mosque No. 2. He was in exceptionally grand shape to be his age—fifty-one—and had only put in work in killing when there was cause for him to be a necessary evil to destroy a greater evil. He was a mentor to Nightmare, Ricky, Teddy, and many other young street cats that lined the ranks of the Vice Lords, through his street academy in the West Side of the Chi. Minister endured many street battles and wars and acted as hired muscle—carrying out contracts and putting people in the dirt, if the ends justified the means.

Nicole's mother, Pauline, welcomed Minister over to the home of her parents, and this was when he'd spotted Nicole there with her family, preparing to bury a loved one. He knew exactly who she was, but she had not too much of a clue—or cared to know—who in the hell he was. It had been so long. She thought Minister to be just another man her frolicking mom brought along to meet her family, similar to the many she'd invited before.

Minister observed Nicole on numerous occasions, as he'd visited their places of living through the years, upon meeting Nightmare there for business or otherwise. Mostly late nights. Minister was connected to Deno, another associate and the guy who Nightmare appointed to lead the newly formed regime of his. Deno was the middleman between Nightmare and Minister. The three were still on the same team but operated under different protocols than they had previously, due to the original team being split and Ricky moving on about his business as he were.

Prior to Minister being a preacher in the religious ranks and way of life with the FOI—which his father raised him to be—he was a strong associate to the Vice Lords. He earned his stripes as a freelance hitter who had taught Nightmare a thing or two in the craft. Minister traveled from Chicago to other major cities that dotted the United States, most notably Philadelphia, and put in work. He and a partner of his named Eddie—a dude who represented Junior Black Mafia (JBM) and then later returned to Islam—handled business. Eddie was known in the streets as 'E-Rock,' but in religion, as Jabbar El-Amin.

Minister reached out to Deno and asked that he get with Nightmare and relate that he had some news for him—that they needed to talk ... ASAP. Deno did so, and Nightmare called Minister to see what his once-mentor and executioner had to share with him. Nightmare sent a coded text message at first to alert Minister that it was indeed him and that he was about to call.

Minister answered, "Talk to me!"

"Minister! What's good with you, my guy?" Nightmare greeted.

"I'm well, youngsta. How you?" Minister replied.

"Likewise. How's life been treatin' you out there, old man?" Nightmare joked.

"Don't nothin' get old but the clothes on me, baby boy. That's a fact," Minister shot back to tease further.

"Deno tells me you got some news for me? Real news I can use." Nightmare wasted no more time outside of wanting to know what the business was.

"Yeah, that's right. I do."

"Okay. Hit me with it."

"One of your problems that you weren't able to solve before or after the trial," Minister said.

"Which one?" Nightmare was eager to know.

"The one that was real personal to you. The pretty young tender you had close by your side," Minister reminded. "The daughter of one of my old flings," he added.

"Nicole?" Nightmare stated, to know if or not he answered correctly.

"The one and only, junior. They got death in the family. Grandma died. She came out of hiding to lay her to rest," Minister informed Nightmare.

"Is that so!" he responded and became excited at the prospect of knowing he could now finally have her ass touched.

"I was at the house with Pauline just yesterday. She don't know me right off or doesn't seem to remember me. Not even if they offered her a billion bucks to do so," Minister stated.

"Damn. Shit is that easy?" Nightmare responded, questioning the words of his assassin, as the information took him by surprise.

"Like a few in the past. So sweet. But guess what? This one here is gonna be on the house, baby boy. Because any act of treason is to be punishable by death," Minister spat.

"This perfect timing too, Minister, because I just got this lawyer to argue my case on appeal, and she advised there's a good chance I could see the light of day. So, hey, take care of this for me, and my path to freedom should be clearer of potholes and blocks in the way," Nightmare stated.

"So, we can look forward to the family being united again?" Minister inquired.

"Strong possibility, my guy. Strong possibility. This your number here, right?" Night asked.

"One of them, at least," Minister replied.

"Good, because I've got something in the making for you down South in Miami," Nightmare informed. "It's a favor that need to be done for a real nigga who I connected with. And it's gonna set us up for a bigger play with him and his crew at some point in the future."

"Anytime, baby boy. Anytime," the old head responded.

"But damn! I only wish like hell that I could personally do this one myself, or at least watch it as it goes down," Nightmare said.

"Shit, nigga! Is this what you want?"

"That would be nice," replied Nightmare to Minister.

"Okay. Say no more. Ain't no need to wish for things that you could already have. I'll put some of my new spyware to work and record the entire affair, and then I can get it to you in your email. This'll be the newest version of *Nightmare on Elm Street* for you. The long-awaited conclusion," spat Minister.

"Ha-ha-ha-ha! You always have been a super-producer and some type of director in the game, Minister. I like the sound of that. But yeah, go ahead and handle this for me, and I'll get back at you with the details of the other work," stated Nightmare.

"Salute," replied Minister.

"Salute," Nightmare responded.

They ended the call.

***

Nightmare felt good as ever in knowing that his once main sleaze, a female that he liked and took very good care of, was in the throes of death—on its brink—and was soon to be sent to meet her maker. She had a grave penalty to pay, for flipping in the way she did, and snitching on Nightmare and about all else she knew.

There was something personal that needed to be settled between the two, and Minister couldn't have been more on time than he was. Nightmare was on the eve of approaching court litigations, and the possibility existed that once the process got going good, the government may attempt to re-contact all of the witnesses, especially those that were key. But, 'No Face, No Case,' would leave the prosecutor in a helpless predicament, without being able to utilize the tools that were previously at their disposal, and such a thing would better enable Nightmare in getting the type of relief he had long awaited to have.

***

The day after Nicole's grandmother was laid to rest proved to be the perfect opportunity for Minister to do what it was he had to do. Nicole's granddad was a borderline dementia patient, and the agreement by the family was that Nicole and her mother, Pauline, would look after and care for the old man. Mister Clarence Beverly was situated in bed at the home he'd bought and had lived in for many years. Pauline and Minister rented a room at one of the low-budget motels on the West Side, not too far from her parents' home. They wanted to be together intimately, so as to make up for lost time.

It was a late Sunday night, and they were in the process of leaving Nicole and her two-year-old there at the house with Mister Clarence, at least until the next day. Pauline put her father to bed and readied herself to leave with Minister. Before walking out the door, Minister had to go use the bathroom and relieve himself of all those cups of Gatorade he'd drank, being he didn't consume alcohol as did Pauline and Nicole. He only had the duty of going to the store to buy what they wanted, and then pour their servings for them. Nicole herself called it an early night, as she was given a little assistance by the hand of Minister. He'd slipped a powerful sleeping agent into the bottle of what Nicole was drinking from.

While in the bathroom, he was sure to unlock the window so that he could have easy access back into the house on the upper stair level. He drove himself and Pauline to the motel and they fucked like two jack rabbits. He knew that once he'd put it on her really good, in the way that only he could— ol' Bobby Joe Floyd (born name)—she'd take her worn-out ass straight to sleep, just like always. He wasted no time in laying down the pipe and then was to be on his way to carry out a hit.

One hour later, Minister was back at the residence, climbing up the drainpipe that led along the backside wall of the house, and easing through the window like a stealth cat burglar. Minister was armed with one of his favorite killing tools of choice: a two-foot-long piano wire string cord, along with an ice pick and a nine-millimeter pistol. He had also brought along a mini spy camcorder to document the deadly affair and later forward to Nightmare, so that he'd have the pleasure to see the rat-bitch being murdered behind the dirty deeds she'd perpetrated against him.

As Minister crawled fully into the space of the bathroom, he heard heavy sighing, yawning, and footsteps approaching. Just as the door to the bathroom was opening, he quickly hopped into the bathtub and behind the dark-colored curtain. Someone turned on the light and yawned again. Minister recognized that it was Nicole. He stood as motionless as possible to prevent blowing his cover. She sat on the toilet, took a piss, then she wiped, flushed, and stood at the sink to wash her hands. This was the perfect time to make his move.

He tapped the button to activate the camcorder and then lunged forward at her from behind the curtain in a swift and decisive fashion, looping the cord around Nicole's throat and tightening it faster than she could blink.

Minister was a bit on the tall side—six foot four, to be exact—and as he tightened the cord securely, he lifted the five-foot-even body frame of Nicole off her feet, causing her to kick, squirm, and frantically try to break free from the executioner's stranglehold. It was all to no avail. Nicole was helpless. She'd been condemned to death.

"Yeah, you little bitch! You gon' learn today not to rat on another muthafucka ever again in your goddamn life, you little piece of shit, you!" Minister spat. He yanked her around like a rag doll in mid-air.

He then tossed her to the floor and straddled her from behind, so as to go ahead and viciously strangle the last breath of life out of Nicole. She gagged morbidly as the wire cut deep into her throat. Then she stopped moving altogether, and her body twitched one last time before she was to be no more. Minister still clutched the wire tightly for another two minutes after the fact of murdering her. He'd always ensured to 'overkill' on any of his hits, as not doing so in the beginning of his career as a killer almost cost him his own life. He learned the lesson from that encounter: to overdo it at all cost. He had to suffer a hollow point to the back and one to the ass in order to know better. And the evidence of this is found in the slight limp he has in his normal walk. The lesson was learned.

Breathing semi-heavy and near winded, he spat epithets at the corpse once he unwrapped his wire and began to wipe the blood from it.

"Goddamnit! You little fine bitch, you! I done bust a muthafuckin' nut on myself killing you! Now I guess I'll have to go fuck ya momma again to end this well," he concluded, put the rolled-up wire in the pocket of his black wool overcoat, stepped over the dead body, and exited the home out the back door. He tapped the button to stop the recording and made his way back to the motel to fuck Pauline yet again.

Love and murder was the game Minister played. He was a superstar while in action, and a well-skilled veteran at his craft.

Chapter 7

Six Months Later...

This was the tenth attorney-client visit between ReeRee and Nightmare over the course of seven months, as he wanted to see her at least twice every thirty days leading to this point. She had not a problem with his request—none at all—being that he tipped well, wrote fairly decent letters, and thoroughly complimented her in those personal letters he forwarded through Tomeka. Atop all of this, she had a deep attraction towards him. She liked the guy.

You could only suppress the amorous nature of a woman for so long before she gave in to the whims of her desires. This be especially true for a woman who has a duty to be in the presence of a handsome man—one that she's infatuated with.

Nightmare had reasoned with himself that this particular visit would be the one where he would hit the gas full-throttle, with all he had to sway her with. He felt he had to have her. And by continuing to hold back, he was doing himself no good.

ReeRee had always been flattered and taken by a well-to-do man—especially someone who knew how to woo her with words and was determined to have what he wanted and who he wanted. That part of her nature had been shaped and groomed by Nate during the time he had her. No one else had filled this void in her life after him.

And so, she toyed around with the reality of being involved with another woman, and the personalities—along with a high level of jealousy—began to clash with hers, until she found herself trying to get away at any available opportunity. This was why she took pleasure in the frequent visits to see Nightmare. She also had duties and desired to visit with a female client of hers in Federal lockup in Connecticut, and her own family on the East Coast during these trips. So, it all went hand-in-hand. Everything worked for her.

Nightmare was able to trigger something within ReeRee that caused her to be reminiscent and relish her 'glory days' as a college girl—the time when she began to sell sex while under the foot and the applied pressure of the all-powerful and 'God-like' Cadillac Nate.

As Nightmare talked and responded to her, she stood at times and paced here and there. She finally took a seat in the chair reserved for her, directly across from him, only two feet away, and had gotten silent as a nun in a convent during prayer hours—displaying a humble and pleasant smile.

She propped her right hand under her chin with her elbow mounted on the table and allowed Nightmare ample opportunity to spew his intoxicating and mesmerizing lines of pimp-laced philosophy all over her neonatal soul. ReeRee literally soaked up every letter, every word, every phrase, and every mind-tantalizing expression that he'd articulated in this visit.

Nightmare felt more so than anything that he had convinced her, in a good sense, to no longer hold back herself—and at least establish some form of meaningful contact that the two of them could have without the use of a middle person, as the personal relations began to gain strength.

"Jettica! Is it okay for me to call you that? Or would you prefer ReeRee in private?" he asked.

"Whichever one you choose, Michael, is *perfectly* fine by me," she replied, placing emphasis on the word *perfectly,* now knowing he'd be able to read between the lines.

"That's good to know. I'm sure it's no secret to you by now that I find you to be a very attractive woman. So much so to the point that I'd go out on the limb in the way I have, in my pursuit of you," he revealed. This was a confession, basically. The first and only one he'd ever made in his life.

"Your letters and your gifts have done all the talking for you, Michael. And I adore you in every aspect of the word. You have nice taste. And you know how to make good choices in the type of women you desire, I must admit. And I took a liking to you the very first time I laid eyes upon you. You're such a magnificent specimen of a man and handsome as ever," ReeRee responded.

"Well, I thank you dearly for the compliments. Can't say that I get this too often, with the exception of a few catcalls from these female staff members who work here every now and again," he said to her.

He touched on something with his remarks of other women. ReeRee, hating to be the one not to have the full spotlight on her, became pissed at the thought of other women lusting on a man whom she's interested in—and also providing the most meaningful help for. She replied in a way to clearly let Nightmare know that he was hers to have, and he shouldn't concern himself with no other woman other than she—or maybe her alter ego.

"Michael, look! I'm gonna make this plain and simple as I can for you, okay? So listen carefully and internalize every word I say. Because I won't repeat myself at no other time afterwards. Understand?"

He produced an illustrious smile that spread from ear to ear. "I gotcha on this. But go ahead and speak your peace."

"Good! But ... other than your mother, whom I've had the pleasure to meet already—bless her heart—I am *the only* woman that you need to be placing any and all of your focus on, all of your energy on, and all of your attention on. You got that? Thou shall not put no other woman before thee!" she proclaimed, strongly stating her own commandments with a stern look about her face. She flinched not once.

Nightmare continued to smile excitedly and then finally responded, "It's been a long time since I last had a woman to tell me what I need to do. But I like that though. And the one and only thing I want to know is ... what exactly do you intend to do in order to keep me locked in on you and with you? Now tell me that," he demanded to know.

"I promise, you'll be the first to know in due time. Just get with 'Meka, and she'll give you everything. She'll thoroughly spell it out for me, because I don't have the time nor the full privacy to do so," she replied.

"That'll work, since you already strongly seem to suggest what I need to be doing. But I do believe you to be the one to take good care of my wants, my needs, and possibly, my desires," he stated to her.

"I'm a phenomenal woman, Michael, in all my wiles and ways. I shall do my part exceptionally well. And that's all you need to know for right now. Stay tuned," she confidently spat.

"Well damn! I feel like the luckiest nigga in the world at this point."

"If you keep up the good work like you are, you just may be," she responded and provided all the hope that he could ask for.

ReeRee had never been the one to mix business with pleasure up until recently. She had not so much as given it a thought, to entertain anything romantically with any of her clients—male or female. But ... there were qualities about Nightmare, and certain sublime aspects to him, that pushed and pulled on her in such a special way that it became impossible for her to ignore. The thoughts of him on a personal level, that is.

He was an enigma to her. Something of a special kind. And she found herself getting more and more involved with him as things progressed. Nightmare was in a win-win situation.

***

Once ReeRee was to return to LA, she would eventually open a post office box exclusively for her and Nightmare to communicate by letters. She was also intent on buying a separate phone, so they could talk more often, and do all other things to ensure that he had effective means of keeping up with her. She now demanded *all* of his attention. It was like she became obsessed with him in a sense. Like she was eager to prove something to him and to herself.

ReeRee only had to be sure to keep any of her business with Nightmare out of the way of Jackie at all cost. Jealousy is definitely a deadly emotion, one that is subject to destroy any bond, any relationship, any marriage, any friendship, or otherwise. What ReeRee and Nightmare were to embark on, was no different than anything a man and a woman in free society had going on. There was no exception to the rule. In fact, this may have made it worse. For those in the free world. Because, if a man with life in prison has what it takes to captivate and gain the attention of a woman, that's already deeply involved, professional, and of high value, this may ignite a fire in the other partner in the relationship. Or possibly instigate a war, even.

***

Maybe This Is Best...

Over time, Nightmare and the friend Ricky had found common ground between one another and had come to an agreement to peacefully part ways and move on about business on an independent basis. All that Nightmare wanted was his fair share of the empire he'd played a part in building: a few million dollars in cash or assets, and the freedom of choice for the soldiers who wanted to line themselves amongst the ranks he had Deno actively expanding. Ricky, on the other hand, wanted to usurp the throne, which he felt he had the right to inherit at the death of his brother, the former leader.

Nightmare and Ricky were once the best of friends and still maintained a bond besides the head-bumping they encountered through the years. The truth of the matter is that Nightmare held animosity towards Ricky behind the fact that Ricky and the other three directly close to him were acquitted at trial, and he—with his close people—ended up getting found guilty. Something didn't sit too well with him in this. Because how could he and all of his close people get found guilty in a joint trial, while Ricky and all of his close people knew to become wise enough to have separate trials—and all be acquitted? And how did the government know exactly who was who, and whose back each other had? This was how they managed to get two separate indictments as well. Nightmare was super determined to know the full truth—even if it took the remainder of his natural life to do so.

Nightmare felt in his heart that Ricky had assisted the government in being made aware of dearly important aspects of their group—the kind of stuff only he and Ricky should've known about. No one else. Nightmare held in his spirit that Ricky may have turned informant at some point along the way. Especially so, being him, of all people, was the first to get convicted. He was the first to fall. The government had him listed as the leader. Therefore, all the RICO charges and the Kingpin laws immediately applied to him and his punishment.

Of the twenty-plus millions of dollars the crew made through the years, Ricky only cut Nightmare about

$900,000. Nightmare demanded five million in installments, and a clean cut of ties for all the members who sided with him and Deno. Ricky reluctantly agreed but made the argument that his brother hadn't technically declared anyone the successor to the throne at the point of him dying twelve years before their arrest. And to prove his point, Ricky copied pages into a journal of his own from the one his brother left behind. It was the 'Will' and wishes for the gang, so to speak—highlighting and specifically detailing the structure of the gang, the names and list of the members, the amount of money they had and were making, literature of the gang, gang protocol, and the whole nine yards. Ricky had only needed a trustworthy person to get this essential journal into the hands of Nightmare, so as to settle their dispute once and for all.

Nightmare intended to pay a guard very good money to pick up and deliver the documented journal to him. But then, along came ReeRee—an even better option. He and Ricky had a conversation leading up to the day that ReeRee was to meet him—Ricky—to pick up money, along with the journal. Nightmare opted to send her and not his parents. He didn't want them getting involved and possibly being caught on surveillance with a drug Kingpin. He couldn't risk this. And as with Nightmare, Deno passed Ricky the phone number. Ricky was so ready to talk.

He texted a coded message to let Nightmare know that, in fact, it was he. Two hours later, Nightmare called back.

"Rick, here," he answered.

"Chief Ricky! What's good, Lord?" Nightmare greeted.

"The usual, Lord. Just keeping things prosperous—business-wise, at least. What's on your mind these days, bro?" Ricky responded.

"Just being sure to uphold the oath that I swore to and keeping in contact with you. We haven't had the chance to get up with one another lately. What's really good?" Nightmare said.

"I've been staying on the low and out the way, Lord. While at the same time, continuing to build on the empire that bro brought me into," Ricky mentioned.

"That's word right there. Big time, it is. But anyway, I hired this lawyer chick to litigate my case for me," Nightmare let Ricky know.

"Oh yeah? What she talking like?" Ricky asked, so as to know the legal status of Nightmare.

"It's too early to call it right now," Nightmare mentioned, and dared not let Ricky know anything about the possibility of there being a *Brady Violation*—a major issue that could potentially free him sooner or later.

"It's too early to call it, huh? What was the ticket for her?" Ricky asked.

"About three hundred and fifty K. She part of the firm I hired, but she's the lead attorney," Nightmare let Ricky know.

"You say about three hundred and fifty K? Shit ... for that type of paper, she better be worth it. So where she located?" he asked.

"She based out in Cali. Twice a month, she fly out to see me. I've had her for several months now. I was referred to her from a chick I know on the home turf," Nightmare let him know. "We've made a few personal ties too, Lord," Nightmare added.

"Oh yeah?" he replied.

"That's right. You already know I couldn't resist the thought of shooting my best shot. I believe I've struck gold."

"Like that?" asked Ricky.

"Like that, Lord. But on the business side of what I wanted to talk with you about—the both of us agreed that it would be best to part ways and do our own thing, right?"

"That's correct, so as to save the bond between you and I, and to also keep the peace. Maybe this is best," Ricky said.

"Understood. But you slowed down on fulfilling the terms of the agreement. The money been slack. What's that all about?" Nightmare wanted to know.

"Lord, to be honest with you, there never was a timetable as to when all the money had to be paid. We only agreed that it would be—eventually. And not only that, I had to fish around for a new connect once I got free. This was behind everything going downhill with the old supplier. Your people got ghost. And much of the money that once again started to come had to be kicked back out to keep things rolling. I did get almost a million to you, and let your soldiers go do what you nccdcd thcm to do behind your guy Deno. But you do know that my brother left behind one hell of an empire. And we added onto that in a major way. So what I'm saying is ... what type of niggas are we, to fuck up what all we and the Vice Lord family has created?" Ricky stated in a sorrowful way, in his attempt to reconcile the differences he and Nightmare had caused to the team with their beef.

"You know something, Rick, you make sense in a lot of ways. But the reality of it all is that—we too big to continue on and follow behind each other. It's only right that we have our own team and lead our own people. And if I get lucky to be set free, then we could possibly unite again. Because ain't no beef or bloodshed gonna take place between us. Only egos and clashes in personality may happen. That's about it. You feel like you could do it better your way, and I feel as though I can do it better how I see fit. But maybe one day, we'll get it right," Nightmare said to Ricky and awaited to know what all he had to say to what he'd stated.

"Oh yeah," Nightmare interjected and began to speak more. "I almost forgot. You haven't kept me up to date with the recent lit, the protocol, and also on all the business transactions and order of affairs in a long time. You know it was customary that we brief the team at least once a month— on who we added, who we let go, who we got rid of forever, and you know, the overall order of affairs. Although we oversee our own unit now, we still under the same structure, Lord," Nightmare acknowledged.

"Absolutely, Lord. Absolutely. And at all cost, we got to respect that. Look, here's what I'm gonna do. Being that I change my number a lot and we may lose contact again—I'm gonna leave you with a post office box address, and I'm also gonna copy over everything you've asked for on the order of affairs of ours, dating back as far as I can. I'll put everything in a journal for you, and then get it to you at that point. I was intending to do this anyway. So, how trustworthy is this lawyer chick of yours?" Ricky asked.

"Obviously, I trust her with my life."

"Good. So you should be able to send her my way at some point soon, right?"

"I was thinking along these lines already. You took the words right outta my mouth," Nightmare stated.

"Okay. Bet. And I got about four hundred K for you, and I'll have the journal ready by the time she gets here. She can do all you need her to do with the money, and eventually get the journal to you. Then, a few months later, I'll send more money—and then more material. Bet?" Ricky stated, doing all he could to keep Nightmare calm and not instigate a war.

"Bet. That's what's up, bro. I'll be sure to send her your way at the earliest time possible. You can link her to one of your nieces and they'll be our go-between people for you and me. Teddy's daughter Alana, maybe. I've also been busy trying to formulate and structure our nation here on the inside too. But, I'ma let you go. I know you busy as hell these days, Lord. I'll be in touch," Nightmare stated.

"That's a bet, Lord. I'm out. One," Ricky responded.

"One," lastly said Nightmare, and they ended the call.

Nightmare held other agendas outside of all Ricky had going on, but had to make it sound legit to Rick, so as to get him to turn over more money to finance the moves he so desired to make. Of the $900,000 or so Ricky had already passed off, he was down to about $275,000 after lawyer fees and buying a home for his parents in a faraway city from Chicago—but still in Illinois.

Nightmare could definitely use all the money he could possibly get to build his very own personal structure how he saw fit. He would soon convince his attorney/newfound friend to travel to Chicago to pick up money and the journal.

Chapter 8

Keeping Friends Close...

ReeRee maintained steady contact with Tomeka, and supplied her all the personal information she needed about herself Tomeka hadn't already known, so that she could be reached by Nightmare once Tomeka provided him with everything. Tomeka wasted no time in reaching out to him so to provide the information ReeRee wanted him to have. And so, the personal relations of the two—Nightmare and ReeRee—had gotten stronger, as he had a direct line to her now. He contacted his newfound female interest about one week after being provided the information from Tomeka.

"ReeRee, what's been good with you, lovely lady? I miss you already," he greeted.

"Hey, Michael. I've been well. Just been busy working my caseloads down to a respectable low number. I can't allow myself to be overwhelmed with my work," she responded.

"I know what you mean by that. But what we looking like on your end?" he inquired.

"Everything going accordingly. I've got another hearing to attend in about three weeks. A conference call won't do on this one. I've got to fly to Chicago and make oral arguments to the court. That'll be my best opportunity to argue Brady Violation then. At the beginning of placing things on the record. No doubt, I should be able to prove my case," ReeRee mentioned.

"That'll be perfect, because there are a few things I need for you to pick up for me while you there," he said.

"A few things you need me to pick up like what?" she retorted.

"A few things like ... a tip for you ... additional funds I need for you to put in an Escrow for me, and a literary journal I need for you to bring to me at one of our future visits. One of my business partners and I have severed ties, and he's paying me my cut from the company. I don't want to have it put in the bank just yet, because I know that the government will more than likely freeze my accounts, or that of my parents. And I'm not trying to go through all that anymore. Besides, you all I've got to fully trust and to rely upon. I trust you with my life. And now, I've got to trust you with my money and the arrangement of my business affairs as well. I also need you to bring three thousand in cash on your next visit, okay? Are you willing to help me? I hope so. It's something in it for you," Nightmare uttered with a bright smile into the camera lens of the phone. They were on video call.

"Michael, I'm your attorney and your female companion. I have no choice but to assist you in your affairs. That's what I'm legally and now personally assigned to do," stated ReeRee.

"That's good to know. That's very good to know. Once you get to Chicago, I'll let you know who to meet and where. But in the meantime, what's really good with you? How has your day been? How has life been treating you?" Nightmare asked to initiate stimulating conversation between the two of them. "And ever since those two counseling sessions with the psychiatrist you had me undergo, for some reason, I feel so much freer, and better, and at ease. Talking with dude and speaking my mind was therapeutic. I may wanna do more of this in the future. Especially so when you get me outta this muthafucka! I'm just saying."

"That's real good to know. And I knew that those examinations and having the psychiatrist to talk with you would help you open up more and appear more human. You present a totally different energy about yourself already. I'm witnessing the results."

"Oh yeah! I feel super good. And I'm no monster like the government tried to make me out to be, either!" he emphatically stated.

"No Michael ... no you're not," ReeRee responded.

They began to converse deeply now, as ReeRee did have time to talk, being she'd gotten out of the house momentarily from Jackie, and took a ride to go treat herself to a fruit bowl and a smoothie.

The two of them did have moments here and there of which they would relate personal matters of their lives and history, but hadn't seriously talked as they wanted to. ReeRee hadn't yet let Michael know personally about Jackie, and he only had information of her through Tomeka. As they talked this night, she felt the need to let him know what caused her the brief bouts of stress and frustration she would sometimes experience. It was her so-called significant other bringing drama into the equation.

He brought up the particular subject. "So tell me something," he said.

"What would you like to know?" she replied.

"This Jackie female. Who is she?" he inquired.

"Jackie, yeah, Jackie. I never told you about her?" ReeRee responded to him.

"Nope. I was made aware of her by Meka."

"Well, she's someone I connected with in law school, and we started dating from that point. We graduated and decided that we'd explore the opportunity of living together. It's nothing too major, though. She do her thing and I do mine. The relationship we share is an open one, because we work on certain occasions together and also live together. But up until recent, everything had been going lovely, but then she began to get jealous and become controlling in a way. That was the purpose of establishing an open relationship—to keep nothing concealed and to try to prevent what she has become. I began to lose interest in what we had and communicated those feelings to her in a way she'd clearly understand. She tightened up with her behavior for a time being, and then went back to it. That was when I said, you know what, fuck it! I deserve muthafuckin' better than this shit! And I'm gonna let my guard down and allow the next best person the opportunity to get to know me, whether that be a male or a female, because affection is affection, and it doesn't matter which sex you get it from. Just so long as you get it! You feeling me on this?"

"That was well put. How long you've been rehearsing that?" he asked jokingly and with a smile.

They both laughed at his witty remark and she went on, "At the time I made the decision to make myself susceptible to be taken by someone else, you came into the equation."

"Is that right? Sounds like perfect timing to me. What you think?" he responded.

"Maybe so. We are off to a good start though. And I find myself liking you," she said.

"What's all that noise in the background?" he asked.

"Oh that ... I'm close to the LAX. I love to park near the end of the runways and watch planes land and take off. It's a particular spot where I park just outside the perimeter fence. I needed to get a peace of mind, and this is one of my main spots, if not the main spot, where I come to in order to have this. I love to come here when I need to reset and get between my thoughts," she related.

"Oh, okay. That's very thoughtful and unique," he responded, and they continued in deep conversation.

The time was about nine forty-five on a Saturday night and still sort of early for the both of them. Nightmare took this to be the best opportunity to probe her further and know more of her personal life—her likes, her dislikes, the things she cherished most, fond memories she possessed—the whole nine yards. They were sure to get thoroughly acquainted with one another from this day forward, at least conversation-wise, and then proceed further as time passed.

It's very amazing how a man can compel a woman, with words, to give into him and allow him the chance to be in her life and lead the way, in all they may decide to do. Nightmare's charismatic wit and charming personality he presented through conversation had ReeRee enchanted and captivated beyond her wildest imagination. She relished and adored the promise and the potential he presented.

ReeRee couldn't overcome the thought and the feelings she'd become affected with—those of how good of a man he would be upon being granted a second chance at life, and no longer buried alive with life in the Feds. His approach and the way he went about doing things with ReeRee was magical to her in many ways.

Nightmare had old-school values and principles still in his possession. Qualities which ReeRee absolutely loved and respected. Besides this, he was a little older than she, and she was fond of these types—hence Cadillac Nate, her father, her boss she worked for at the law firm, and Andrew. These tended to be the most meaningful guys. They all had years over her in living and knowing how to navigate their way through life.

She was extremely excited at the prospect of all that Nightmare presented, and she could hardly wait to assist him in all he wanted to do. She was so ready and eager to prove a point in how thorough and real she was willing to be to someone, anyone, who she was truly feeling, and wanted to explore the possibilities with. ReeRee surmised that she'd found everything in Nightmare. Everything she's ever wanted and desired in a man—she found it with him.

Two Weeks Later...

ReeRee made the trip to Chicago to meet with Ricky and pick up the money, along with the journal he'd prepared for Nightmare. It was a Thursday, and the intent was to stay the weekend in the Windy City, as she was to be paired with one of the nieces of Ricky and forge an acquaintance. The two of them were to be the people Ricky and Nightmare would rely upon for pick-up and delivery services in the future. And if they developed something more, the better.

Alana Nechelle Isaacs, the daughter of Teddy and the niece of Ricky, was prepared to meet ReeRee later in the evening for the two to have a night out on the town and begin a weekend which was to be filled with fun. ReeRee arrived in Chicago at about eleven that morning and wanted a little rest before she was to get out and about. She'd checked into one of the ritziest hotels in downtown, The W, as this would be where she'd rest each night. She took a nap as intended, and had set the alarm clock for six p.m.

Upon waking, ReeRee took a shower, brushed her teeth, put on some music, and pampered herself as she stayed nude under the robe she had on. She then sent a text to Nightmare to let him know she was in his hometown, and asked that he call whenever he became available to do so. He did thirty minutes later.

"What's good, ReeRee? I see you made it," he greeted her in the screen of his phone as the video call began.

"I'm doing wonderful, Michael. You okay?" she asked.

"I am. Just chilling, and was about to watch a few movies once I'm done talking with you. Has Alana called yet? Rick told me he would introduce you two," he inquired.

"Yeah, we spoke briefly when I made it here. I let her know I'd call once I was ready for her to come and pick me up. You familiar with her?" she asked.

"I am," he replied. "Don't forget, sweetie, Ricky and I were once best friends. I know his entire family, and they all know me. We grew up together, basically. We were about sixteen or so at the time we became friends," he advised ReeRee.

"Got ya on that. The reason I asked is because she speaks of you in a way that clearly lets me know you are a friend of the family. But maybe more for her though," she said.

"That's because I am family. And her father was someone who I was really close to. But I assume you two intend to have a busy weekend, huh?"

"Oh yeah, we are. She told me that we'd be going to some of the best spots in the city, the ones that grown and sexy women like ourselves visit to socialize," she said.

"Alana is a real socialite. She loves to visit mature spots. I can't blame her for that, because Chicago could get a little chaotic from time to time," Nightmare said.

"I'm reminded of that on the news almost daily," ReeRee responded.

The two of them talked about thirty minutes more before she got dressed and then called Alana to come and pick her up.

Alana appeared at the hotel maybe forty minutes later, and was dressed to kill. She was the type of female who was infatuated with top brand-name clothing labels, as her outfit for the night exemplified her taste and fetish for this desire she possessed. She had on a form-fitting, plum-colored dress by Christian Dior, which had an opening in the front to show extra cleavage, and an elastic choker-type collar. There was a diamond-shaped opening to the dress as well, near the small of her back, revealing her caramel-complexioned skin tone. The dress extended down past her knees and to the halfway level of her shins. She had on a pair of matching pumps by Dior as well, and was holding a clutch purse by Perrin that was black in color. Her hair was fabulously done, like always, with the best quality weave that her money could pay for. It had been styled in a way that was pulled to the right side of her head and pinned behind her ear so as to reveal both her earrings by Lugans. She actually had on the full jewelry set—a bracelet, a necklace, a ring, and the earrings. Alana accentuated the dress with a thin scarf, laced across her shoulder.

She reached the front desk of the hotel lobby and requested the clerk buzz ReeRee's room to let her know she was there.

"Good day, ma'am! How may I help you?" the pretty young white female clerk asked of Alana.

"Yes, I'm here to see a Miss Jettica Jackson, please," Alana requested.

The clerk clicked and keyed on her computer at the name provided. "Miss Jettica Jackson, you say, right?" the clerk asked of Alana.

"That's correct, ma'am," Alana replied.

The clerk then picked up her phone and called ReeRee, so to receive permission to send up her guest.

"Hello," ReeRee answered.

"Yes, Miss Jackson, I have a guest here to see you, ma'am. A '*Miss Alana Isaacs*,'" the clerk read from the ID card she'd been handed.

"Yes, please send her up. Thank you."

"Okay, I will do," lastly responded the clerk. She hung up the phone and advised Alana what room ReeRee was staying in.

"Yes, Miss Isaacs, she's in room Four Nineteen, ma'am," said the clerk.

"Four Nineteen, okay. Thank you," Alana responded, and then sashayed to the elevator, tossing those forty-two-inch hips and ass of hers to each side beautifully.

On the elevator ride up, she pulled out her cellphone and called ReeRee.

"Hello," ReeRee had answered.

"Yes, ReeRee, I'm on the fourth floor now. If you can, be standing at the front door for me?" Alana had asked.

"Okay, not a problem."

Alana got off the elevator and rounded the corner where room 419 was located. She was two feet from the front door when ReeRee opened it to be greeted by the smiling face of Alana. She returned one of her own as she looked Alana twice over, silently lusting from within at the stunning allure and sex appeal the chocolate bombshell possessed. The two lovely ladies had instantly connected then and there, as though they'd known one another all their lives.

"Jettica?" Alana had asked.

"Yes, that's me. But please, call me ReeRee. And you must be Alana," she asked in reply, matching the voice to the one she'd heard on the phone.

"The one and only," Alana responded, and extended her hand to shake that of ReeRee's.

"Again, please, call me ReeRee, okay? I'm more comfortable with that," she said to Alana, so as to initiate a down-to-earth and easygoing vibe between the two.

"My pleasure ... *ReeRee*," responded Alana, as they shook hands and also caressed the forehand and palms of each other.

Chapter 9

Alana took instant observance of the dual rose gold rings ReeRee had on her left and right index fingers. The rings signaled an esoteric about the person wearing them, along with the feminine vibe that went hand-in-hand with the way they both gazed deeply into the eyes of each other. Only females who were a part of this life would understand.

Still smiling and locked deeply into the eyes of one another, ReeRee finally managed to break free from the fantasizing moment she'd enjoyed, long enough to welcome Alana into the suite.

"I'm so sorry. Please do come in, will you? I was just about done getting myself together," ReeRee said as she flipped her hair and continued to smile, radiating pure estrogen and sex appeal like she never had.

ReeRee was now already dressed and had only to complete putting on her eyeliner and peach-flavored lip gloss she loved so much. She flaunted one of the dresses and diamond-studded jewelry Nightmare had provided her with as a tip. The dress was metallic blue in color, similar in design to that which Alana had on, but not in totality.

ReeRee's dress and heels were both by Prada, and her jewelry—a pair of ruby, diamond, and rose gold designs, with beaded tasseled earrings, and a tassel satori rose gold necklace—all by Nina Runsdorf.

Alana couldn't help but compliment the class and sophisticated taste that ReeRee had.

"Life as a lawyer must be really nice, huh?" Alana said.

"It has its perks and its benefits to go along with the profession. Thankfully, I've been on the receiving end of the benefits more so than the stressed-out and overwhelmed end that many do experience," ReeRee stated.

Alana admired with a smile and a complimenting remark, "I see." She then caught a hint of the perfume that ReeRee had dabbed on. It was Curve Crush for Her.

"So where you got in mind for us to go?" ReeRee asked.

"It's a nice and very upscale lounge that offers a diverse crowd. They have jazz music, soul, R&B, and also have a few aspiring poets come out to do their thing. Trust me, you gonna love it," Alana had said.

"I truly believe I will," responded ReeRee, and they were out.

Alana reminded ReeRee so much of one of her stablemates who she paired well with in her days of being under the management of Cadillac Nate. She was a Creole female with an amazing body and lively spirit. Her name was Holly, and she and ReeRee had really loved and adored each other as no other female duo had. They did almost everything together. The only difference ReeRee saw between Holly and Alana was skin complexion.

Holly became the replacement in ReeRee's life at the time when Tomeka left for Texas. In all actuality, Holly and ReeRee had become closer than ReeRee and Tomeka. They had a bond unmatched and made a ton more money for Nate, being that Holly had extraordinary sex appeal and charming skills to keep all of their top-paying customers completely satisfied—even more so than ReeRee had.

Alana had first taken ReeRee to meet her uncle Ricky and a few female members of her family—her mother, Emma, and her sister, Jalisa, were among the few. Then they made a quick stop by Alana's house, and they were on their way to the lounge after that.

ReeRee and Nightmare briefly exchanged text messages, and so did she and Jackie. There were also a few failed attempts by Jackie in requesting video chats, and that had her pissed in a way. She felt ReeRee had a little more going on than a business trip and a meeting with a potential client, due to the type of clothing she'd packed, along with the jewelry. Jackie had done a little snooping around the house, but nothing too heavy, as she didn't want to give ReeRee the wrong impression and reveal the possibility of the fits of jealousy she was having—and left ReeRee alone to handle her business in Chicago.

■■

ReeRee and Alana both ended up back at the hotel suite later that night. Alana had one too many cocktails and was unable to drive from the lounge back to the suite, let alone home afterward. So, ReeRee took the wheel to safely get them back. ReeRee knew to exercise a high level of discipline and not drink too much. This had to be done at all cost. She was there on business and so happened to also meet a female friend she could grow and become really close with, in due time.

But the bottom line was, she was there on business and to take care of affairs to benefit herself and the guy that she wanted to possibly establish a future with. But, for the love of God, she couldn't understand that, of all the men—all of the qualified men that were available and made advances at her—why was she so attracted to Nightmare? And why was she so infatuated with a dude that she represented, a nigga who had life in Federal prison?

There was some type of wicked bravado and intriguing aura that Nightmare possessed about himself. This had a certain effect on her—one which she couldn't shake. *Voodoo maybe? Or some form of Black Magic even?* She actually thought over.

Was it a possibility that Nightmare found a way to put Roots on her? He did practice the Ifá religion, and probably held special powers in the spiritual world, to move and control elements in the metaphysical realm as he saw fit. And maybe this was what compelled her to give in more and more as time progressed, and they got to know each other deeper through conversation. After all, there's nothing in the world that can't be negotiated. Not to mention the gifts, the money, and the charming features of Nightmare. This made it no easier for her to escape, and with each request which were to come, she would make herself his lady on a stronger basis.

The Sunday of the weekend ReeRee had spent in Chicago was a day her and Alana shared briefly, touring the city and capping the evening at her Uncle Ricky's house, enjoying family and a dinner. Ricky invited his niece and ReeRee into his private chambers of the house—a sanctuary where he held high-stakes meetings, brokered deals, ordered hits, and spoke easy. It was in an efficiency basement which had a bar area and was equipped with high-end upscale appliances and seating. A 'Man Cave,' if you will.

"So ReeRee, I assume that this is another of many meetings that the both of us are to have on behalf of my guy, Michael?" Ricky had questioned.

"Yes, it is to be. And I look forward to us keeping the business affairs and all else in proper perspective for him," ReeRee responded to the words of Ricky.

"I like the sound of that, ReeRee. I really do," Ricky replied. "And I see you and my niece here took to one another pretty well," Ricky said, as he glanced over at his niece and smiled.

"Oh yeah. The both of us are two of a kind. I see our bond going a long way in the future. She's full of life and energy, and we have so much in common between one another," ReeRee related to Ricky.

"That's good to know as well. You got two things going good for you in this regard: my guy Michael trusts you enough to have you meet up with me to pick up the package I've got for him; and, I trust you enough to have my family keep you company on your trip. I also welcomed you into my home," Ricky mentioned.

"I'm glad to know that my level of trust is being earned by all means, Ricky," ReeRee replied.

"Okay, now that we've gotten that part out of the way, let's move on to the business at hand, shall we?" he said, and then reached and grabbed the strap handles of an all-black mini duffel bag.

"Inside this bag is four hundred K for Michael. I'm sure you already know how to appropriate these funds to make everything proper, right?" Ricky asked.

"Absolutely, I'll be sure to handle my part," ReeRee replied to the remark Ricky made.

"You do speak and appear to be capable of making it back to Los Angeles safe and sound with this type of money. Also, I have this for you to personally place directly in his hands at the next meeting you have with him," Ricky stated, and palmed tightly with both hands the six-by-nine-inch journal that was filled with very important and critical information to be conveyed to Nightmare directly from him—information related to the organization which was held by Teddy, and now, by the current leader he deemed himself to be.

"No need to worry, Ricky. That too shall be in good hands," ReeRee assured him, at least with her words. "I should be able to get this to him with no problem. But it won't be so until the next thirty days. I'm only allowed two visits every month, and I've already exhausted them for this month."

"That's not a problem. Just please, get it to him," he replied.

The meeting between Ricky and ReeRee had went very well—just the way she liked it. ReeRee had the opportunity to meet Ricky's wife, Loretta, his eldest son, Donavan, his youngest son, Zack, his daughter Yasmine, his second daughter by Loretta, Jasmine, and one of his other nieces, Xena, as he'd hosted a small family get-together this day, and they were the ones—other than his wife and kids—to have remained.

SECTION TWO

Chapter 10

The H.N.I.C...

Without dispute, Ricky was the head nigga in charge of his family, as everyone looked up to him for everything. He had three brothers and three sisters still living, and they respected all that he stood for as a man and a leader—of both the immediate family, and the gang people he held responsibilities to lead as well. His brothers and two of his sisters had been members of the Vice Lords organization for many years, and they still had a deep love and a level of respect for the group, at least the set that was headed by Ricky.

The Isaacs family history was deep"y ro'ted In politics and the Christian faith, as the grandfather of Ricky, Alfred Robert Isaacs, had been a preacher, a civil servant worker, and a city council member on the West Side of Chicago. Ricky's father, Jerry Sr., had been a community activist, an insurance salesperson, and a city council member himself, who had ties and connections to Jesse Jackson Sr. and many other Black political figures that operated in and around the Chicago area. Jerry Sr. took control of the education of his two oldest sons, Jerry Jr. and Teddy, to groom them for what he wanted them to be—focusing on political skills and knowledge related to organizing and planning events—being he desired them to one day seek political office on some level. He wanted his progeny to be strictly involved in politics from an African-American perspective, perhaps the Congressional Black Caucus.

Teddy and their eldest sister, Maxine, found success in a few political ambitions at their father's wishes. Maxine acquired a seat on the Cook County Board of Education, and worked her way up to being a prominent member on this entity. Teddy, on the other hand, started out on a good foot once he was honorably discharged from the Army. While there, he studied Political Science, as this went particularly well with Military Science. This was also in addition to all his father had taught. Teddy did make a run at a municipal office, to no avail.

Teddy personally knew Jeff Fort, Benny Lee, Walter Wheat, Freddy Gauge, and yes, the ever-flamboyant Willie Lyles, as he had gone to school with family members of the future street legends and leaders. However, it was Lyles who held the greatest level of influence over Teddy, due to his personality, style, and shot-calling abilities. It was also Lyles who was the 'Chief' at the time over the particular set he represented, and held the unofficial title of 'Underworld Mayor' of Chicago.

Lyles had political connections, judicial connections, business connections, and of course, a solid narcotics connection, which had all helped to transform the Vice Lords under him into a cash-strapped and heavily armed street juggernaut to be reckoned with.

Teddy definitely wanted to be down with the VL family, party hard, and run with Lyles. He wasted no time in making the fact known. Lyles was the one to oversee the ceremony of initiation, and he made Teddy one of them. Once the business of narcotics dealing had been fully learned firsthand for Teddy, his leader, Lyles, situated him over his own crew and supplied them with kilos of product, along with the territory to put it down.

Ricky ended up following in the footsteps of his brother and became a member of the crew by the blessings of the sibling. He quickly became the first lieutenant and a brilliant hustler that made outstanding and wise moves from the money, the power, and the many bricks of narcotics that passed through his hands and that of his enterprise.

The beauty of Ricky's mind was that, although he had a blacker-than-normal complexion of skin, suffered from inferiority complexes and insecurities, he had a knack and a taste for the finer things in life. But he loved to have sex with and be involved with females from the lowest rungs of society, contrary to his rise from the gutter. Atop this, he saw himself as someone much more than a mere gang-banger, drug dealer, street nigga, or hood figure. With each and every deal he made, move he put together, and dollar he acquired, it all went towards making such ideology and mentality manifest in his everyday living.

Ricky's diplomatic skills were of an impeccable nature. He'd linked up with business persons of Jewish descent, Italian syndicate figureheads, Black political leaders, street legends, Arab merchants, and white intellectuals—not to mention the male and female counterparts he dealt with from all other walks of life not named.

Ricky and Nightmare got acquainted at an early age. They were part of the same Boy Scouts Club division, and had also been to the same summer camps as teenagers, through the years growing up. As young adults, Ricky and Nightmare came across one another on many occasions in the clubs and dance halls they frequented in Chicago.

Over time, after Omar was killed, Nightmare would journey from the suburb city of Park Ridge more often than usual, and away from his interracial parents who struggled and fought—hair, tooth, and nail—to keep their dear Michael out of the inner-city hellholes and confined to the upper-middle-class sanctums which they'd raised him in. This was to no avail. Michael loved the functions and the lifestyle of the city, as opposed to the slow movement of the suburbs, and became infatuated with the appeals of street/hood life, especially with those little ghetto bold-behavior Black girls and Latina chicks he lusted over. He held an undeniable obsession for hip-hop music as well.

The more and more Michael entered the city to play basketball, date girls, club hop, and socialize, the more and more he got addicted to the streets and being a hoodlum. He became a natural with the girls, as they favored him and adored his genetic features and physique. That was how he gained the edge and psychological advantages to manipulate and dictate to the many females that he experienced brief moments with in the life of being a pimp, a Mack, at the early age of nineteen.

■■

ReeRee returned to Los Angeles from her trip to Chicago, New York City, and Philly, to handle business and to visit with family. Of the $400,000 that was supposed to be appropriated and put away for Nightmare, she stashed $100,000 in New York at the home of her mother, and let her father borrow $100,000 to handle his business with and get a few of his affairs in order. She knew her dad would pay her back the money in due time, and the funds she left at the home of her mother were in safe hands—the same as the many thousands of dollars she'd situated there in the past, in the event that she ever needed money on hand for emergency situations. The mother had growing responsibilities to take care of for ReeRee. This was literally and figuratively.

Jackie developed a bit of an attitude, in a sense, towards ReeRee due to the amount of time she'd all of a sudden begun to utilize in taking trips and visiting with "clients." ReeRee seemed to not want to provide the quality time with Jackie now more as they had in the past, prior to Nightmare becoming her new client.

Jackie was upset and fumed within at the thought of ReeRee no longer being interested in all they had and built up to be over the past five years or more. She really felt some type of way and had made the decision to question ReeRee about it upon her coming home.

Jackie wanted direct answers, and anything short of that wouldn't do. Especially not so with the fact that ReeRee ignored all of her calls but one, and didn't reply to any of the emails while away. There was no way in all of hell that Jackie would allow her to not answer up to ignoring her the way she had and disrespect her so blatantly.

"ReeRee, I'm so glad you're back, sweetheart," Jackie said upon returning home from work to find her lover there as well. She tried to lean in and kiss ReeRee, but ReeRee really wasn't up for it. She only stepped to the kitchen to get some juice and a quick snack, then she was to return to bed for rest at the time that Jackie walked through the front door.

"Jettica, didn't you hear me, sweetie? I said I'm so glad to see you and that you made it back safely," she said again, with a look of anguish and disgust on her face and hands straight down by her side behind the snub ReeRee had put upon her.

ReeRee had just awoken, was groggy, and had only gotten up to relieve herself and make a pit stop to the kitchen to replenish. Her shirking of Jackie was not intentional by any means. She was simply tired and wanted to get some sleep. Jackie felt otherwise.

"You know what?" Jackie began, as she followed behind ReeRee en route back to the bedroom. "I've gotten sick and tired of you with this new and funky attitude you've developed towards me. You been doing some fucked up shit lately, ReeRee, and I want to know what is really going on!" Jackie spat.

"What do you mean I've been doing some fucked up shit lately?" ReeRee challenged.

"Just like the fuck I said! You been doing some fucked up shit lately! You ignored my calls. You returned none of my emails. And now you on some bullshit with how you trying to talk to me and handle me. You know I ain't with none of the bullshit, ReeRee, and I want to know what's gotten into you! Why all of a sudden you acting this way?" Jackie demanded of her.

"Maybe I was too busy in the midst of handling business when you began blowing up my damn line. Maybe I didn't want to reply to all your emails because I knew the only thing you wanted in them was to know why I wasn't answering my phone. You act like you couldn't simply let me be for those few days I was away. Like you couldn't let me get back home first to say all you needed to say or relate all you needed to relate. Jackie, damn! Your ass behaving just like a fucking petulant child! You get on my goddamn nerves with that needy shit! I'm about to go back to sleep, so please let me rest and leave me the fuck alone, if you intend to continue and throw bullshit my way," ReeRee pierced Jackie with her words.

"What the fuck you just say to me? ReeRee! Who the fuck you think you talking to like that!" Jackie retorted.

"Jackie, please, I'm trying to go back to sleep and you making it hard for me," ReeRee said and pulled the blanket over her head.

Jackie snatched the bed covering completely off ReeRee and tossed it onto the floor. She then kicked off her shoes, clenched her fists, and readied herself for a fight, because she felt for certain ReeRee was about to hop up and give her what she wanted—just like the last time they'd scrapped—a good reason to beat her ass. Jackie was too much physically for ReeRee. She was no contest.

"Jackie, look, okay. I ain't with this shit. I'm tired. I've been on an exhausting trip to meet up with my client. I have to return to the office tomorrow. And you making it so difficult for me to rest. This for no reason at all," ReeRee stated as she got up out of bed, walked over to the closet, and began to get dressed in one of her sweat suits so she could leave the house—possibly for the night and not return until the next day. She knew it was important to allow a cool-off period between the two of them before it really got heated and they began to fight.

As ReeRee was putting on her sneakers to head out the door, Jackie fast-stepped to the living room and grabbed ReeRee's phone to keep her from taking it with her. She figured that if ReeRee had no phone, she couldn't ignore her calls and would definitely return home a little faster than anticipated.

"I'mma hold this for you until your ass come back. And now I ain't got to worry about you not taking my calls or staying gone longer than necessary," Jackie said to her as she confiscated the iPhone.

"You see what I mean now? You behaving so immature right now, Jackie, that it ain't even funny. Just keep the goddamn phone. I'll be okay for now without it," ReeRee said, and then hurried and got her car keys before Jackie decided to get those too.

She left the house, hopped in her car, and drove away towards Andrew's low-key place while retrieving her second phone out of the glove box, powering it on, and calling Andrew to let him know that she was headed over. He was still in LA, assisting an artist to complete their soon-to-be-released album.

Earlier that morning while home alone, ReeRee had put away $150,000 of the money she'd picked up from Ricky for Nightmare there in the house. She had a stash spot down in the basement of the home in the laundry room. This was also the location that she kept all of the cash she and Jackie maintained at home, to keep from making multiple withdrawals when they needed on-hand funds. Together, they had about $250,000 at their residence, in addition to the $150,000 ReeRee included.

ReeRee had taken the journal Ricky insisted she put directly in the hands of her client and photocopied each page. She placed the copies in a legal envelope to make it appear as if it was case documents and was far easier for Nightmare to return to the dorm with him and not be scrutinized, as he would be if he were to attempt to take a journal itself back. The journal was then wrapped up along with the money and placed in the cubbyhole down in the laundry room.

She would later make Nightmare aware of all she'd done and why. But for the moment, her intent was to stay the night over at Andrew's place and get back into the groove of working the next day, in the hopes that Jackie would be a better person upon her return. If not, then she'd planned to stay away until she became so.

Chapter 11

In The Meantime...

Over in Chicago, Ricky had been called on to meet up with two of his most trusted guys—those who he had working on the inside—who kept him in the know of all relevant matters which pertained to him. They were agents of the DEA that held positions in the special department which placed focus and attention on taking down kingpins, criminal enterprises, and other high-profile underworld organizations.

The dirty agents, Doug Lopez and Scott Pollock, were paid by Ricky on a monthly basis to keep him abreast of all the activities and on many other matters which he could benefit from. Ricky had even played the game raw on a few occasions, by having his two double agents investigate, turn in information on, get indicted, and knock off rival competition in the heroin trade—those he faced and eliminated. In most cases, this would be the end of the competition—either by federal lockup or by being killed.

He'd managed to connect with the double agents through the new Italian connection who supplied his product. Mister Dominic Francesca wanted to ensure that anyone he dealt with would be able to properly distribute and sell all material he provided with no problems. And he made sure that his customers had the type of protection from arrest or indictment like he and his people enjoyed.

At any time Ricky was called to meet the two, it would be at different locations, and never the same place twice. He had to appear alone always and was not allowed to bring any communication devices. Doug and Scott set up this meeting to be on a small sailboat that was docked on Lake Michigan. They were to sail out about four miles into the waters and conduct the sit-down in the cabin of the boat.

"Ricky, you've got a small problem that has the potential to escalate to something bigger at some point or another," began the tall, skinny Chicano one of the two, Doug.

"And what do that problem consist of?" replied Ricky.

"It's one of your people, who was moved to Detroit from here—from what I've been told by our people. One of my people related this to me, that the guy who they got is spilling his guts on all he knows about you, and has done for you specifically through the years. He says he was a part of your Vice Lords drug organization," Doug said.

"Oh yeah? Spilling his guts on things he's done and knows like what?" Ricky demanded to know with a stern face.

The second of the two said, "Things like the people he's murdered for you ... the amount of drugs he's sold for you ... and on how you conduct and handle your crew in the line of business you're in—that which you are the CEO of. The guy has provided some pretty accurate details on a few things too. The one that stands out most, which causes the greatest level of concern for us is, a killing he says you ordered him to do," injected Scott in mentioning to Ricky.

"How would you know that this random and anonymous snitch ain't lying and simply making some shit up to put me in the middle of it?" inquired Ricky.

"To be honest with you, Rick, this fella don't appear to be random and making up something. He provided specific details about a kidnapping that later resulted in a murder, which he and one more of your top boys committed. So he's related. He says that he and your lieutenant—who he was under—his 'capo,' Greg Suggs, aka 'Puncho,' took hostage of a guy that owed you money and also owned a small-time bar, which has an apartment situated atop it, where you sometimes hold meetings. He said that the guy didn't have your money for you when you sent someone to collect. He also refused to sign over the deeds to the properties that so happened to be in prime territory on the West Side of the city, in the area you'd looked to expand, near West Washington," Doug related and then paused briefly.

"If you were wondering how we got involved in all of this, it's because when Puncho and the C.I. kidnapped the victim—Smitty Nixon—they took him across state lines into Wisconsin when they killed him, as they were en route to distribute kilos of heroin—your product, so says the C.I.—to a dealer you heavily supply in Milwaukee," Doug attached in a matter-of-fact type of way to Ricky.

"They buried Nixon along the way," chimed Scott, "which brings in the Feds, if a kidnapping takes place and a victim is taken across state lines. Besides, the guy ran directly to the Feds for help. But luckily for us, it was two of our guys we work with in extracurricular activities who got a hand on him long before some career-oriented and politically-seeking fuck got to him."

Ricky had a very disturbed, angry look about his face that said it all to the two agents, because he knew that the information they related had deadly detailing facts to it that he couldn't refute. He remained silent as he attempted to brainstorm and try to think of who it could've possibly been that Puncho took along with him to handle that particular piece of work.

Puncho commanded a crew of twenty-five or more soldiers over the four trap houses and locations he held power to run. But Ricky was not in doubt about it being someone very close to him, since Puncho took the guy along on such an important mission.

"Who is this 'confidential informant' that you tell me about?" Ricky demanded to know.

"I'm sorry, Ricky, we can't tell you that at this time. It may cause more problems than we can handle. After all, you pay us to protect you, right? We got your back. We're not going to let you go down for any of this. Our guy is milking this rat for all he knows on a few people in other cases that they are working. And in exchange for immunity from prosecution, he's fully cooperating. He's helped us bring down a few people and has also helped us solve a few puzzling cases which took place before you and that Nightmare crew got pinched, and after the fact of you being acquitted and rebuilding the organization. He's too beneficial right now. But in due time, I'm pretty sure that we may be the ones who have to do him for you at some point, if the price is right," stated Doug.

"You care to hear more, Ricky?" asked Scott.

"Why not? This is why I hired you two, right?" responded Ricky.

"The C.I. also gave up the guy you supplied those kilos of heroin to in Milwaukee. And the field bureau in that jurisdiction ended up busting him. He mentioned your name and offered to try at setting you and that Puncho up, in exchange for a lenient sentence. Didn't anything ever appear fishy at some point with that guy ... City Blue?" asked Scott.

"Yeah, he disappeared for a time being, then showed back up talking reckless and trying to do funny business. I got leery and eventually stopped dealing with him," responded Ricky.

"Yeah, you did. But not so that Puncho. Your guy Suggs—who's connected to you and equally poses the threat of a RICO coming down to bust your ass if he ever got knocked. They got him on surveillance and on wire doing deals with Abrams," said Scott.

"Abrams?" retorted Ricky.

"Yeah, Colin Abrams, aka 'City Blue.' Damn, Ricky! You don't know the names of people you deal kilos of smack to?" Doug asked sarcastically.

"I'm slipping bad, ain't I?" Ricky responded.

"You bet your ass you are, buddy. But here is the more disturbing news that will really piss you off," Scott proclaimed.

"Damn! There's more?" asked Ricky.

"Oh yeah! The shit that makes me want to whack the little piece of shit myself," said Scott.

"And what's that?" Ricky inquired.

The dirty agent paused. Then, reluctantly, he let it spew. "The guy has been socking it to your little daughter, Yasmine, ever since she was fourteen and in the eighth grade," blurted Scott.

"What the fuck you just say to me?" Ricky spat.

"I said ... the C.I.—the one we share back and forth—has been screwing and sodomizing your little daughter Yasmine you have with your wife Loretta, since she was fourteen years of age," Scott repeated clearly for Ricky.

"We made him hand over his phone out of the blue one day, and also forced him to give up email account information, social media info, passcodes, and all other information to unlock his phone. He'd recorded videos of him FaceTiming Yasmine, nude photos of her, and also videos of the two of them sexually involved—both oral and by way of intercourse. Not to mention the shit he had of her stored in his main email account. Yasmine had skipped school on several occasions, and the C.I. would pick her up to go do the things to her that they used to do," added Scott.

■■■

He paused for a minute and then continued with the bad news. Scott stated, "Yeah, Ricky, Loretta or one of your nieces would drop her off, and she would stall long enough until they were gone. Then, shortly thereafter, he would swoop in to pick her up. She's even stole from you on a few instances to treat the C.I. to some of your valuable possessions," he further revealed.

"Dude, my daughter only sixteen years old. How in the fuck am I not to get pissed off at the shit y'all now telling me?" Ricky said.

"I know what you mean, dude. I've got a teenage daughter myself. But we can't give up our guy right now. He's too valuable. Obviously, he's been exposed to a lot of activity in his years of being in the streets," Scott said.

"And how old is this guy?" Ricky asked.

"Can't tell you that either, Ricky. We may as well just give him up if we do that. But if you want to know if he and Yasmine are still involved—no. I wouldn't doubt that at some point in the future he wouldn't try to sneak out of hiding and try to go be with her again. If and only if he's ever freed again. If he is, and does, and you catch him, then he's fair game. But if he doesn't, then we have to keep him concealed. He hasn't touched her in a couple of months though—I can tell you that much. So you may begin to breathe easy. In order for him to receive immunity and not be part of any prosecution once those RICO indictments begin to get unsealed and arrests are made all over the place, he had to cease and desist with any criminal activity he's doing, and to also reveal all crimes that he's committed. To my surprise, the prick seems to be really serious about being in the Witness Protection Program," Scott stated.

"He's scared shitless for his life!" added Scott.

"Other than all you've let me know, what other advice do you have, or maybe suggestions y'all wanna make?" Ricky wanted to know.

"Just have your boys slow down with some of those fucking murders they've been committing! It's like the Wild Wild West over on your side of town. They need to find a better way to settle disputes and deal with their problems.

That was the thing which drew too much attention to your other partner, Gentry—that Nightmare fella. You gotta also remember, Ricky, that under a RICO statute, any and everything your boys do will fall on your head, no matter if you gave the order or not, know of it or not—you will be to blame," Doug warned.

"I'm already familiar with that from the last time around," Ricky said with a sad look about his face. He recollected on the downfall of Nightmare, with murder counts pinned to him, and Ricky considered himself blessed, by all means, to get acquittals due to all the blame being on Nightmare.

"One last thing, Ricky," Doug tossed out to get his full attention before he stated what needed to be stated.

Ricky didn't say anything and had only stood ramrod with a look of disgust, concern, and anger smeared on his face all at one time. He looked Doug straight in the eyes and awaited the revelations.

"Please, do not go busting your brain trying to figure out who this child predator is that's doing all the ratting, and become impulsive yourself, then go out to do something crazy. You don't even have to press your daughter or force her for answers. We strongly suggest you not say anything to her about it, and continue to act as though you know nothing. Just tighten up your loose ends and prevent your people from doing sloppy work," Doug said.

"Will do," Ricky replied, paid his dirty agents $50,000 in cash, and departed the sight of the corrupt Federal workers.

On his drive back home, Ricky thought over everything he'd been told by Doug and Scott. Of all the information, quite naturally for a father, the most disturbing was that which concerned his teenage girl, Yasmine. He felt as though he had her thoroughly protected and out of harm's way from any sexual predators, but apparently not. He knew that the person who had manipulated and molested her from the age of fourteen had to be someone close to him—someone he had welcomed to his home. Not only this, the same dude was also someone who worked for him and must be numbered amongst the rank and file of the Vice Lord Nation.

"But who?" he questioned himself in soliloquy. *I know how to find out who this nigga is. I've got to figure out a way to question Puncho and get it out of him without making that nigga too suspicious and fearful of what he knows I'll do to the person once I find out exactly who he be. It has to be a nigga close to him, possibly one of his family members, for this nigga to take them along to kidnap that stubborn fuck, Smitty—kill his ass—and then proceed on to Milwaukee to deliver the work I sent them with.*

Yeah, it had to be someone very close to him for whoever that C.I. is to not implicate Puncho to the Feds, or reveal that he was responsible for some of the things told to the people that's juicing him for information. Doug and Scott mentioned that the snitch nigga pointing the finger at me! But I know how to get it out of Puncho who the rat is, without him thinking otherwise. And I'mma also deal with Yasmine's little hot ass too! That little cunt! She's really done it this time. Had it not been for the good work of Doug and Scott, I wouldn't had known shit! I'd still be in the blind. But I've got a trick for her little ass. I really do, Ricky thought to himself on the drive back home from the conclave.

Chapter 12

Ricky continued to ponder heavily and fume on all he'd been told and warned of. It took him roughly three hours to finally grasp the real message Doug and Scott conveyed and urged him to do before his problems got too far out of hand. The first thing was that, in an indirect way, they suggested he whack Puncho! This was without actually saying so, being that the informant was someone close to him. And by Puncho being dead, that would clean up some of the mess he'd made and prevent additional sloppy work In the future.

Puncho was a lot like Nightmare in so many ways—dangerous and a vicious motherfucker. They both had a penchant for murder and had a cold-blooded nature about themselves. Puncho had no problem killing, as Ricky knew this all too well. He'd put Puncho to task on several occasions to knock people off. But the killing of old man Smitty could potentially come back to haunt Ricky, if it came down to it—being that murder is the only crime which don't have a statute of limitations on it.

Doug and Scott revealed everything about the killing of Smitty, so it was, by itself, mandated that Puncho had to go. To eliminate Puncho would be to essentially eliminate some of the threat of prosecution behind dishing out the order to do Nixon. Also, being that they mentioned him—Nightmare, Puncho, RICO statute, and murder—all in the same paragraph, which meant he'd gotten his warning before the storm, required him to take heed and do as told. It also let him know that the powers out of the control of Doug and

Scott were possibly hot on his trail, and it was only a matter of time before disaster strikes.

But before Puncho was to be killed, he had to get him to reveal who the person was that tagged along with him to take out old man Smitty. And if anything, Ricky would have to take out Puncho all by his lonely, being that Puncho was well alert and capable in smelling a trap with no problem.

Next, Ricky would immediately sell the bar and other properties he'd muscled old man Smitty to sign over the deeds to, before having him killed. This would cut any and all ties to Nixon and his death. And if pressure mounted, would be hearsay at best and wouldn't stand in a court of law. He had the perfect guy in mind to sell the bar to. It was one of his pals named Roscoe. He'd long dreamed of the day he'd own his personal bar and no longer had to bootleg from a makeshift one he'd constructed in the den of his house.

Ricky used to enjoy going over to Roscoe's place on Saturdays and Sundays to watch football games, make bets, talk shit, and have a good ol' time with the boys before he made his rise to power. He also would sometimes sneak off to the bathroom or to one of the back rooms of Roscoe's house to trick with one of the girls there and get his dick sucked or fuck something quickly. That part of being a hood legend and street figure he really adored.

The part about dealing with his daughter, Yasmine—he would send her ass off to go and live with his sister, Maxine, and her daughter, who was about five months older than Yasmine, until she graduated and went off to college someplace. So thought Ricky. Maxine, her husband Craig, and their two kids—Justin, who was eighteen, and Kaitlyn, who was sixteen as is Yasmine—lived in the suburbs of Chicago, in Park Forest, Illinois.

Ricky's plan was to suddenly make Yasmine get up early one Saturday morning, leave everything but the gown she may have on, devices—phones, tablets, etc.—get in the car, and be taken to Maxine's house without any explanation whatsoever.

He would have Maxine buy her all new everything, and at some point, Ricky would pin her down, beat her ass if necessary, and force her to come off the passcodes to every account that she has. Then, he would unlock her phone—if he hadn't found someone by then to do so—and make her reveal who the guy was she'd been sexually manipulated by since she was fourteen years old.

Ricky had planned to beat her bloody, if it called for it. The bottom line was to force her to give him those recorded videos of them FaceTiming or having sex, and also to come off those nude photos that he now knew she had stashed on some email account.

Yasmine was Ricky's sweetheart and also daddy's little princess. She could do no wrong in Ricky's eyes. But how gravely mistaken was he at all the mess his baby had going on behind his back, under his roof, and in her room. The things that kids—teenagers—get caught up in these days and age are simply unimaginable and a nightmare for parents. If only Yasmine knew the type of mess that she'd gotten her father tied up in by being underage and having sexual relations with whoever the guy was that she'd been with for two years ongoing.

Ricky was forced to really restrain and control himself from the beating he had in mind to put on Yasmine before he made the mistake and killed his very own daughter. But who knows how it may turn out, if she refused to tell him everything he needed to know? And not only that, Ricky had to ensure that his daughter was isolated and restrained well enough to prevent her from getting her hands on another phone, reactivating all of her accounts, changing passcodes, and finally contacting her lover and making him aware of all that's going on—sending him into a panic and in total fear for his life. He didn't know if or not they were still able to communicate.

Who knows, the chump may flip the script on Yasmine and do something to her to prevent exposing himself to her dad—or to the police, Ricky thought. The little teeny bopper had serious problems on her hands and knew not the slightest of how serious it truly was. May the angels of God be with her.

Chapter 13

Two Months Earlier...

His six-foot two-inch frame was stretched out the long way across the bed. He was propped on his elbows and laid back atop the thick fluffy pillows. He had his head tilted, with his eyes rolled to the rear of his skull as the result of the sensation and ecstatic feeling he was receiving.

She passionately slid up and down, from front to back, and gyrated her hips and waistline atop the nine-inch dick of her lover man. For her to be a sixteen-year-old nearing the age of seventeen, she'd certainly learned a lot from the first time he'd taken her virginity and popped her sweet little cherry. This was their eleventh time together in the two years he'd been sexing her, as Everett had taught Yasmine everything she knew about how to have sex and on how to please a man in this way.

He had not long before the day turned thirty, but could easily pass for twenty any day, with his lean body, bi-racial background of being Black and Arabian, clean-shaven boyish facial features, and youthful haircut and demeanor. Not to mention his sweet words and charming behavior. Yasmine had a crush on him and fell in love the very moment she'd seen him and they locked eyes at a family get-together her dad had hosted.

Everett was the boyfriend of one of Yasmine's cousins. She was the one who had brought him over to meet the family and enjoy their company after a year of them heavily dating, but mostly infatuated with the sex of their relationship.

Yasmine's female cousin, Alana, had always favored her of all the younger female cousins of the Isaacs family, as Alana had kept Yasmine with her and around her the majority of the time. Ricky would give Alana all the finances necessary, to take Yasmine shopping at the malls, to get her hair done, their nails done, and to do all the other things that girly-girls do.

Ricky entrusted Alana to keep his daughter over the weekends and through the summer months when school was in vacation for many years prior to the niece meeting Everett. Yasmine absolutely loved and adored her cousin, and had always desired to be grown, sexy, and independent, just like her beloved flesh and blood, Alana.

The reason she favored Alana more so than being with her own mother was because Alana allowed her to be free-spirited and do all the things she wanted to do—unlike her mother, who was moody, strict, and wouldn't let Yasmine have her way or be herself as a young teenage girl growing up. Alana let her talk to boys on the phone—boys she might've met on social media or at school. She would also allow Yasmine to meet up with her boyfriends at the mall for ice cream or a movie—of course, always in her presence. But as for her mother, Loretta, Yasmine would not dare let her know anything about any type of boyfriend, let alone meeting up with them in person. She'd kill her dead with her own bare hands if she knew anything about this.

"Ah yeah, work that shit, my little sweet thing. Ride this dick like you really mean it, baby. Ah shit. Hell yeah. This little tight pussy of yours feels so good to me. Damn, I love the way you've learned to ride on this dick," Everett moaned in pleasure and proclaimed to a smiling Yasmine.

Her little vagina was gripping and snatching so well on the thickness and length of his dick, that each time she arched her back and slowly raised her butt from his pelvis,

"That's what it supposed to do, *hurt so good*," he said and then did it again, as she stood to her feet and began to assume the position of doggy style.

She got atop the bed on her knees and elbows with her breasts flat to the mattress and a deep arch in her back, just as she'd seen one of her favorite female porn stars do on one of those XNXX videos and noticed in the e-book version of the Kama Sutra she'd downloaded.

Her pretty little perfectly shaven pussy was too irresistible for Everett to pass up tasting, as he always had. He buried his face deep in her love box and used his tongue as a spear, stabbing between her wet lips and sending a shocking feeling of tantalizing pleasure charging through her young and tender body. This was the third time Everett had orally fondled Yasmine throughout the time that the two had begun to sneak around.

***

In Everett's mind, he believed as though he were teaching Yasmine how to be a grown lady in the sex-hood department, by the both of them pleasing one another in multiple ways. And it never occurred to him that he was, indeed, having sex with a barely legal teen, way before reaching sixteen—an underage minor. Never mind the fact that Yasmine did blatantly lie to him in the beginning about her being seventeen, when in fact, she was only fourteen, soon to turn fifteen the same year. He should have known better and asked to see some ID; or at best, upon being made aware of her actual age, he should have stopped any and all dealings that they had, especially the sexual relations.

But Yasmine was too good to him and he absolutely loved the supreme feeling he'd experience each time he penetrated, ravished her, and ejaculated on her body. She had filled out proportionately as if she actually were a fully grown woman with all of her feminine features. Yasmine was *32-22-34*, and

ensuring that she didn't move or try to pull away as he climaxed.

Everett howled ferociously, like he were a vigorous young wolf, as he exploded and blew a thick robust load of semen inside of Yasmine. He remained hung deep inside of her, for the better part of two minutes. He slowly withdrew as she pulled away. His load was so plentiful that it ran out of her and oozed in large amount, down her leg then onto the mattress.

She cat-crawled her way to the headboard of the bed, pulled the blanket back, got under, and then drew it back up just past her breasts to cover her naked body from the cool air of the motel room. Everett went to the bathroom to take a quick piss, then returned, hopped atop the bed, got under the blanket and lay beside Yasmine as they were face-to-face and began to pillow talk.

"E-Nice, let me ask you something," she referred to him by his nickname.

"Go ahead, I'm listening," he responded.

"Tell me exactly, what am I supposed to do, or better yet, what do 'you' intend to do, if you get me pregnant?" she asked.

"What do you mean, 'what do I intend to do if you get pregnant?' I intend to be the best man I can be, and take care of my baby. That's what I intent to do," he retorted. "Besides, it's perfect timing. By the time you have the baby, you'll be seventeen years old, going on eighteen, and I should be safe from that point," Everett added.

"That won't be good for business, pretty boy. Do you not recall who my daddy is? Nigga! He'll personally kill the both of us dead if, my cousin don't find out and get to us first," Yasmine stated.

"Ain't no need to worry about Alana. I got her right where I want her to be. If that ever happened and she found out, she'd probably want all three of us to be in a relationship as one big happy family," he said to her.

Yasmine sucked her teeth. "Boy, please! Won't none of that shit be good for business," she responded.

"Why you say that? And where all of this talk come from about you getting pregnant?" he demanded to know.

She locked eyes with him and developed this peevish look about her face before she continued. "Well, for one, you been fucking me since I was fourteen years old," she spat.

"And? Your little hot-ass been enjoying every inch of this dick ever since," he fired back.

"That's beside the point, E."

"Well, what is the point?" he retorted.

"If you lct mc finish without cutting me off, then you'll know," she said emphatically.

"Well ... go ahead, I'm listening." He got really silent and allowed Yasmine the chance to say what was on her mind.

"Like I was saying, E, you got two kids already, one by your first baby mama and one by my cousin. You don't have a job, and you're not stable. You a worker for your uncle that is himself a worker of the boss, my dad. You got to be better than that, because your pretty looks and Godly-blessed dick you got on you not gonna continue to get you by," she said as she caressed the side of his face with the tips of her fingers and pulled on his dick under the cover with her other hand.

"A'ight! Your little ass better stop now. You gonna make this anaconda come back to life," he joked with her.

"Nah, but on the real, Everett, I've come to realize that we've been playing a really dangerous game, sweetheart. If we gonna continue to be together and truly do this, then we got to do something to make it right. And not only that. Nigga, you done nutted in me the last two times we've been together! It's like you asking for trouble," she stated.

"If you want to know the truth, you became too good to me, and I was unable to control myself. I can't stop nutting in you now, not even if you paid me a million dollars to," he said as he leaned in and kissed her on the forehead.

"I'mma ask you again, E. What do you intend to do if you got me pregnant?" Yasmine reiterated her question. "And don't give me any more foolish answers without thinking them all the way through," she attached.

"Look, Yabby, what's with you and this thing about getting pregnant?" he questioned.

"If you really want to know, Everett, I missed my period last cycle, and it was supposed to be on the last couple of days, but it ain't. I'm scared. That's what this all about. I'm scared as hell. Not for me, because I'm good. My dad or mom won't be able to do nothing to me even if they wanted to. My fear is for you, of what I know my dad will have done to you, and I'm in love with you, Everett. I always have been since I was a little girl and you took my virginity. I'm yours forever, and we got to do whatever it takes to make this work," Yasmine said to Everett.

"Are you serious, baby?" he asked.

"I'm serious as ever, Everett," she replied with a very innocent and concerned look in her eyes.

"You took a pregnancy test yet?"

"Nope."

"Why am I asking you stuff like that anyway? You too damn young, little girl, to know about any of that stuff anyway," he spat.

"Everett, please, it's the New Millennium, my nigga. The youngest of us youngsters are up on game," she stated.

He got out of the bed and began to get dressed.

"Where you going? We still got about three more hours before school's out."

"I'll be right back in about ten minutes. I'm going to the drug store to get a pregnancy test," he let her know. Everett exited the motel room to go get the test so that he'd know the results himself directly. He was determined to find out.

Twenty minutes later, he was walking back through the front door with a test in a bag. Yasmine was in the shower upon his return.

"Baby, I'm back," he said, to let her know of his presence.

"I'm in the shower, E," she responded, to let him know where she was.

He walked into the bathroom and began taking the test out of its package. "Lil baby, you gotta get out that shower and dry off real quick so we can handle this business," he said to her.

"Okay, sweetie. Not a problem," she replied. She got out of the shower, dried off thoroughly, and stood in front of Everett ass-naked, tempting him further and trying to arouse his nature yet again. She put on this love doll innocent look about her face to indicate her love and obedience to him.

"I took a pee already when you left. I had to get your baby-making juice out of me to the best of my ability. But, I do have to pee again," she let him know.

"That's good. That's so good," he replied.

With the test in hand and ready to get down to the business, Everett instructed her to have a seat on the toilet. "Well, you know what to do. I ain't got to tell you," he said to her as she stood in one place with her hands on her hips and her mind on being stuffed again with the nine-inch beef sausage Everett had dangling between his legs.

Yasmine took the test from him, sat on the toilet, situated the test between her and the water in the bowl, and urinated, heavily drenching the absorbent area of the pregnancy test. Once complete, she sat the test atop a thick pile of tissue and began to talk with Everett as they both anxiously awaited the results.

They stepped back into the bedroom area, out of the bathroom, and laid on the bed, kissing and frolicking around to kill time and not be so impatient.

"Baby, what we gonna do if the results are positive?" she asked of him.

"They shouldn't be, because your little ass been taking your birth control pills like you suppose too, right?" he retorted with a question of his own.

"Everett, I been stop taking those pills about three years ago. I had my first period at eleven and my mom put me on birth control at twelve going on thirteen. About six months into being thirteen, I started flushing them damn things down the toilet and lying to my mom about my use of them," she revealed.

"Why the hell you do that?" he questioned.

"Because those damn things make you eat like a fucking pig, and cause young girls to pick up so much weight. All of my friends at school and at home had gotten fat as ever, unattractive, and began to have health problems behind those pills and eating like crazy. I knew my mom wouldn't have any understanding, so I never bothered to say anything to her about it. I went to my cousin—your baby momma—for advice, and Alana told me what to do. She said, as long as I'm not having sex, then there was no need to be taking those pills."

"But, you *were* having sex wasn't you?" Everett asked.

"Not at the time. You and I didn't get going until about a year after the fact. You were my first, remember? Then, once we did begin to have sex, you wouldn't cum inside me, so I never had to worry about getting pregnant, up until the last two times your muthafuckin' ass began to do otherwise," Yasmine spat and pinched Everett hard in the manhood area.

Chapter 14

Everett flinched and laughed it off, hopping up from the bed to go retrieve the test out of the bathroom. He took a piss himself, extending his stay in the restroom.

Yasmine's little grown and sneaky-ass had already known what the results would read, as she'd taken a test at the time she missed her period. It was indeed positive. She only wanted to wait until the right time to tell Everett, or better yet, allow him to find out in the way that he was about to, so as to not be in doubt.

While holding his dick and pissing with his right hand, Everett picked up the test with the other and stared at it in a deep state of mind. All of his feelings and emotions raced through his body at one time while holding the test and trying to aim.

DAMN! I done fucked up and got this little bitch pregnant. Ain't this a bitch! That nigga Ricky gonna definitely send somebody to try and kill my muthafuckin' ass if he ever found out I've been fucking his little girl, let alone, got the little bitch pregnant! Alana is gonna certainly call the police and have me locked up. So now, I gotta do something! I'mma make that little bitch have an abortion. That's what I'm gonna do. That's the only way out of this to live to see another day and have the opportunity to be able to fuck her more in the days to come. That little pussy of hers is too tight and too good to just let it go like that. We got to do something and the plan I got in mind is the thing we gonna do, Everett thought long and selfishly.

He exited the bathroom and dragged his feet, returning to the bed where Yasmine sat.

"So you not gonna tell me the results?" she asked.

"It's positive. You pregnant, lil baby. I messed around and got you pregnant," Everett replied.

"You wanna know something else?" she asked.

"What's up?" he responded.

"I already knew that I was pregnant. I took a test when I first missed my period," she revealed.

"Yasmine, you ain't tell nobody else, did you?" he demanded to know.

"Of course not, stupid. I know better than that," she replied.

"How we supposed to hide this shit, Yasmine?" Everett asked.

"We'll figure something out soon," she said.

"I already done figured something out. You ain't gonna have it. You gonna have an abortion," he emphatically stated.

"Oh no the fuck, I ain't! I'm not about to fuck my body up! Are you crazy, nigga?" she spat.

"Oh yes the fuck, you are!" Everett spat angrily behind her defiance at his position on what he wanted to do.

"No, I'm not!" Yasmine returned fire and rolled her neck as she spoke to Everett.

"Yasmine?" he said her name in a way to get her attention.

"What?" she fired back.

"Listen, do you not understand that I could lose my fucking life or my freedom for a long time for this behind this shit?" he questioned.

"Everett, I'm not a dumb stupid little girl, bro. I know what I gotta do, baby. I'm more than sure if I let my momma know, she's gonna try to make me do the same thing you talking about. And I can't tell my dad. He's gonna force me to terminate my baby and then probably beat me silly to tell him who got me pregnant," she stated.

"So what you plan to do?" he asked.

"I plan to hide my pregnancy for as long as I can, until I'm too far up in months to not be legally able to have an abortion, so they can't make me go through the process of having my baby killed. Then, I'll make up a name to give them if pressured to tell who my baby daddy is," she related to him.

"You got to be gone crazy if you think Rick will believe that shit! Oh man! What in the fuck have I done!" Everett loathed and slapped his hand atop his head.

"Maybe this'll cheer you up and not have you so worried, baby," Yasmine said and presented him with a high end watch by Bell and Ross and a diamond pinky ring. She pulled out $2,500 in cash as well and begged Everett to think positive, at least for the moment, while they were together.

"Here," she proclaimed. "Stop being so worried, pretty boy. Everything gonna be alright. I promise you," she said upon appeasing Everett with her gifts and money.

He'd stopped with the pity, gave her a very surprised look of satisfaction, accepted the gifts, and finally took a seat on the bed again, after tossing the test in the trash. "Your little ass too fucking much, you know that?" he said, cracked a smile and kissed her.

"I know I can be sometimes. But we gonna see to it that the rest of the day turn out good. Just like it began," she stated.

"I know that's right," he responded and then began to get undressed as he was prior to going to the drug store.

He sexed her more that day and returned her close to her high school. Everett knew that he had made a grave mistake which was impossible to correct, other than with the abortion he had in mind. But, there was nothing he could do about it. He'd planned to put some distance between the two of them, and fast. But before doing so, he wanted to gain the upper hand on Yasmine's father, by getting him on video and audio recordings, with any type of incriminating interactions with Ricky and his uncle as possible. He would go on to have his phone recording at any time he and his uncle were together and had conversations, or whenever he was to meet up with Ricky with the uncle.

And if any true pressure really came down on him, he would reveal to the Feds all he knew of Ricky's organization, turn in narcotic products that he would be supplied with, and at worst, reveal the exact location of where he and his uncle Puncho had killed and buried old man Smitty Nixon. So if Ricky were to get really stupid on him at some point about Yasmine, a point that may eventually come about when Everett would go insane on him, by running to the Feds. He had his strategy for survival laid out and ready to be put into effect on a moment's notice. He had only hoped that Yasmine wouldn't spill the beans and do something immature and expose him and all that they had going on. But how reliable could a sixteen-year-old be at containing the fact of being pregnant by a thirty-year-old man? A very difficult task for a teenager.

***

Two Weeks Later...

Yasmine contacted her cousin, Alana, to seek some advice on a few things. This was after making the fact known to Everett that she was pregnant.

"Hello," Alana answered.

"Hey, big cuz. How you doing, girl? I hadn't seen you in a few days. What's been good with you?" Yasmine said.

"I'm good, Yabby, I'm good. I've just been going through a few things lately with my boyfriend slash baby daddy. But other than that, I've been great. What's going on? What's on your mind?" Alana asked.

"I've got something serious I need to speak to you about. In person. You not busy tomorrow, are you?" she asked of Alana.

"Not really. You want me to pick you up and we can go to the mall or something?" Alana replied.

"Yeah, that'll be good. We can talk then," said Yasmine. "You know you're the only one I can truly talk to," she added.

"Okay, that's a bet, my little cousin. We can do that. No problem," responded Alana.

"I want to thank you, Alana, for being so understanding towards me," Yasmine complimented.

"You're welcome. That's what family is for, right?" replied Alana.

"I'll see you and talk tomorrow, cuz," said Yasmine.

"Okay. I'll see you then," responded Alana, and they ended the call.

The next day, Alana showed up to visit family at Yasmine's house before the two were to go shopping. Yasmine was the oldest female Loretta gave birth to. She had two additional brothers by different female parents who were older than she, ages twenty and twenty-two. Then there was Donovan, Ricky's eldest by another woman. He was twenty-eight. In total, Ricky sired seven.

Alana brought along her two kids, one by a guy named Kendrick—a son. He was four. And the baby by Everett, Bella Monet. She was one, almost two. Yasmine's mom, Loretta, absolutely loved and adored baby Bella. She always wanted to babysit and keep her, anytime that Alana wanted to go out and needed a nanny.

"Hey, Alana," Loretta greeted.

"Hello, Aunt Loretta. How you been?" Alana replied, and the both of them hugged each other with a kiss on the cheek.

"You look good, girl. You better be sure to keep that figure of yours in shape," Loretta giggled out and pinched Alana on the butt. "Let Auntie have that pretty baby of yours," Loretta said and then picked up Baby Bella and began to load her with pleasant kisses and smiled very excitedly at the pretty toddler that Alana and Everett produced.

Yasmine came from upstairs, dressed and ready to enjoy a day of shopping with her big cousin.

"Hey Yabby," Alana greeted happily.

"Hi cuz. How you doing?" Yasmine replied, and the both of them shared a hug.

Yasmine looked on in jealousy as her mother so energetically and delightfully kissed and played with Alana's baby—Everett's seed. This left Yasmine with a deep thought: *I know my baby is gonna be just as cute, if not more cute, than Baby Bella is. And I certainly hope that my momma embrace my child, her very own grandbaby, the same way she does Baby Bella. Maybe better.*

"Momma, I need a few extra dollars to go shopping with," Yasmine asked of her mother.

"Girl, please! As disrespectful as your little ass have been of late, and those fucking grades keep falling—you won't be getting a damn thing from me no time soon. You better spend whatever your daddy already gave you," Loretta replied.

Truthfully, Yasmine didn't need any extra money. She had about $1,000 of her own that she'd saved up and what remained from her cutting out the money she'd stole from her daddy to give to Everett. She only wanted to see and know what her momma's attitude towards her would be. She found that out quickly. Yasmine didn't take it to heart. She just moved on past the bullshit energy her mother gave off at her.

"Never mind. I'll be alright with what little money I do have left to shop with," Yasmine said.

"I know you will, because I ain't got nothing for you, sweetie pie," Loretta proclaimed in shooting back at Yasmine, then proceeded to walk to the back of the house with Baby Bella in arms.

"I'll see y'all later," Loretta lastly stated, then Alana and Yasmine left out the house on their way to the mall.

***

Thirty minutes later, they were strolling through the mall, taking a look at the nice material that was for sale and making small talk before Alana popped the big question to turn the subject to something more serious.

"So what's on your mind so important you wanted to talk about, lil cuz?" Alana asked.

"Alana, you already see how my momma be acting and treating me lately. And I ain't got nobody to talk to that I trust or deal with, other than you," Yasmine stated.

"Whatever your secret is, you know it's safe with me," Alana replied, clearly reading between the lines to know there was something serious on Yasmine's mind.

"Come on, let's take a seat for a moment," Yasmine declared, and they sat in the food court area to talk.

"What's up?" Alana looked her little cousin square in the eyes and asked, serious toned.

"Cuz, I done messed around and let my little boyfriend get me pregnant," Yasmine revealed.

"You got to be bullshittin', right?" Alana responded.

"No girl. I'm dead-ass."

"You right about that! Because if your daddy or momma finds out, that's what you're gonna be—a dead ass!" Alana made what was already a thought a current reality in the ears and mind of Yasmine. "Damn, Yasmine! Why you had to drag me into this bullshit?! You already know that they gonna swear up and down that I taught your little hot ass how to be grown! And exactly how you know you pregnant?" Alana asked.

"Cuz! I'm not no little girl no more. I ain't stupid!" Yasmine spat, as she felt insulted by Alana. "I missed my period and then took a pregnancy test."

"By yourself?" Alana asked.

"Cuz, please stop with the insults, will you?" Yasmine demanded. "Of course by myself. Nawl, I did like you told me you had done, and I took a test with Everett when I found out I was pregnant," Yasmine attached sarcastically and really caught Alana's attention long enough to force a stop with the insults.

"Nah, seriously, cuz. I took a test twice, and both times, it was positive," she further said upon finally having Alana's total attention following the remark that included Everett's name. She actually told Alana the God honest truth, if only she'd comprehended the shot made.

"Well, what you got in mind to do?" Alana asked.

"What you mean 'what I got in mind'? I intend to have my baby," Yasmine declared.

"Yabby, now you know damn well that your momma and daddy ain't going for that. You not even out of high school yet," said Alana.

"How they supposed to find out? I don't intend to tell them. My life would never be normal again. So, I plan to keep this between us until I'm up in pregnancy, and then let them know. At that point, they can't force me to have an abortion. And if they give me too many problems after that, I'll just pack up and run away," Yasmine related.

"Yabby! Listen to yourself, girl!" stated Alana.

"You got any better ideas? That's why I wanted to talk to you—so you can give me good advice. My damn boyfriend talking about having an abortion. So much for advice from him," Yasmine stated.

"My advice to you is to go ahead and let your damn parents know what the deal is, and for you to just accept the consequences that come along with it," spoke Alana.

"Yeah right, Alana! For the last time, cuz, I'm not gonna get rid of my fuckin' baby! I'm not gonna let my parents force their will upon me, okay? That clearly will be the consequence—force me to abort and kill my baby ... and then beat me senseless once I heal. I may as well go ahead and pack up right now and then run away, if I'm gonna let my parents know," Yasmine stated.

"Well ... you got two options ... let them know now and be forced to abort, or, do what you just say you would do to avoid killing your baby and being killed yourself, because Uncle Ricky damn sure gonna fuck you up, lil girl!" Alana had said.

"And you don't think I already know that?" responded Yasmine.

Alana expressed a gravely concerned look on her face as she continued to stare at her little cousin. "Yabby, why you stopped taking your birth control pills?" Alana asked.

"It's a little too late for that now, cuz. But can I come stay with you?" Yasmine asked of Alana.

"Hell fuck no! And be pregnant all up in my place? We both will be dead, then! No-no! That's out of the question! And who knows, your damn momma and daddy might be accepting and understanding that you made a mistake like many other little teenage girls your age. You won't know till you tell them."

"And then have my daddy ask me a thousand questions, trying to get me to reveal who I got pregnant by? No deal!" Yasmine spat. "Not gonna work. That's alright. I'll figure out something of my own. All I ask you is that you not tell my parents, cuz. Okay? Please don't," Yasmine begged of her cousin.

"Don't worry, I won't. That'll cause me too many problems," Alana declared. But in the back of her mind, she knew that if it came down to it, she'd immediately let Ricky know what's going on with his little girl—or if it became a situation of where Alana would have to save Yasmine from herself. That would be the right thing to do, Alana maintained in mind.

Chapter 15

Later that night, Everett had come over to Alana's house, possibly to stay the remainder of the weekend as he'd most often done. He and Alana were laid back, chilling and watching a movie after they'd just had sex. She initiated the conversation with him about all she and Yasmine had talked about earlier in the day.

"Everett, you not gonna believe this shit," she began.

"What that?" he replied.

"How about, me and my little cousin Yasmine go shopping at the mall today, and that little bitch got the nerve to tell me her little shrimp-dick boyfriend done got her pregnant."

"Say what? Ain't no way. Ricky and her mom gonna kill her," he responded.

"That's the same thing I said to her," Alana said with a chuckle behind her remark. "She so-called herself coming to me for advice," she added.

"And what advice did you give her?" Everett asked.

"I told the little hot-bitch to just tell her momma and daddy what's up, and that she'd made a mistake like many other girls her age. Hell, they even got reality TV shows dedicated to little girls who'd made those same mistakes called *Teen Moms*. Ricky and Loretta might be understanding and go with the flow. But Yabby had sworn me up and down that no matter what, they gonna make her have an abortion and then beat the living shit out of her once she healed from the procedure."

"And what you think?" he asked.

"I believe there's a lot of truth to that. Because Ricky gonna be too busy trying to force her to tell him who the little nigga is that got her pregnant. I believe eventually he'll get it out of her too. Then, he gonna send somebody to go deal with the little nigga that got his little girl pregnant," Alana stated.

"Damn. That sound scary," he responded to what he knew to be the mentality of her uncle.

"You damn right it do. Because I know my uncle. And that nigga mean business! But the crazy part about it is that Yabby sccmcd to bc very determined to keep her baby. She told me she'd run away if she had to, in order to keep her baby," said Alana.

"That's crazy," Everett responded. "Absolutely crazy," he added. "How she plan to support herself if she so-called 'run away'?" he questioned.

"The little bitch said that, on top of the money she'd saved that her daddy had given to her, she's been stealing money from him, and watches and jewelry. My Uncle Ricky crazy about those expensive-ass watches too," Alana stated, causing Everett to become seriously startled upon the thought of Yasmine giving him the watch and pinky ring. He took a glance out the corner of his eye while Alana paid no attention. It was the first watch Yasmine had given to him, and it sat on the table along with the diamond pinky ring by Harry Winston. The timepiece was a *Richard Mille Lotus F-1 Team–Romain Grosjean,* a watch worth anywhere north of $50,000.

Everett became paranoid as shit behind all that Alana related to him—especially the parts about the watch and Ricky beating Yasmine to get her to confess who she'd been sexually active with. He was so shaken, to the point of not being able to sleep. He got up, redressed, lied to Alana about having some important business to take care of with his uncle, and left her house, headed to the motel where he normally met up with Yasmine for play time.

He checked in for a two-day stay. Once inside the room, he immediately began to text and call Yasmine, to know why she ran her mouth to anybody the way she had. She was asleep and unable to readily respond. Everett became infuriated by her not being available, then began to send nasty, ugly, and disrespectful text messages and voice-mails to her phone. His impatience forced him to check out of the room at first daybreak, to go hide at some other locale in fear Ricky finding out of her being pregnant and forcing the truth out of her—if Alana didn't tell them about the pregnancy first, as she revealed she'd do, if it came to it.

***

Yasmine finally woke up. She was stunned at what she saw in her phone. The text messages left her feeling terribly bad at Everett's choice of words. She called him to find out why he was tripping the way that he was.

He answered, "What?"

"Hey-Hey-Hey! What's your problem, dude? Pipe down, pretty boy, and talk to me," she responded.

"Yo. Why the fuck did your little stupid-ass go and tell Alana what the fuck going on with you?" he spat. "Don't play dumb, you little stupid bitch!" he blasted her.

"Whoa now! You gone too far. Why you got to talk to me like this, E?"

"Because that's what the fuck you are, dumb-ass! What you thought, she wasn't gonna say something to me? My bitch tells me everything, little girl. Everything. I told your little dumb-ass that the shit could do me harm and put my life in danger. I could possibly go to jail! But your little ass don't give a fuck. I thought I made myself perfectly clear, Yasmine, for you not to say shit to nobody," Everett scolded her.

"And I understood you about that. I didn't say anything, E. I only asked a question, she responded."

"Oh, you only asked a fucking question, but she was able to tell me everything! The only thing she left out was the fact of who it is that got you pregnant. Your dumb-ass even told her about you stealing watches and money from your daddy. Now how dumb was that? Look, I ain't got time to keep going back and forth with you on this phone. I need you to meet up with me later. I was at the motel a few hours ago, but I ain't know if your dad done found out already, because Alana say she plan to tell your people, so you don't do anything stupid like continue to steal from Rick and then later run away from home. She say Rick gonna definitely put the press down on you to tell him who you pregnant by. And I already know you gonna break and tell on me, so we can't meet up at none of our old spots. I'm gone drive to pick you up from somewhere. When will you be free?" Everett asked.

"I'll be up and free at about twelve today, maybe one," she replied.

"Good. I'll hit you back up at that time. But until then, don't call me or text this number. I'll call and text you. I'm about to change my number ASAP! Alana not even gonna know it. Look, keep your goddamn mouth closed, okay. Don't say shit to nobody. Not Alana, not nobody, alright?" he ordered.

"Alright, E, alright. I love you," she lastly stated, but he didn't hear not one word of it as he'd already ended the call.

"Hello. Hello. Hellooo! Damn! That bastard," Yasmine spat into the phone.

Immediately following him ending the call, Everett changed his phone number and deactivated all of his social media accounts. An hour later, Yasmine attempted to call Everett back at the last known number of his, but learned that it had been changed. It angered her to no longer have a direct line to him when it became a must that they increase all forms of communication due to her now being impregnated with his seed. She took to social media only to learn that all profiles no longer existed.

"What the fuck?" she thought out loud. "So this nigga trying to bounce on a bitch like that, huh? A little heat comes and he can't stand the pressure. It's not like we can't get over this small bump in the road and be able to move on to a better life together. We should be good at some point soon, I imagine. Hopefully we gonna get it right," she spoke in a low voice to herself.

***

Yasmine showered, dressed, and was in the process of being on her way to meet Everett, but had been cut off from her mission by her father.

"I see you all dressed and ready to go, baby girl," he said.

"Yeah, me and my girls are about to go out to eat and take some pics together at the mall or at some other event for teenage girls," she responded to her father.

"Oh no. That's not gonna happen today. You know we all supposed to go and meet up at your Aunt Maxie's place for dinner and family time, after we leave your grandfather's grave for the memorial celebration of his birthday today. So you may as well cancel that, baby girl, and plan your outing with those other little girls for another day, or next weekend. It's almost time to go too. We supposed to all meet up at two. It's now one, so it's good you already dressed. And I can't seem to find my daddy goddamn pinky ring around here nowhere. You happen to see a men's diamond ring around here anywhere?" Ricky had asked of his daughter.

But his instructions to her about not being able to go anywhere were without the slightest form of her rejecting.

"No. I haven't," she responded about the ring.

Ricky walked away at that point.

She knew that Daddy's words were law, and there was no way to reverse anything he'd declared—especially not so, being that it was something that had to do with his father, her grandfather. Everything was out of the question.

Everett called her back from a restricted number. She didn't answer at first because it was not known who the caller was. But on the second time, she'd done so due to her becoming aware that it could possibly be Everett on the other end.

"Hello."

"Hey, it's me again. You dressed yet?" he asked.

"I am. But—"

"Good. Look, meet me at the Burger King that's close to the motel where we always hang out at, okay?" he said.

"Everett, I'm not gonna be able to make it," she replied.

"What the fuck you mean, you not gonna be able to make it?" he demanded to know.

"Because my family supposed to have a get-together in honor of my granddad's birthday, and my dad already got the press down on me about being ready," she related.

"Man, whatever! I ain't going for that bullshit! You lying and I know your little ass is, you stupid lil bitch! I knew I should've stopped fucking with you a long time ago. But it's all good. I live and I learn, don't I? Bye!" he spat and clicked the call to an end.

"Everett. Everett!" she called out his name twice into the phone hoping he was still there. He wasn't.

Yasmine began to cry at this point in the fact of how Everett had talked to her. He had never done so in such a disrespectful manner. That attitude from him didn't begin until after the fact of her revealing that she was pregnant. Although she was telling the truth, there was nothing she could have said to make Everett believe it.

She began to cry, and the tears poured from her eyes at the realization of her predicament. She contemplated the thought of going against what her father had said and meet up with Everett anyway. But she knew she'd be dead by sunrise the next morning had she done this. So she simply cried and cried and cried her poor little eyes out, with her hands covering her face as she held her head low and sat on the edge of the bed.

The thought hit her again to up and go meet Everett, but quickly died out once she remembered that he'd changed his number and killed all forms of her being able to contact him. The level of fear and paranoia he began to experience was for real. He was in full panic mode.

***

Three days after his attempt to meet up with Yasmine to go over a few things to no avail, his supreme level of fear had forced him to get in contact with the FBI to make a few reports on the drug lord and gang leader he and his uncle worked for. The hope was to possibly give up enough information on Ricky to have him arrested and remove him from being a threat to the person who got his little teenage daughter pregnant. He'd seen more than enough episodes on the History Channel, A&E, and other networks about the mob, gangs, and conspiracy, and had observed how the RICO law worked.

Everett knew that the Feds didn't want small catfish like him. They always aim to snag the big tuna of a criminal enterprise, and then pin all the crimes of their underlings on them on the pretext that "the boss or the leader ordered them to do it or they would be dealt with for not following orders." That was the exact same line that Everett put to the Feds. He told them that he no longer wanted to be part of the gang, the Vice Lords, didn't want to sell anymore drugs, and that he was being forced to go and kill somebody. His uncle fingered him to carry out a contract on a dude that owed Ricky—the leader and Big Homie of everyone—a lot of money. He was sure to keep away from Yasmine and Alana in the process.

Based on his statements, signed affidavit, and other detailed relations, the Feds had to take him in under their protection. They took the advantage to squeeze him for far more than he would have initially given.

Everett felt safe to wear a wire and to also wear a mini camera to record many functions and activities that the gang had going on. He was successful in getting Ricky on footage as well, but had nothing incriminating to show the Feds. After about one week of having Everett wear recording devices, they pulled him from the street, whisked him away out of state to a safe house, and continued to milk him further for any and all information that they could, even that against himself, in exchange—potentially—for immunity from prosecution.

It was at this point that the keepers of Everett had to report to their field office in Chicago, for purposes of jurisdiction, and the two dirty boys—Doug and Scott—had gotten the inside scoop on all that was going on from two other dirty agents and provided Ricky with full details, just not a name, and not the full truth of how they came about capturing Everett. At least not at the particular time.

Everett not only lied to Yasmine. He'd lied to Alana and his uncle as well. The lie he put to Alana was that he and his people were looking to expand, and he had to go down South and maybe out West to put it together. She found some truth in his story because of prior times he and some of his people had actually gone out of state to other locales setting up shop and putting in work. But he made sure to always keep in contact, as they'd talk periodically on the phone.

This time around turned out to be a little different. He had not contacted Alana on any accord, and she had no way to get in touch with him, being he'd killed all contact between himself and everybody but the Feds. Alana feared the worst—that Everett had possibly been killed or something—since he was prone to relate stories to her about the many shootouts and other street encounters that they frequently ran into. She didn't know what to think or how to find out what was up with the father of her baby girl.

And on the other end, Everett told his uncle Puncho basically the same lie, but in a different type of way. Everett expressed an ambitious mindset to his uncle. He told him that his little clique outside of the main body he was a part of had scouted out some territory that they could put it down at, and he needed Puncho to spot him a kilo or two of his heroin product to go and serve in these new ghetto havens.

However, Everett took the narcotics that his uncle gave to him, along with recorded conversations, and turned that shit over to the Feds to help support everything he had already related to them and to help them build a strong case in exchange for protection. You talk about being cutthroat and conniving—Everett played the game raw. But nothing was working for him.

Chapter 16

Presently...

ReeRee made the trip out to Lewisburg Federal Prison to visit her client/man again. They had been holding heavy video call conversations leading up to the day. Nightmare had always liked to have people recap all that they had taken care of for him, in terms of business. ReeRee had no problem providing him the full details on her trip to meet Ricky, get the money and the journal, then head back home to LA and be forced to go through the bullshit she would with Jackie.

Whether she knew it or not, she'd brought delight to Nightmare's ears anytime she related the domestic problems that she and her lover were having. He figured that the more problems they'd have, the better his position would turn out to be with her in the long run. By providing her with the things he quickly learned she loved so much—money, expensive gifts, affection, constant attention—and a man who had capabilities to soothe and control her intellectually, and in more ways than just with his dick—the entry into her heart became easy.

The hardest part about the relationship they carried on was being able to maintain a strong level of control of themselves in person and prevent from revealing that there was more to them than "a lawyer coming to meet up with one of her clients." It was the role-playing in the eyes of prison officials that they'd put on, which required more discipline, so as not to blow their cover.

"I'm so glad to see you made it, sweetie," Nightmare said to her as he extended his hand to shake hers and play it off about any possible dealings of the two on a personal level.

"I'm so glad to be here myself," she replied. "I wish like all hell that I could hug you and kiss you, Michael. But unfortunately, I can't," she added.

"Well, we'll just do some foreplay for the time being and make love to each other's mind for these three hours or so and heighten the level of anticipation for the time in between," he said to her.

"What's the name of that damn philosophy book you've been reading and studying on? Because you seem to have the right thing to say almost every time," ReeRee replied to his remark as she smiled in delight and tingled on the inside due to the stimulation his talk game caused.

Nightmare returned a smile of his own and displayed those pearly white expensive set of teeth he possessed. To be a diehard street nigga he deemed himself to be, Nightmare had an extreme obsession about his teeth and oral hygiene. He didn't play at all when it came down to his mouth. Before his arrest, he had put $90,000 into his grill for veneers, two implants of molars, whitening, and the whole nine yards. He was a serious advocate of preserving everything that rested perfectly behind those feminine-like lips of his.

"Let's get down to business, shall we? What's good on the business side of things?" he asked about the money and the journal.

"I took great care of all there were to do. Ricky came off the four hundred thousand as he said he would. I brought along the three thousand you asked for and copied pages of the journal," she related.

"Copied pages?" Nightmare questioned in a confused state.

"Yeah, copied pages. I knew it would be best and easier to get everything to you this way than to risk trying to pass you a journal that's loaded with what you say is supposed to be on those pages. I don't know. I didn't review anything. I simply opened, made copies, and packaged it like it's legal material," she let Nightmare know.

"That was smart on your part."

"Thanks. And not only that," she had more. "The originals are kept in a safe place at my house, in the event that some unfortunate mishap occurred with the copies you got. I could simply make another copy and get it to you, if you're not out by then," she said.

"So we do have a good chance to get this conviction tossed?" he questioned.

"Michael, I don't know if or not you are aware, but almost all cases in federal court that are reversed on grounds of constitutional violations occur because of 'Brady,' the withholding of evidence by the prosecutor."

"I trust your knowledge on the law. Just get me out of this motherfucker the best way you know how, sweetie, so I can finally show you how I really get down as a man," he said.

"I got you, no doubt. Just continue to be patient with the process, okay. Now about the money, I've got three thousand stashed in this envelope right here," she tapped the legal folder which had the thirty $100 bills of cash flattened out inside it. "I did it just like you told me to," she stated.

"Okay," he replied with a smile again.

"Also, of the four hundred thousand, I stashed two hundred in two different locations—a hundred thousand in New York and a hundred thousand in Philly. And I've got a hundred ninety-seven grand out at my place in LA. So that's my mom's place, my dad's place, and my place. I like to keep things spread out. I've learned that's the best way to roll when you're the type of attorney that I am and have the type of clients I represent," ReeRee mentioned.

"So you got a stash spot in New York, Philly, and LA? Your mom from the Big Apple, your dad from the City of Brotherly Love, and you now live in the City of Angels. That's fascinating, ReeRee. I never knew that about you.

How come you know everything about me, but I know nothing at all on such a level about you?" he wanted to know.

ReeRee leaned in and got really close to Nightmare's face, then locked eyes and stated, "It's because, Michael, I'm your lawyer, I'm your lady, and I'm also a woman. And it's very important that a woman find out and be made known of everything about a man long before she gives into him and gives herself away to a man with her life. And not only that, Michael, I'm used to dealing with men that hold positions of power, and you're not the only high-profile client that I've represented. You may be the only one that moves me and causes me to feel really good and special inside about you with your words, but certainly not the sole high-profile figure," she stated, then smiled gleefully at the end of her remark.

"You something else, you know that?" Nightmare complimented.

"And so are you," she replied and moved onto the legal aspects of their meeting.

"I'm set to appear back in Chicago for oral arguments on a few points of law. I mentioned this to you already. But basically, it's only a bunch of legal mumbo jumbo that you wouldn't understand. So I waived your right to be present, because I felt it wouldn't be necessary," she related.

"Again, I respect and adhere to any and all the judgments and decisions you make on my behalf. By the way, while you're in my hometown at the court, I need for you to meet up with Ricky again for me. He's got about a quarter million more for me, okay? I recently spoke to him and he told me what the deal was. So just hit his niece up and y'all do what y'all do for that time being. You get the cash and then be gone after that," Nightmare related.

"Not a problem. I've just got to schedule and reserve a train ticket from Chicago. I can't be trying to risk it like that going through the airport loaded with that type of cash. But no need to worry. It's done," she said.

The meeting went on about two more hours and she hit the highway back to New York to be with her family for the remainder of the weekend, prior to making her way to the Windy City. The closer she and Nightmare had gotten, the more money he began to get out of Ricky and place in the trust of her.

If there were two things that a man could do to keep her attention for the long haul, it was to lay money on her to manage and save, and to also be dependent upon her to take care of his business for him in the proper way that she knew how to do as a woman and a lawyer. It was her mission and duty to do so—and very well.

Chapter 17

Not To Be Played With...

Back at the residence of ReeRee and Jackie. The house had been torn apart little by little and piece by piece at the hands of Jackie. ReeRee was still away on her trip to handle business for Nightmare and to visit with a second client, in addition to visiting him. In Jackie's frantic and desperate search to locate any incriminating evidence that she could find—so as to bring up charges against ReeRee in the love affair that they shared—she completely tossed the house upside down and felt no type of way about it.

Jackie dug through all of ReeRee's personal belongings, legal papers, and other effects, seeking to find out if or not ReeRee were in fact cheating on her, as she'd suspected. Jackie had come to such conclusion after ReeRee vehemently denied her the quality time, love, affection, attention, and all other sensuous pleasures that the relationship once had to offer. She noticed a huge change in her from the way things once were, up to now—how they'd presently devolved into, Jackie felt.

Through her plundering, she'd stumbled upon the personal letters that Nightmare mailed to her, a few of the high-end gifts he'd bought, the trinket boxes that the gifts belonged in, and an article or two of the exquisite and rare jewels that he'd bought for ReeRee. There were rings, necklaces, earrings, and a watch or two.

As Jackie thought to herself, she figured there had to be more to it than the eye could see. ReeRee had to have more someplace else in the house stashed away, according to the content of the letters that Jackie discovered.

She began to really destroy the house at this point, as she got more enraged by the second. Jackie's intuition kicked in and suggested to her to think long and deep on how ReeRee had done things in the past—and to put herself in the position of a woman that absolutely had something to hide from her lover.

Where would something be placed in the house she felt secure to hide, other than in the walk-in closet atop a shelf and at the bottom of the storage drawer where she located all of the newly found valuables? It then hit her. She snapped her finger upon the mental revelation. *The laundry room,* she thought.

Being that ReeRee had been the one to always do the laundry when needed and had spent more time in the laundry room than she had, Jackie had never washed, dried, nor folded not one piece of garment of theirs. That's where she went to look. All of these responsibilities had been the primary duty that belonged to ReeRee.

Since the two had been in a relationship for years on end, and they shared a deep love, they had a good idea on how the other thought when it came to certain matters. They kept an emergency nest egg on a straight *cash-only* policy so they would be ready in the event of any crisis arising. Together, they had about $250,000 put up. But the catch was, at the time when they'd agreed to put money away, the duty was on ReeRee to situate the bread in a proper hiding spot. She did make mention to Jackie on exactly where their money would be tucked away, but Jackie seemed to not pay any attention through the years—up until this point.

This black bitch sprinted down to the basement and pushed the dryer to the side, since it was the easiest to move. With a flat-head screwdriver, Jackie dismounted the panel board that was at floor level on the wall, where the lint tube from the dryer was connected to, and moved it out the way. She ripped the insulation off from the panel board's square-sized space and discovered stacks of miniature rectangular-shaped objects there that were wrapped in black trash bag-type plastic and sealed with electrical tape. They were all layered finely, as if a brick mason had done so. Each stack was about the size of a clay brick—the standard size that houses are built with.

Jackie took each stack out of the stash one by one and placed them atop the washer. The last object she removed was something flat and thin, with slender edges, as if it were a *book* or a *journal* perhaps—maybe one of ReeRee's diaries that she'd "told all" or some sort. It was also wrapped in the same fashion as the brick-like objects.

"Jackpot!" Jackie exclaimed loudly.

Without doubt, she knew she'd located the money, but didn't expect to find as much as she had. *Has ReeRee been putting up more money through the years without me knowing?* Jackie further thought. *Or has that cheating, no-good cunt been keeping money for that guy Michael she's been involved with?* she questioned more in thought. *The guy that bought her those gifts, that jewelry, and had written those letters? And what is this flat thing along with the money? Hmm ... let me see.*

In addition to the ten stacks of money that were the same size, there were four stacks that were larger. She peeled the tape and plastic from one of the larger brick-like objects and found a handwritten label that read, *$50,000* on it.

Wow! I cannot believe what I'm seeing. I can't believe it, Jackie thought on.

She had bombarded herself with a multitude of questions regarding everything. She was in absolute shock to find out all ReeRee had going on behind her back. *Why?* she wanted to know. *Why take the easy road to glory and fame?*

She snapped from her daze and got back to the duty at hand, unwrapping and counting up money. *Okay, where was I?* she further spoke to herself. *There is fifty ... one hundred ... one hundred fifty ... and two hundred. That's two hundred thousand there,* in the four larger stacks of money, Jackie acknowledged. Actually, the money she'd picked up and counted was that from Ricky for Nightmare. The $200,000 ReeRee brought to Los Angeles with her from the $400,000.

Jackie then counted the $100,000 of their money they'd saved together. *That sneaky bitch been laundering money!* she spat. *ReeRee been committing a crime from our home! Ain't no way she's turned out to be this,* Jackie thought on. *She's got to have gone nuts or something. I've got something for her no-good ass. Oh yes I do. I'm going to keep every penny of it, and the gifts, along with the jewelry too!!! What's that bitch gonna do about it? All of it is mine now! Since that bitch wants to cheat and then launder money for a criminal. It's on now. For real it is. I had a hunch she'd been up to something funny, or has been cheating. But now, I've got the proof. And not only that, the bitch has the nerve to be involved with a no-good nigga that's in prison! A fucking jailbird she's in the process of trying to help get free. Fuck that! How she going to accept someone like that over me? There is no way ReeRee is going to have me going out bad like this. No fuckin' way! I definitely plan to do something about this shit.*

***

The part that really pissed Jackie off and alarmed her was about the content of the journal she'd read. She felt that her dear ReeRee had taken a turn for nothing other than the worst. That she'd been manipulated to do things for her client which were against the law and bar rules of being an attorney. With all the information discovered, Jackie knew there was no way ReeRee could back out of the dealings she had become involved in, even if she tried to.

She placed her and Jackie in harm's way by being exposed to the inner workings of a criminal enterprise, and also making moves for them at the risk of their freedom—hers and Jackie's. A no-no for a lawyer.

Jackie's psychotic-ass did have something in store for ReeRee the very moment she was to return from her trip to visit her boyfriend client. She knew that there was no way she could go to the authorities over the money or about the other ill gains ReeRee had accepted. Such honesty would place the spotlight on the both of them and would have inadvertently subjected the lesbian couple to severe scrutiny and investigation, or worse, possible disbarment and prison time. She felt betrayed by the actions and unfaithful nature ReeRee had taken on. But Jackie had not been hurt nor scorned to the point of her wanting to see her sweetheart behind bars. She thought that maybe if they were to talk about a few things, ReeRee may provide her with some solid answers. And also, she loved ReeRee too much to hurt her in any type of way. She only wanted some answers. And ReeRee was qualified, before anyone else, to give.

Jackie was hopeful that their love would be able to stand the test of time as it always had since leaving college. After all, ReeRee did owe her an explanation, being that honesty was always the best policy, she assumed.

Jackie attempted to reach out to ReeRee with repeated phone calls. They were flat out ignored. Text messages the same. Not replied to. And emails that were sent to no avail. Five days lapsed between the last time the two had contact with one another. Being ignored infuriated Jackie. She became unhinged in a way at being shirked, and then she went off the grid, just as ReeRee had planned for ahead of time in anticipation of her to do.

The problem was that ReeRee didn't know Jackie had found the money, the gifts, and most of all, that journal.

Jackie left repeated and unapologetic threats and remarks on ReeRee's voicemail and in text messages and emails. It was mentioned about the discovery of the affair of her and Nightmare. Jackie held back from telling about the money, the gifts, and the "gang book" she found. She wanted to save this for when they were face-to-face, and then they could air out any and all their dirty laundry—each and every issue that they may have.

ReeRee disregarded everything Jackie came at her with, as she wanted to keep focused on the litigation at hand and not be disturbed nor thrown off with Jackie's antics. She didn't want to get angry. To keep level-headed and on point, ReeRee simply turned off her phone and ignored the emails, due to the intense level of harassment which was thrown her way by a newly created arch-nemesis. This turned out to be Jackie.

Jackie threatened that "it was on once she were to return home!" via voicemail. The threat was real. And the very moment ReeRee walked through the door, it would be brought into reality.

Chapter 18

And so, when she returned to LA and entered into their home, Jackie stormed from the bedroom at a fast pace—in her *Stomp the Yard* strut—and aggressively approached ReeRee to confront her about all she was now knowledgeable of. ReeRee was in the act of going to the bedroom to put up her clothes. She had the $250,000 that Ricky recently passed off to her in a Gucci tote bag. She'd been cut short in her path. Jackie had something to say.

"Bitch! Who the fuck you think you playing with, ReeRee? Huh! How the fuck you gonna be out there cheating on me like this and doing me the way you are, and thinking I wasn't gonna find out?" Jackie ranted and raved at the top of her lungs. She offered ReeRee no room to speak, as there wasn't a break in all that came out of her mouth.

"And not only that ... bitch! Not only do I question you being faithful! Not only are you disrespecting the relationship. But you not even keeping true to the creed of being lesbian! You stepped outside of the life and began to deal with a low-down, no good, and dirty dog of a man that the both of us supposed to hate so much," Jackie said.

Her accosting ReeRee was utterly laughable in a way, as Jackie still possessed a strong hint of her African accent, which may give an unknowing person the impression she was younger than she actually was in age, and that she may not have meant business like they would expect a serious woman would, due to the teenage-like tone of her voice. But mind you and believe this—she was a fierce black bitch when she wanted to be. A warlord or an African strongman in the person of a female specimen. A girl version of the late African dictator, Idi Amin Dada.

ReeRee was finally able to try and offer a response, as she began very calmly and nonchalantly, giving the impression to Jackie that she was still ignoring her or just really didn't care.

"Look, Jackie, okay. I don't care—"

Jackie cut her words off and dropped a bomb on her by revealing the fact that she'd found the jewelry, the gifts, and had also taken all of the money. If Jackie hadn't ever gotten her attention before, in all of their years of being together, she damn sure had it then.

"Yeah, bitch, I found all those bullshit letters and shit you had stashed up in the closet. And guess what else? I went down to the laundry room and also found that money you had tucked away behind the dryer too, bitch," Jackie stated.

By the time the last two words left her tongue, ReeRee darted to the bedroom closet to check and know if she was telling the truth. She frantically searched for her belongings in the closet, hoping that Jackie had only placed them in a different spot. No luck. Jackie had relocated everything to another place. ReeRee knew not where. In the trunk of her car maybe?

Chapter 19

ReeRee then ran down to the basement to check on the money and the journal. She pushed the dryer to the side and noticed the panel board had been removed and the bread was gone. Jackie had waited in the living room and snickered like a motherfucker as she anticipated ReeRee to return—then, she could really tell her about herself.

ReeRee rushed Jackie and demanded that she hand it over or else.

"Bitch, where the fuck is my damn money and my other shit? Where the fuck is it? Give it to me, Jackie! And I mean it! Because you don't know what you are doing. You don't really know what you are about to start. I'm going to ask you one last time—"

"Or else what, bitch?" Jackie cut her off and said. "What you gonna do? You can't go to the police. They'll lock your ass up for sure for money laundering and other related crimes. And you'll have your license taken and no longer be able to practice law. So what can you do about it?" Jackie taunted.

"Jackie, where the fuck is my money and my other shit at, bitch? Give me my shit! I'm so sick and tired of you and all your drama!" ReeRee stated to her.

"It's not here anymore," Jackie responded.

"What the fuck do you mean, '*it's not here anymore*'? Where the fuck is it?" ReeRee shouted. She then grabbed Jackie by the arm and shirt, then yanked on her in an attempt to force her to turn over the goods.

In Jackie's mind, everything she'd taken from ReeRee would be charged to the game as the "spoils of war"—valuables and finances that would be utilized for the common good of humanity and for all of the causes that she stood for, as opposed to the desires of ReeRee.

Jackie considered keeping ReeRee's belongings to be compensation for the bad behavior her lover had been committing throughout the times leading up to the moment. Although Jackie had been convinced by ReeRee to take her practice of law into the area of post-conviction, her mentality as a prosecutor had went into full effect without fail—even so, against the woman whom she loved so dearly. Jackie couldn't let up, and she couldn't show any mercy in her decision to teach ReeRee a lesson.

Jackie tried to free herself from the clutches of ReeRee's grip to no avail. She refused to turn her loose.

"Bitch, let me go!" Jackie stated.

She still refused and continued to tug on her, demanding those possessions back. Jackie then forcefully yanked her arms free, and within the blink of an eye, she'd stolen off on ReeRee with a hard sucker punch to the right side of the jaw and a mean left hook. The fight was on. ReeRee fired back with a punch of her own to the rib cage of Jackie and grabbed her by the arms again as she kneed her in the gut. She then grabbed two handfuls of Jackie's dreadlocks, yanked her head low, kneed her in the face and then again to the forehead.

ReeRee must have experienced a flashback of some sort—of one of those terrible beatdowns that Cadillac Nate had put on her in the past—because it appeared that she had literally snapped and possibly had lost it. She had not been placed under such circumstances and forced to duke it out in battle like this since the night she had to free herself from the near-death experience that Nate had threatened, before she pumped two hot pieces of lead in that nigga's ass. She taught him a lesson or two, and in the scrimmage that was being fought out with Jackie, ReeRee wanted to do the same thing—teach this bitch a lesson about fucking with her.

Jackie was briefly dazed for a second or two, but then she shook it off and regained the focus to fight more, as ReeRee continued to pummel her with vicious haymakers and manic blows of rights, uppercuts, left hooks, and knees—all about the head and body with precision and accuracy. Jackie finally managed to get a good shot off of her own and landed a nice blow to the eye of ReeRee, taking away her sight.

Being thirteen pounds heavier than ReeRee, Jackie went all the way the fuck in on her physically, overpowering the Dominican half-breed and putting her in a chokehold from behind as she maneuvered to gain such position to better fight.

"You see what you making me do to you, bitch!" Jackie spat. "Huh! I told you your weak-ass shoulda never been so stuck up on that 'pretty-girl' shit and strutting around on compound like you had a fucking tiara on your head or something! Now look at you, bitch. Look at you! You silly bitch!" Jackie had snarled and spat all types of fight theme slogans and remarks as they scrapped like they'd never been in a relationship before and had always been bitter foes for years on end.

ReeRee struggled to get free from the submission hold and grasp of Jackie as she gasped for a breath of air while being held in such a choke-out tactic. She'd almost been at the point of blacking out as she fought, twisted, squirmed, and scratched in her efforts to get free from the hold. But she clearly was no match for the athletic and Grace Jones muscle-bound type woman that Jackie was.

Jackie's African culture and tradition required all females be circumcised at birth, and this such practice altered the hormonal balance and stripped away much of her feminine side—being that she rumbled thoroughly and went to war as if she were a dude of some sort. This bitch worked ReeRee ten times over.

All of a sudden, ReeRee came to her senses and remembered that she still had on a pair of heels, as she'd just walked through the front door when Jackie approached on the bullshit. She didn't have any time to kick them off, and that probably served her well—as Jackie had already beaten and damn near strangled her to death out of one of the heels from the jump. The left shoe remained—her strong leg.

ReeRee came down extremely hard on the bare foot of Jackie and caused her to loosen the python-tight coil grip she had around her neck. She then grabbed her by the same arm that almost caused her to be a dearly departed, and sank her teeth into it.

With a lock from hell, as if she were a female American Pitbull Terrier, she ripped a chunk out of the right bicep of Jackie like a rabid dog that had never been domesticated.

Being nimble on her toes and thinking faster than Jackie, as the fighter and survivor she was, ReeRee hurriedly made a break for the door in an effort to get the fuck out the house before she wouldn't be able to. But Jackie had blocked her path and offered no way of escape. ReeRee grabbed her laptop from the coffee table and with both hands holding it, she knocked Jackie upside the head with the first blow, then along the right side of the face with the second—sending her falling to the side, downward onto the glass table, and breaking it in the process.

ReeRee snatched her keys from the wall ring holder and darted out the door. She got into her car and sped off down the road, burning rubber from the tires in the process. She was en route to check into a hotel far away from the house, until she would be able to have a restraining order put in place and return by police escort to get her belongings.

This particular cat fight between the two turned out to be, by far, the worst and the nastiest they'd ever gotten into. The very last one, to be exact—as ReeRee had absolutely zero intentions on returning, or with being involved in such a relationship that she no longer wanted to be in.

***

A firestorm was ignited, and all sorts of aggressive actions and behaviors by the crazy heifer Jackie were in the process of going down from this day onward. The stupid love-sick bitch had a crazy, never-ending list of shit she sought to do to avenge all of the wrong, the hurt, the emotional pain and suffering she'd been forced to endure by ReeRee—and Nightmare, of all people.

Not only this, but when ReeRee had run out of the house to get away, she'd left behind the $250,000 in cash in her bag that she'd picked up from Ricky for Nightmare. She'd completely forgotten about it and had only been reminded once she began to recollect all Jackie had taken. This only added fuel to the fire and caused the situation to heat up like no other.

Chapter 20

Just To Let You Know...

The day after their fight, Jackie initiated her first personal attack and declaration of war against Nightmare. It came in the form of an aggressive and threatening letter that contained hateful words, spitefulness, and a few derogatory epithets which clearly let Nightmare know that the bitch was an absolute psychopath who despised men on all levels, and to the core. She'd made him completely aware that she had intended to stop at nothing to do him harm, and in a major way if necessary:

To: Michael Gentry
From: Jackie

Dear Jailbird,
It's a fact we don't know one another, nor do I have any intentions to get to know you. But just to let you know, the reason for this letter is because I wanted to personally let you know that you have offended and wronged me in a way that's unforgivable and unapologetic, in my view. It's to the point that I absolutely couldn't resist the temptation to write to you and express how I feel. You criminal and disgusting waste of life. You are a despicable bastard. Are you aware of that? How dare you take away from me the only love I've ever wanted and the only love I've ever known affectionately? At no point in my life have I ever been with a

man in a relationship, or otherwise, and I never will either. I will never experience what a traditional relationship is like, because I don't care for it.

Michael, please, allow me to be very frank and blunt about this, okay. So again, just to let you know—Jettica is my lady, okay? She's mine! She belongs to me, not you. Do you understand me, motherfucker? You are a scumbag and a worthless piece of shit. Jettica and I were in the process of getting married, and everything else that goes along with us being a happy couple. We shared a happy space until your dog-ass came along and fucked everything up. Again— you've offended the wrong bitch, buddy. And now, you must pay. I cannot let you get away with the bullshit you've caused. It's on and popping, dude. Just be ready.

And to also let you know, I found all of those expensive gifts you bought for Jettica, along with everything else. I've got your letters—that's how I was able to get your information. What else would you like to know? Oh yeah, all of the money you had her travel to Chicago to pick up for you? I've got that too. It was almost a "half million" in cash. How do you like that? I have that "gang journal" too, the one you had her pick up, and I guess at some point soon, she was going to try to get it into your hands—but that won't be possible any longer.

My first instincts told me to turn all of this shit over to the Feds—the cash and the journal. But I figured that I could make good charitable contributions with the money to help a few people that need it instead, and then turn the journal over to the Feds at some point if you don't back down. About the money going to better causes—you are repaying your debt to society, right? This, along with you not being able to get free, should be a great start. I plan to spend every penny in a useful way, because if you must know, I am a law-abiding citizen and an officer of the court—someone that you will never be, nor know anything about.

You have the remainder of your natural life in prison, so you won't be missing the money any time soon, and there ain't a thing you are able to do about it. Had I not feared the wrath of the government coming down on us and placing Jettica and me on a list for investigation, and putting us at risk for being disbarred, all of that dirty money would have been turned in and you would have been subject to another prosecution and had time added to the life term you already have. That would literally mean a life term in this life you now live, and a life term in the one to come. How do you love that—life now and life later? Smile for me, will you.

Anyways, I don't know how in the hell you were able to convince and influence Jettica to not only break the law, but to continue committing high-crimes at your behest. I'm still trying to figure out why you and she had the audacity to detail all of your business in those letters y'all exchanged— her trip to Chicago, the visit with some guy named Ricky, the amount of money she laundered for you, and everything else. Why would you two be so foolish to do that? Just wait until the United States Attorney's office gets their hands on this shit. I'm going to have that no-good cheating bitch housed in a Federal prison that's specifically for whores, right next to the one you're in. Watch.

I guess that the old saying is true: "Once a whore, always a whore." A whore that's hot in the ass at that. Jettica has clearly reverted to her old ways. But that's okay—I plan on fixing this.

All I have left to say is—back the fuck off, okay. Or else. Don't forget that I am an attorney myself, and I do know people on the inside who can connect with other people and touch you, if that's what it takes. I have that kind of power, as my people may need a little help on their legal issues from time to time by a lawyer. So "a favor for a favor" can work out well, if you get my drift. They do a job for me, and in return, I do a job for them. It's just that simple.

You make the call—O.G. Jettica, or your life? It's all on you. Bye.

After reading the letter Jackie had sent to him, Nightmare then and there came to the conclusion that, indeed, the bitch was psychotic—for real. Little had Jackie known that Nightmare was not the type of nigga to take threats lightly, and she had been the one to fire the first shot that was heard around the world. Nightmare had planned and prepared to make a preemptive strike, but Jackie had already taken precautions and decisive measures ahead of him.

Did she not know, nor take into account, that Nightmare was a street general himself and had retained a certain level of power and muscle on the turf? What had she been thinking to go so far as to threaten a nigga like him? He had always been capable of smelling a trap that may have been laid for him.

The thing that made matters worse with his newly created foe was the fact that she had robbed ReeRee of those jewels, those gifts, and all that cash. Not to mention the danger she posed by having possession of that journal. It was the money she took which really instigated a war and caused snakes to really jump out of birthday cakes, in the mind of Nightmare. He was serious about his money.

Nightmare may not have been so offended at the bitch had she left the money and the journal alone. But no—this bitch had to get fancy and step all the way out of line on the bullshit. And for this, Nightmare hatched a plot in his mind to have the bitch whacked, and then permanently removed—for the old and for the new, for ReeRee and for himself.

Jackie had plots of her own as well. Nightmare just didn't know it.

Chapter 21

Crashing Out...

Ricky finally made up his mind on what to do with his daughter in order to press her into telling him who it was she'd been sexually involved with, being that this anonymous guy was the key figure to all that the FBI had on him. They were building a very strong case on the information which was being provided, courtesy of the confidential informant, the same dude that was sexing his teenage daughter.

Ricky had already talked to his wife on what he intended to do, as he'd mentioned bits and pieces to Loretta. But gave no details. Also, he mentioned on what his paid inside guys had related to him. He'd sent Loretta and their other kids away for a weekend vacation, down to Disney World in the state of Florida, but prohibited Yasmine from going, by making the claim that she had failing grades in school, a capped up lie he utilized to ground her in the house so that he could make his move.

The time was three thirty A.M. this Saturday morning. Loretta and the others were not due to be back until the upcoming Monday afternoon. Yasmine had been up all night, until about two thirty, talking on her phone to her girlfriends and playing on social media. She was sound asleep when Ricky made his move. He barged into her room unannounced and headed straight to the nightstand that had her cell phone and tablet charging on it. Yasmine had awakened from her sleep to find her father unplugging her personal devices and securing them in his hands.

"Daddy! What are you doing, dude?" Yasmine asked.

"Get up! Get dressed, now! And don't question me," Ricky demanded.

"Daddy! Wait! Why are you taking my phone and tablet?" she cried out.

"This ain't all I'm taking. I'm about to get everything from you," Ricky responded. "And I just told your ass, don't ask me no damn questions! Now get up and put them damn shoes on right there," he gestured in pointing at a pair of Nike's she had at the side of her bed. "And let's go. We got somewhere to be," he stated with some aggression in his voice to let her know he meant business.

Yasmine angrily jumped out of the bed and immediately reached for her phone and tablet, due to the thought shooting through her mind of all the sensitive information she had stored inside. Ricky paused momentarily and gave his daughter a stern look that almost had the potential to cause her to have a miscarriage right there on the spot. She reluctantly pulled away, then slowly began to put on her sneakers as Ricky got back to pocketing her phone, watch phone, and clutching her tablet tightly under his arm.

As he waited for her to put on her footwear, he stood over her and mean-mugged the entire time. "Now let's go," he said and directed she lead the way downstairs to the garage. Ricky hit the remote to disarm his Tahoe, indicating to Yasmine what vehicle they would be leaving in.

"Daddy, where are we going?" Yasmine asked in a demanding way, as she reached for the door handle of the SUV to get in.

"If you ask me that shit one more muthafuckin' time, Yabby, I know something," Ricky responded more serious now than he had the entire time. "Now shut your goddamn mouth until told to talk," he added as they both got situated in the truck and he pulled off.

Yasmine knew from this point to keep quiet because her daddy seriously meant business and was subject to go off on her at any moment's notice. She didn't have the slightest clue in the world where they were headed and Ricky kept silent the entire one-hour ride.

They arrived at a very secluded house in the woods of the Illinois country side, northwest of Chicago. The home was a modest, three-bedroom, brick house that had a carport and a basement to it. It was a residence that no one from the family or crew knew about but Ricky alone, as he'd bought it about four months earlier and had added security features to it, like a 2,500-pound steel door to the master bedroom, the same as he had at their family home in Chicago. He also had the basement outfitted to a setting he literally was dying to put to use at some point soon, at the first available opportunity.

He pulled into the carport and let down the doors by remote. "Get out," he ordered his daughter.

By the time she'd exited and made it to the front, Daddy met her at the hood of the truck and grabbed her by the wrist tightly, escorting her to the door of the house. He unlocked it and they entered with him immediately locking the door securely behind.

All windows and doors had bars on them, so whatever Ricky had in mind, Yasmine would not be able to readily escape his wrath. He basically dragged his daughter to the master bedroom and they entered with him securing the 2,500-pound door behind.

"Daddy, why are we here? What is this all about?" she asked.

"Sit your ass down on that bed and I'll tell you what this all about," he barked as he sat the tablet on the carpeted floor by the door and out of reach of Yasmine. He still had the phone and the watch in his pocket. "Now, you ready to start talking? Because your ass ain't going nowhere until you give me some answers, you little bitch, you!" Ricky cursed his daughter like he didn't know her from a runaway hooker

171

who'd robbed him in the past, and he now had the capabilities to punish her for it.

***

Yasmine was taken aback at her daddy's words towards her and began to tear up as her father had never talked to her like this. Ever.

"Daddy, why you cursing me?" She wanted to know.

"Yabby, you done really fucked up, baby. You done *really* fucked up, you hear me!" Ricky spat.

"What have I done, Daddy?" she asked.

"Baby, you've gotten your daddy in a lot of trouble, sweetie," he said to her.

She dropped her head and began to cry.

"Don't cry now. I haven't even begun to ask you nothing yet," he stated to her.

She held her head up and then asked, "Well, why you got to take my phone and tablet and stuff from me? And why we got to come way out to this place this early in the morning for you to talk to me? We could have did this at home, Daddy."

"Why I took your phone, tablet, and watch is because I paid for them. And in a minute, you gonna put in your pass-code to unlock everything for me. And why we had to come out here instead of staying home is because I had chosen to do this my way and far out, so no one will hear you scream, if it came down to it. Now, I'm the one who's supposed to be doing all the questioning. So let's begin," he said and pulled a chair up close to the bed, directly in front of Yasmine as she sat on the edge.

"Yabby, who the fuck is this older guy you been skipping school to be with, and been having fuckin' since you were fourteen years old?" Ricky demanded to know.

"Daddy, I ain't been with no older dude. And no I'm not going to tell you who my boyfriend is, so you can send someone to beat him up. And who mentioned something to you anyway? Alana, didn't she?" Yasmine spat in defiance to her father.

Whop!

Ricky slapped the shit out of Yasmine, knocking her over onto the floor where she lay curled up in the fetal position, holding the side of her face.

"Get the fuck up!" he demanded, then yanked her up by the arm and pushed her onto the bed again. Her face had begun to swell and she cried like there was no tomorrow.

"Now, let's try this shit again, you little disrespectful bitch, you! I'm gonna treat you just like what you are, until you show me otherwise. You not no daughter of mine right now, so stop saying that," Ricky stated serious-toned so as to leave no room for what the intent was he had in mind. "Once again, who is this guy you been fuckin' since you were fourteen? And not only that, he got all types of videos of the two of you fuckin', of you sucking his dick, and of you shaking your ass, popping your little hot pussy open for him, and the whole nine yards. Not to mention the pictures of you naked he got too," Ricky blasted his daughter with his words.

He'd obtained the videos and photos that there were of his daughter, from the two dirty agents, Doug and Scott. Videos that they selected to hand over to him from the collection of material that they had Everett cough up. The footage didn't show the face of the person doing the recording, as they'd blocked out the identity of their C-I, but clearly showed the face of Yasmine, her private parts and all that she was doing, whether that was having intercourse, performing orally, or playing with herself for the camera.

Ricky asked for proof that indeed his daughter was doing everything that they'd claimed she'd been doing, so the dirty agents provided him with all the information to log into an email account that had the videos and photos stored onto it.

Ricky knew, without a doubt from that point, that the boys on his payroll had been relating the truth and not making something up to try and juice him out of more money. Ricky did eventually end up paying a hefty tip for the intel, to enable him the chance to get the mess cleaned up long before he would be forced to pay a major price with his life or freedom from the penalty behind the mistakes his people had made; of all people, his very own daughter.

"What's that part about Alana supposed to be knowing something to tell me?" Ricky stood over Yasmine and asked.

Still holding the side of her face, tears in her eyes and whimpering, she said to her father, "I had talked to Alana about a few problems I was having ... basic female talk that two girl cousins would have—"

"Un-huh! And what else?" Ricky butted in and asked.

"And I told her a little bit of what I had going on. I only said something to her to get her advice and I begged her please not to say anything to you or momma, to prevent this type of behavior from you. But obviously, she broke her promise and ran her mouth to you anyway," Yasmine said.

"And what was that conversation all about between you and Alana?" Ricky demanded to be told.

"I ain't telling you that, Daddy. That's woman talk and my personal business," Yasmine defiantly stated and rolled her neck as she stood up to the demands of her daddy.

Whop!

Ricky slapped the shit out of her again, sending her back down to the floor once more. The blow he put on her this time was far worse than the first. He stood over her, leaned down, snatched her hand away from protecting her face, held her by the wrist tightly to keep her from blocking her face, and began to vehemently slap his daughter silly as if she were one of his worst enemies.

Ricky literally blacked out and began slapping his sixteen-year-old daughter senseless.

Whop-Whop ... Whop ... Whop ... Whop!

174

He hit her blow after blow, and lick after lick, backhanded her and all, until he was near out of breath. He paused to catch his wind and huffed out a few words to Yasmine.

"Now ... is ... that enough to let you know ... that I really mean business, you little bitch, you! Get the fuck back up!" he snarled at her.

Barely conscious, she reluctantly got to her knees and eased up onto the bed, then rolled over to lay down.

"Sit your muthafuckin' ass up, bitch!" Ricky spat and called his daughter out of her name yet another time. He snatched his phone from his hip, rapidly logged into the email account which had those videos and photos of Yasmine stored on it, and turned the screen of the phone in her direction. "Look at this shit, Yabby," he demanded and showed her ten to fifteen second snippets of her sex videos, where she'd been getting banged from behind in some, and sucked on a penis in the others. He also showed her the photos too.

***

Lost His Mind...

Everything was visibly clear, and she'd seen her face on all her daddy presented to her. Yasmine simply sat there and didn't utter a word. She had her lips poked out and both hands on the side of her face, with her elbows propped on her knees. Her face was badly swollen, but Ricky expressed not a concern in the world behind any of this. He literally didn't give a shit.

"What you got to say for yourself now?" he asked.

Yasmine had not the slightest clue in hell how her daddy had gotten hold of the material he had of her.

"You can't say that it's not you," he added.

She felt betrayed because she thought Everett had maybe posted the photos and videos online for the public to see, and her daddy had gotten them from there. She also thought her father might've paid someone to hack into her accounts or something of that nature. The bottom line was that he had evidence to everything he'd accused her of—but didn't know who the guy was that she was with. She thought it might be possible to endure the beating her father was putting on her and make it past that point without revealing who the guy was she made those videos with.

But man, was she sadly mistaken.

"Here," Ricky stated, as he threw her phone at her, hitting her hard in the chest with it.

"Unlock that goddamn phone, right now, bitch!" he spat in anger.

Yasmine had really begun to cry now, as she knew shit had gotten real. She knew without a doubt that if she unlocked her phone and exposed to her daddy all the things she had inside, he would beat her to the very brink of death—if not literally kill her by mistake in overdoing the ass-whipping itself.

She hit a button or two and fidgeted around on the screen of her phone, absolutely refusing to unlock it. Then, she became extremely defiant and went against her father by blatantly refusing.

"No! I'm not gonna unlock my phone and show you nothing, because it ain't none of your business to know what my business is!" Yasmine spat.

"What?" Ricky exclaimed. He then lunged for her throat with both his hands.

He was unable to get a hand on her due to Yasmine weaving out of the way and making a break for the door of the room. It was locked, and she was trapped on the inside with no way out from behind the 2,500-pound steel door.

Ricky ran her down and cornered her at the door of the room.

"You little bitch! I'm gonna fuck you up, you hear me!" he spat and clutched her by the throat, then began to choke her uncontrollably.

He lifted her off her feet and into the air by the throat, then slammed the poor little girl down hard to the floor. He shook her left to right like a rag doll, then stood and put his foot in her ass two to three times.

"You little bitch! Now who the fuck you think you talking to about 'what you is and what you ain't gonna do?' I brought you up in this muthafuckin' world, and bitch, I'll take your ass out if I have to!" he spat, as he slapped her hard against the side of her face—she'd forgotten to cover and block.

"Daddy, why you doing me like this?" she asked.

"I don't want to hear that shit! Just do what the fuck I tell you to, that's it!" he said and slammed the phone down on her head for her to unlock.

Yasmine remained lying on the floor, curled up and defeated by the blows and action her daddy put on her. She reluctantly unlocked her phone, then passed it back to him. He snatched it out of her hand and attempted to access the gallery app, which had the videos and photos in it. Yasmine had an app lock security feature on all of her apps.

Ricky kicked her hard in the gut and demanded the passcode.

"What the fuck is the passcode? What the fuck is the passcode to this app lock shit?" he demanded.

Yasmine had thrown up from the kick and could barely breathe at the moment. She managed to mumble out the app lock passcode, due to the fear she felt of her father possibly kicking her in the stomach once more—guaranteeing a miscarriage of her baby then.

"God please, don't let my daddy kill me in this house right now," Yasmine prayed.

"Your muthafuckin' ass better do more than pray to God to help you out of this shit. Because if I go in this goddamn phone and find more shit than I already know, I'mma kill you dead my damn self, you little bitch," Ricky had warned.

He finally had total access and was sure to keep memory of the passcode. He couldn't risk placing the phone back into the hands of Yasmine, as he feared she might get bold and dial 9-1-1 to report he was in the process of killing her.

Ricky absolutely could not believe his eyes and ears at all he had seen and heard. Yasmine lay on the floor crying and crying and crying about everything she knew her father was subject to see and hear on her phone.

Ricky had taken his precious time in going through one video after another, one photo after another. She had an album in her gallery titled *Video Diary*, which had recordings of herself speaking very freely about everything—her being pregnant, how much she loved Everett, how much she hated her parents, what she was intending to name her baby, and everything else.

She had another album titled *Me and My Love Making Sweet Love*, which essentially was all the videos and photos of her and Everett having sex or her sucking on his dick. The videos on her phone clearly revealed who the guy was that she'd been involved with—and the revelation of who the informant was.

Ricky couldn't immediately make out exactly who the guy was, then it hit him, once he thought on it a little more.

"I know damn well that ain't E-Nice, is it?" he blurted out. "Yasmine! Is this Alana's boyfriend, E-Nice, you been fucking since you were fourteen?" he asked.

But she refused to answer him. Ricky kicked her in the back.

"Answer me, bitch!" he spat. "Is this Alana's boyfriend— Alana's kid's dad—you been creeping around with?" he asked in an angry voice that revealed the hurt and the pain he'd felt in knowing that if it was indeed him, the Feds had all the evidence they needed to put him away forever. His days as a free man—or even a living man—would be coming to an end very soon.

Chapter 22

Tripped Out Ain't The Word...

Yasmine knew she was trapped with no one to help her, so she had to answer up and reveal everything. As bad as she didn't want to answer her father, she had to.

"Yes, Daddy. That's E-Nice—Everett—Alana's baby daddy," she responded.

"Yabby! How could you? Do you know how much shit you've caused me?" he stated, thinking of all the activities that E-Nice had been exposed to. He'd been to Ricky's home too many times to count and had inside information on the entire Vice Lord operation that Ricky headed.

Right in that moment, it hit Ricky—E-Nice is Puncho's nephew. This the nigga the Feds got all their accurate information from. About homicides, kidnappings, drug deals, trap locations, and everything else. This the nigga Puncho trusted the most to go do hits with—his sister's son. This the nigga he took with him to take out that stupid, stubborn old bastard Nixon, who owned the bar, he thought.

He turned around and looked down at his daughter with a grimaced expression on his face as he continued to go through the phone. He then kicked Yasmine hard in the back again and punched her in the rib cage, possibly breaking a few in the process.

"Get the fuck off that floor, bitch! And tell me right now what the fuck you were thinking when your little hot ass started to fuck your cousin's boyfriend—the nigga she got a kid by!" he spat at her.

She didn't move. Only balled up tighter in the fetal position.

"Yasmine!" Ricky yelled. "What the fuck were you thinking?"

She began to cry almost nonstop at this point and offered her excuse in the hopes that maybe the beating would stop. "It was wrong. Daddy, I'm so sorry, okay. I wasn't thinking at all. Please forgive me," she begged.

Ricky lost it. He leaned down, punching the shit out of his daughter right in the jaw. He did it again, and proceeded to check her phone more. Just by going through his daughter's device, he was now provided everything he needed to know about who it was supplying the Feds their information. Everett had placed Ricky and his uncle under the gun on two different fronts—all because he'd fucked up and lost control of his sexual desires.

The first instance was that: he could have caused them enough trouble to get the death penalty behind all the murders he held firsthand information about. The second: he could have caused Ricky to be killed from an order by the Italian mob boss who supplied him his product. Being his supplier connected him to the agents—Doug and Scott—they held additional responsibility to report to the Mob Don about any messy activity that could potentially cause him harm or get him into trouble with the law. And Mister Francesca couldn't have this. He'd have that Black monkey in Ricky killed long before Doug and Scott could make it to him to give warning that trouble was lurking—just as they'd warned Ricky in the aftermath of Everett being on the verge of destroying his empire.

"How long were you gonna wait to tell me you were pregnant?" he asked Yasmine as he continued to go through her phone.

"I was gonna tell you. But you probably done killed my baby now, when you kicked me in the stomach. You probably killed your own grandbaby. This would've been your second behind Donovan's son," she responded.

"Huh. You think so? Please, forget it," he replied to her remark and stopped on a video album titled *Me Blessing My Boo.* Ricky clicked onto the album and observed Everett showing off cash and jewelry while talking shit into the camera. The crazy part about it—all the jewelry that Everett had on looked exactly like the jewelry he once owned before he'd "misplaced" it.

Then Everett made a statement that clearly revealed he'd gotten the watches and other jewelry from Yasmine. "Yeah, I got these top dollar watches and pink diamond pinky ring from my little boo thang today. My sweetie also blessed me with two G's in cash for my birthday. I love her so much," he said, as Yasmine leaned into the video and kissed him.

That was the last time they shared at the motel before Everett ran to the Feds. Ricky had the volume up loud enough to where Yasmine was able to hear all that the video played.

"Yasmine! I know good and muthafuckin' well that those were not my watches and my pinky ring I've been missing all this time! And my money too, huh? You little bitch, you stole from me? I know damn well you ain't stole from me, Yabby! And then got the nerve to give my shit to that nigga! Then you two got the audacity to make a video about how you 'blessed him' with something for his birthday?

"Yasmine, that pinky ring been in my family for ten decades now. A hundred years! And now you steal it from me and give it to that random nigga you been fucking! How could you?" Ricky wanted to know. But Yasmine could offer no answer, and continued to keep quiet from absolute fear.

Ricky felt betrayed more than ever, and really didn't want to do what his very own daughter had literally forced him to. But he had no choice. In his mind, the act of treason to the degree that she'd committed, along with the mess which her dealings with Everett had caused, could only be remedied by one act itself—death to the perpetrator and nothing less.

Ricky tossed Yasmine's phone onto the bed, as he'd seen more than enough. He then ran over to where she was still lying on the floor. He kicked her in the stomach three times—hard as fuck. With great force. There was no regard whatsoever if or not his precious girl was pregnant with his grandbaby. He didn't give a damn. Not at all.

He reached down and grabbed Yasmine around the throat with both hands and began choking her, as if she was supposed to have been dead two years ago when she began having sex with Everett.

***

Gone Too Far...

Ricky began to cry himself as he was strangling the very life out of his daughter—lifting her up off the floor about one foot, then slamming her back down hard, banging her head violently in the process. He straddled atop Yasmine, still choking, with her eyes threatening to pop out of their sockets and her mouth agape. He pressed down harder and squeezed viciously as she clawed and slapped at him, while life seeped from her body with each second of no air entering into her system. She squirmed and kicked as Ricky pressed and held, with no regard nor remorse, until eventually, her body and limbs went limp—and she was dead as a doorknob.

Ricky continued to press on her throat for the better part of three minutes, well after the fact of her being already dead. He finally loosened his clutch slowly, dropped his head to his chest, and cried nonstop, with tears falling, hitting his daughter's body in the face.

Ricky sobbed and asked God to please forgive him.

"Lord, please forgive me, but it had to be done. My daughter, as you know, had turned into a demon and an evil being. She became somebody that had to be eliminated for the greater good of the family. She simply had to go, Lord. Please forgive me, Father God. Please," he prayed.

Ricky had killed his daughter. And by doing so, the cleanup process of elimination had begun—with all the mess that had been caused. He didn't want to, but such killing was an act that had to be done, so he reasoned with himself.

Ricky had committed the unthinkable. He'd blacked out and lost it, with no conscious regard of who it was he'd been choking, nor to what degree he was carrying out the act.

At the point of returning to sanity, he slumped to the floor, sobbed, cried, and whimpered like he'd never done before. But what was done had been done, and there was no bringing little Yabby back from death. He laid down beside his daughter's body and stroked her bangs. He also stroked her along the structure of her chin. He then kissed her on the forehead.

"Oh no. What on God's earth have I done? This can't be reality. This can't be true. What have I done?" he said aloud to himself.

Ricky then pulled out his cellphone, removed the back plate, and took the battery out. He walked over and grabbed Yasmine's phone and tablet and did the same thing. By doing so, any signal that the devices gave GPS tracking to had been powered off. Ricky lay next to his daughter's body and dozed off to take a nap while contemplating what to do next.

He awoke two hours later, just past the crack of dawn, and thought on exactly how to conceal the fact that he'd taken the life of his very own daughter. The home was in a wooded location and had a decent area behind it where thick brush and a lot of trees existed. He utilized one of the shovels in the tool shed, dug a grave for Yasmine's body, and buried her there.

***

Once he was back in Chicago, long before his wife and the other kids were to return, his plan was to call around in a panic frenzy—to Alana, his sister Maxine, and other family members—asking them if they had seen Yabby, because she'd run away from home and he hadn't heard from her.

Prior to doing so, he would go to her room and gather everything a teenager would take with them if they were to run away from the home of their parents. He would then make all the necessary phone calls and have people come over to the house to assist him with locating Yasmine, if possible. After two weeks or so of this, he and his wife, along with Maxine, would then get the police involved and put out a Missing Person's report.

Following this, he would only have his own conscience to deal with and then return to the additional business at hand: killing Puncho, killing a customer of his that turned rat in Milwaukee—Colin Abrams, aka "City Blue"—and then pay whatever price tag Doug and Scott would ask of him to take out that punk motherfucker, Everett. Or better yet, deliver him to Ricky for him to do it himself, since it definitely had turned personal.

Ricky was in a race against time. The faster he could take care of the pressing matters at hand, the better the outcome he would have, versus the agents of the Feds he didn't have on his payroll who possibly wanted to put him away. Although it was his very own daughter, it was one body down and three to go. Ricky had transformed into the same type of killer that he'd personally witnessed his friend Nightmare turn into—a bloodthirsty wolf. A motherfucker who operated as a pretty-faced businessman, and someone who didn't play the radio. Murder became a mandatory duty, and his soul was on ice.

SECTION THREE

Chapter 23

Flexing Muscle...

In keeping true to her threat to do Nightmare the harm she swore she would, Jackie amplified the beef and wasted no time to get at this nigga. She had gotten a subpoena issued upon the BOP, regarding being provided the entire inmate profile of record on Nightmare's institutional history. The task was easy for her, being she was an attorney herself. She was made aware of everything that he'd done, dating from the time of his inception into the prison system. Everything—like how many times he'd made commissary, how many times he'd had money put on his inmate account, how much money he had on his account, how many times he'd been to medical, how many visits he'd had, who all he had on his visitation list, and so on and so forth.

However, the most important body of information Jackie was interested in knowing was regarding the affiliation and other ties Nightmare held part of, as her intentions were to manipulate any of the facts and make life hard as possible for her new foe. She'd plotted and established an angle to possibly have a hit carried out on the almighty and once powerful street Lord, Nightmare.

Jackie done a thorough research of Nightmare on Google, of his life in the streets, and of the gang he was the leader of. She'd discovered that indeed, Nightmare was an exceptionally high-ranking member of the Vice Lord gang—a group that was once headed by the notorious "underworld mayor of Chicago," Willie Lyles. Her research also prompted her to watch as many episodes as possible of the series *Gangland*, the particular shows that were aired about the Vice Lords, which Willie Lyles and Nightmare were included on. Some of those episodes featured Ricky as well, along with a brother or two of his.

She had noted that the bitter enemy and rival foe of the Vice Lords nationwide were the Gangster Disciples—the "GD's"—and the war between the two factions had always been an unending one ... a continued struggle that had not an end to it. At least no time soon. Such particulars was all she needed to know to begin the work she had intentions to perform.

Her mind operated on the notion that caused her to view the battles between the Vice Lords and GD's the same as that between prosecutors and defense attorneys ... Republicans and Democrats ... Crips and Bloods ... Sunni and Shiite Muslims ... Blacks and Whites ... Yankees and Confederates— and hell, God and devil even ... and so on and so forth. In other words, there would always be an issue and beef, no matter what.

Jackie had a potential first client of hers (she now operated as a legal consultant and legal advisor—she contemplated Post-Conviction litigations), who sought her out for legal services, to defend him as an assistant lawyer in his upcoming trial, where he faced heavy charges for firearms trafficking and gun possession. She'd crossed over from the prosecuting side of the aisle temporarily—at least for this mission.

The guy and his crew had been charged and accused of running a ring that sought out vulnerable gun and pawn shops, which had weak security systems. They would break into them, steal high-powered rifles, shotguns, and handguns, then sell them statewide or nationwide to their customers through the black market.

The guy was originally from down south, out of the state of Mississippi, but had been living in California—Long Beach—with a girlfriend he'd met on Facebook. Gang life in Mississippi was rich with both 'Folk Nation' and 'Vice Lord' culture, and the two groups fought it out on the South Coast, the same as they had in 'Chi-Raq' City.

The dude himself, Purdis Lamar Winston, aka 'Three-Hundred' or '300' (he preferred the number version)—a rather plumped and heavy-set fella—had stepped away momentarily from the gang and was no longer on count with his nation until after the outcome of his court situation, he decided. He had an older brother that was still down for his niggaz and knee-deep in the gang, while doing a Federal bid in USP-Atlanta. The brother was the 'I-C' on compound ("The Head G") that had deep connections all around and ties to other gangstas of Folk Nation that were housed at various Fed camps around the country, or had once been through Atlanta with him. Everyone stayed connected by cell phones, emails, three-way letters to family, or on social media, as it wouldn't be a hard task at all for the brother, Walter James Winston aka 'Walt-G,' to reach out to somebody—another Gangsta who had a team of hitters, and who all represented GD—with a job for them. *'On BOSS'.*

***

The legal fees that Jackie had asked of *300* to represent him on his case and to file a petition on his brother's behalf was $85,000. But, if Purdis were to do her a favor and have his brother put his people on a mission to get at Nightmare—let's say maybe stab him up good or possibly kill him—she would greatly reduce the ticket to $50,000, if only stabbed up; or $15,000, if he were to die. Essentially, a $35,000 to $70,000 hit had been put out on Nightmare's life, if the deal was accepted.

300 had to get in touch with his brother first, to know what he wanted to do. If agreed upon, Jackie would reach out to one of her white male companions who operated a bail bond service, post Purdis' bail, and file the paperwork to be the attorney of record on his and the brother's case. He was to get back with her shortly thereafter, to let her know what was good, If or not it was a go.

***

Between the time, 300 had written letters to his brother, utilizing gang language to code all he related. He sent the mail to their sister in Mississippi, for her to forward to Walt-G in an envelope that had her name on it. He'd also called, and she made 3-way calls to Walt on his cellphone, and the two brothers discussed the business at hand. It didn't take Walt-G long at all to make a boss decision on what to do. It was an easy one to decide, being that Nightmare was not at the same camp as him and his boys, and they didn't have to put in any work.

The G's up in Lewisburg that had life sentences and basketball scores in numbers on prison time were the ones who had been available to do "whatever," in the name of Folk Nation. All Walt-G had to do was say who the vic was. That was it.

Roughly sixteen days later, 300 had gotten back in contact with Jackie and let her know that everything was a go.

"Jackie. My brother agreed to everything you need us to do. He said he's got solid connections at the Fed camp in Lewisburg, so they'll be able to touch the nigga you want hit. It's time for you to do your part now, sweetheart," 300 stated.

"I'm gonna do my part. Just as soon as I know that his ass has gotten what was coming to him. So don't worry about that. I keep my promises. And I keep my threats," she came back with.

Afterwards, she managed to get him free on bond, as this was part of the deal. And once he was out, she provided him with every piece of information on Nightmare which she had, and the hit was set. Jackie had been able to clap at Nightmare's ass long before he was to mobilize and bust at her first. Shit had gotten real. She was to get her payback against him—in blood too. But things had to go right, being that Nightmare was a true veteran himself in the game and knew his position well.

If there was one thing about greed, it holds great potential to take someone under each and every time it's ran to for help. And trust, he is a difficult bastard to do business with. Greed I'm speaking of.

Jackie had over a half-million dollars in cash and jewelry she'd taken from ReeRee and Nightmare. She should've left things alone. But instead, she took the initiative to put out a contract on the man, in addition to stealing the money and the valuables. She'd sought to save herself $35,000 to $70,000 and had made far too many mistakes and mishaps in the process than she would have, if she went about doing things in a different way.

Jackie and ReeRee had a joint mediocre legal service they'd incorporated, so as to tackle certain complex situations on cases they'd accepted. At the time she served the subpoena to receive the institutional history of Nightmare, she utilized the title "Elite Law" to do so. The process had been documented in the court and also with the BOP. Also, upon her accepting to represent 300 and Walt-G on their cases, she'd submitted the Entry of Appearance forms by way of this business title as well. This placed on the record that she and "Jettica" shall be formally representing the two gangstas at all phases of litigation—a major mistake she was unaware of that was subject to cost them in the end game.

Jackie fucked up further, as she didn't simply stop there. She contacted the warden of the prison where Nightmare was housed and reported the extracurricular activities that he and ReeRee had going on, opposite her being simply his lawyer.

Jackie spilled her guts and told everything—about the letters, the money, and the possibility that he'd possessed a cellphone, an illegal device for an inmate—and also about him dealing contraband narcotics. Her mentality was situated on the basis that whosoever was to get to him first— the government or the crew hired to ambush him—they would indeed serve her well.

All she wanted was to have that nigga dealt with. The warden didn't readily react so fast, being he was all too used to anonymous people calling in to make reports on inmates. But the people that Walt-G put on the job had no understanding, especially not so against a rival enemy—a Vice Lord, of all foes.

***

It was about six fifteen in the A.M. when the six-man crew went to handle the piece of work they had lined up to do—the work Walt-G put together from his prison cell down in Atlanta. Whatever was to happen was to happen, and all that was to be was to be. The GDs were strapped to the hilt with their ten-inch knife-shanks gripped firmly and wrist-wraps tied tight so as not to slip out once the battle got to going.

Nightmare had no knowledge at all that he was a plate— that he was in the throes of being attacked, that other gang rivals were about to eat him. And it was about to go down. Nightmare felt Jackie incapable of such and thought she posed no threat in any sense of the word. He had underestimated her and assumed her offensive against him was to come from finding a way to make ReeRee focus more on her and no longer on him. But then it dawned on dude that his gifts and money already had ReeRee's attention. And also, she still had to represent him on his case. So he literally wrote Jackie off as being a nobody... simply a dizzy bitch that had lost her grip on her lover to him. Obviously, a miscalculation and wrong judgment of this terrible Black bitch.

Being the Chief, as he always was, Nightmare maintained a security team around him throughout the day at all times. The number of soldiers he kept would vary depending on his movement. The dudes who came to get him had really done their homework, along with being provided a great deal of information on his day-to-day habits.

Nightmare was a vegan and a participant in the Alternative Entree Program at the prison, which required him to report to the dining hall, check in his ID card, and retrieve his vegan meals three times daily, no matter what. He'd been an advocate of the vegan lifestyle for many years, and an early bird who had always loved to rise before the sun in the morning, eat breakfast, then hit the gym to work out or hit the trail to run. This practice was in place long before the prison sentence.

On the particular day of the potential ambush, things were no different, as his favorite breakfast was being served, and he was certainly going to get it. Besides, if he missed seven or more meals in a week's time period, or fifteen meals in a thirty-day period, he would be removed from the vegan list for cause due to failure to report, and he didn't want that. He had gotten too comfortable and complacent at the prison. He honored his vegan privilege.

Nightmare had four Vice Lords by his side as they strolled down the sidewalk, headed to the dining hall. The GD assailants laid low and waited in ready mode on the side of the gym, which sat along the route to the chow hall. A building or two was situated between the dorms and the kitchen. It was still dark outside, and a cool breeze blew, as it was the month of November—perfect for jackets to conceal weapons.

The gangstas seemed to pop up out of nowhere as they rushed the Vice Lord targets, aiming to get Nightmare.

"Oh shit! What the fuck! It's a hit!" Nightmare yelled out to alert his bodyguards.

Each attacker had the duty to rush one of Nightmare's men one-on-one. And specifically, someone had to go directly at Nightmare himself, so as to hold him down long enough for their remaining two hitters to go in and attack him the most.

The fight was six on five, leaving Nightmare and his crew out-knifed. They weren't equipped to buck back. They had the responsibility of literally scrapping for their lives, and for the life of Nightmare, as they were extremely loyal to the ringleader.

The attackers went to work without any hesitation, as they were ordered to do. The more muscle-built and skilled boxer of the hit squad punched Nightmare with a serious right hook. The blow dropped him on contact. As he sat on his back pockets, woozy-headed from the haymaker, he went into a bit of a struggle in his attempt to get to his feet and duke it out. Everything was happening so fast, he'd forgotten the fact that he had his own shank along his waistline.

By the time he began to realize exactly what was happening, musclebound boxed him in the face yet again with vicious combinations of blows back-to-back.

Pap-Pap-Pap-Pap-Pap!

Dude split the bridge of Nightmare's nose and an eyelid in the process. He then kicked Nightmare in the face for good measure, as he tossed and turned on the concrete, trying to recover. As musclebound was getting ready to kick Nightmare yet again, one of the other Vice Lords managed to get a good blow in on him, which startled 'Tyson' and caused him to turn and begin to fight it out with them. The boxer had a pair of homemade brass knuckles that made his blows far more effective and dangerous. It was no wonder how he'd rattled Nightmare in the way he had. The fruit of his work instantly showed on Nightmare's face.

The guards hadn't noticed anything of the scuffle, as daybreak had not begun to show light on the brawl. As Nightmare struggled to his feet from the position of being down on all fours, one of his worst fears came to reality. The sixth attacker of the hit team had done all he'd specifically been ordered to do—not to worry about no one else but to be sure that he stabbed the nigga Nightmare, and to get him good.

He rushed in, poked Nightmare four times in rapid fashion, kicked him, and then hit him twice more. Dude hit Nightmare two times in the legs, two times in the back, and two times in the torso. The wounds to the body were the worst of them all, as Nightmare began to bleed profusely.

Chapter 24

Within the melee, one of Nightmare's men had managed to yell out at the top of his lungs, "*Takbir. Takbir. Takbir!*" This is the Muslim call and alarm for assistance in the time of being in great danger. Within seconds, roughly ten well-armed and trained Muslims, who had exited the dining hall and were on their way back to the dorm, raced over to gain control of the situation.

For the most part, the Muslims to answer the call were from the Nation of Islam—the F.O.I.—but there were also about three to four brothers from the Sunni Orthodox ranks who appeared and gave help to the group getting attacked.

Being that Nightmare and his cohorts were members of the Vice Lord Nation—a part of the growing number of street organizations, much like the Black P-Stones and several others—they had converted to Islam as their religion and faith, as this had been the case all along for Nightmare.

At the time he reached the Fed camp in Lewisburg, he immediately made mention to the Muslim community that, by faith, he was indeed one of them. He had gotten with the inmate Imam of the Orthodox circle, and the top Minister of the Nation of Islam. Also, Nightmare paid his fair dues in a lump sum to both powers that be regarding the Deen, so as to have security from the "Sutra Team," and from the "Fruit of Islam" or "X-Men" by the Nation.

Nightmare thoroughly briefed the Vice Lord faction on the importance of their alliance with the Muslims, and had dictated to all of them what to do if a situation occurred and they needed additional help. Such was the case the morning they'd gotten ambushed.

Once the Muslims approached the brawl, they immediately recognized who Nightmare and the boys were, and they also recognized the other Muslims helping out, apart from the GDs, as the Islamic team had on the kufi headpieces and wrist bracelets that spelled out the words "Allah Akbar" in Arabic calligraphy.

With no hesitation, the Muslims went to work on the attackers. They pulled out their shanks and began to stab and beat the hit squad with might and force. The life and health of their brothers had to be defended, as their blood, property, and honor were sacred to one another.

One of the six GD attackers got it the worst. He got stabbed at least eleven times and was in pretty bad shape as two of the Muslim security forces put the hurts down on him. He passed out there on the spot due to a tremendous amount of blood loss. He'd been hit in the throat, in the back of the neck, and all about the chest area. Both his lungs were punctured beyond repair. The guy had begun to choke on his own blood. He would surely die if he didn't get help fast.

With every bit of twenty men involved in the brawl and knife fight, there was no way the guards couldn't notice what was going on—and that blood was being spilled. There was a lieutenant on patrol of the sidewalk who observed the battle. One of the attackers fled the scene to avoid being stabbed and was caught by the guards.

The code had been called to alert authority of the situation, and the majority of the guards on duty responded to the site of the action. They pepper-sprayed everyone and Tasered a few as well. Guards even pulled out sticks and beat a few of the guys. Everyone was laid down on the ground and cuffed as the guards gained the upper hand. There were at least seven people who needed medical attention right away due to the stab wounds they'd suffered and from gasping to catch their breath behind the use of pepper spray.

All the injured had to be hauled off to an outside hospital. Nightmare and one of the GD attackers were hurt the worst.

***

Reality Strikes...

The reality for Nightmare appeared grim. He'd finally awakened to find himself chained and shackled to the post of a hospital bed in the intensive care unit. The surgery had been a success, as was the blood transfusion. He'd gotten hit with a blade that had been soaked overnight in a concoction of shit, piss, and shaving powder. They intended to do him dirty, one way or the other.

Besides the surgery, Nightmare had an additional challenge to face with the fact he'd been poked in the torso with a contaminated shank. He had to wear a colostomy bag until his guts healed. They stabbed Nightmare just below the waistline, and his intestines had been snagged slightly by the blade, which had hooking ridges designed on it. The impact and the damage caused him to pass out and go into a coma.

Nightmare was lucky, so to speak—but the other guy, one of the attackers, was not. The dude never made it into the operating room, as he flatlined en route to the hospital, leaving someone with a murder charge later down the road. The rest of the people involved had been patched up at the hospital, returned to the prison, and thrown in the hole to be held indefinitely while the investigation was conducted. The entire prison was placed on lockdown, as the warden and his administration had their hands full with all sorts of mess to work out.

There had been three different groups involved in the melee—the Vice Lords, the GDs, and the Muslims—with two of the trio being declared 'Security Threat Groups,' adding to the paperwork.

After the brawl, the guards had to identify each individual, then go to everyone's cell to pack up their property. They also conducted a thorough shakedown to locate any possible weapons or other contraband, as they tried to figure out what the fight was all about. A few cell phones were found, gang literature, narcotics, and other incriminating material to aid administration with the investigation. They even discovered those copied pages of the journal Nightmare had. That could eventually spell trouble for him later down the line.

Prison officials quickly pieced together the puzzle of the events that unfolded and learned who the responsible people were. Surveillance footage of the fight and the GD attacker who ran off first gave admin information to help solve everything. He even spoke on the order that they had from their leader, to put in the work for their gang brethren, Walt-G.

Two days after checking into protective custody—due to his life being endangered by the Vice Lords and the Muslims who took aim to get him, and by his very own people who wanted to whack him for fleeing and leaving them in harm's way, with one eventually being killed—the snitch revealed more to the warden. He put the icing on the cake when he broke it all down, piece by piece, call by call. He provided critical information points to aid the investigation. This set the stage for the hammer to be brought down in the future. He left no stone unturned.

Even though Nightmare was a victim in the situation, he'd already been under investigation by the warden, due to Jackie calling to report about him and ReeRee. Being that she was an actual attorney and registered member of the bar, Jackie held the title of officially being an officer of the court. And so, the warden had to respect her as such, and accept all she related—regardless.

Technically, she was on the same team as he was, and had he not acted on the claims she made, she could've possibly snitched on him, as she held closer ties to the Attorney General's office as an attorney than he did as a superintendent.

Nightmare's cell was searched more thoroughly than anyone else's, due to his higher status in the gang. A smartphone was found, $5,000 in cash, three ounces of meth, and two shanks. Since the stabbing incident had occurred before the contraband was found, he'd been placed in the hole on 'Involuntary Protective Custody.'

Nightmare was now back at the prison from the hospital, long before the warden had the opportunity to stick those heavy write-ups on him and file additional charges. In essence, the warden had literally spared him from having his security jacked up again to a higher level—one that would have been detrimental and possibly landed him on 23-and-1 lockdown at another Fed pen.

The warden must've felt sympathy for the once kingpin, due to him being stabbed and in the fucked-up predicament he was in. So, the warden merely chalked it up as an 'ordinary' finding of contraband around the compound, since they were all too familiar with such activity going on in the prison. Either way, Nightmare was set to be transferred to a different facility, and wouldn't have the opportunity to get back at the goons who stabbed him—or anyone else from their crew.

All of Nightmare's visitation rights had been suspended indefinitely, as he sat in the hole nearly 180 days, healing and awaiting transfer. On the 176th day, the warden finally submitted the necessary paperwork to have him sent elsewhere. He ended up going to the Federal Correctional Institution down in Miami, Florida, which turned out to be a convenient swap between two wardens.

Nightmare figured his security level might be raised, due to the contraband discovered in his cell—but it didn't work against him. Once at the fed camp down in the 305, he asked his case manager why he'd been transferred from Lewisburg to a less strenuous prison. His impression had been the opposite. The counselor told him his move was based on the health condition he was recovering from, and due to 'redistribution of the prison population.' Those were the primary reasons why he'd been transferred.

***

The bottom line was that the warden was going to get rid of him anyway—for protective custody reasons, and also due to the large amount of cash and drugs that were discovered in his domain. The type of influence such a total sum of cash potentially could gain over an *overworked and underpaid* employee that guarded the prison could have spelled disaster for the warden. He already had death and other issues to sort out. Nightmare could not be allowed to return to general population, as this would've posed a threat to the welfare of the institution. And not only that— Nightmare would eventually begin to like the Miami facility, as it was a far better place than the previous spot.

For the six months Nightmare spent in the hole healing and awaiting transfer, he maintained contact with ReeRee through letters and brief phone calls here and there. He didn't let her know about the hit that was put out on him or being stabbed—not until after being transferred. He had no knowledge of why the GDs had chosen to get at him, or who possibly sent them. But he was intent on getting down to the bottom of it at some point soon.

ReeRee told him all about her fight and break-up with Jackie. She had a restraining order put in place to prevent Jackie from coming near her person or workplace, and had moved out and rented a space in a fairly decent apartment duplex near downtown L.A.

"Sweetie, they transferred me from the Lewisburg spot. They got me situated down here in Miami now. I got into it with some niggaz there—me and my boys. They fucked around and stabbed me, ReeRee," Nightmare let her know.

"Oh wow, baby! Are you okay?" she responded.

"I'm good. But I had to have a colostomy bag put in place because I got stabbed in the lower gut," he stated.

"Damn, baby! What was that all about?" ReeRee wanted to know.

"Hell, to be honest, I don't even know. Not yet, at least. Them niggaz ambushed us. Some rival gang niggaz. It ain't shit though. I'm good. What's been up with you?" he asked.

"Speaking of problems, I've had to deal with some myself out here. I've got some things to tell you," ReeRee expressed.

"I'm listening."

"You already know about Jackie, so—"

"Oh yeah, I almost forgot to tell you what she's done," he cut ReeRee off upon hearing Jackie's name.

"What she's done?" ReeRee repeated. "You mean to you?"

"Yeah, to me. How about, I get a letter in the mail. And guess who it was from?" he said.

"Who, Michael? Please don't tell me from her, sweetie," ReeRee responded.

"No doubt. It was from her, Ree. She said all type of shit that's not worth me repeating or paying attention to. She mostly talked shit about you and me getting acquainted with one another. The crazy bitch said something about she found the letters I wrote you, that she got the jewelry, and the money. Sweetie, what is this bitch talking about?" he wanted to know. "And if I remember well, she mentioned something about having the journal too."

"And that's what I wanted to tell you. The issue which led to us fighting and splitting was because Jackie found your letters. She found the jewelry you bought for me. And the crazy-ass bitch found the money I had put up at the house," ReeRee admitted.

"How much of that money she got, ReeRee?" Nightmare asked.

"Michael," she uttered, then reluctantly revealed, "she stole all the money."

"What you mean *all* the money? Be specific, sweetie!" he demanded.

"She found and kept the two hundred thousand I had at the house. And when I returned from Chicago this second time, that's when the fight started," she said.

"What," he exclaimed, vehemently.

"Yeah, baby. I didn't even have the chance to get to the bedroom, because she rushed me at the front door with the bullshit."

"Seriously, sweetie?" he asked.

"You know I won't lie to you, Michael."

"She didn't touch that last pickup of money, did she?" he asked.

"Yeah, baby, she got that too. I had to run out of the house and didn't have time to grab the bag once I made a run for it," ReeRee reluctantly said in response. Nothing to make matters better.

"I mean, I don't understand. What's her intent? What do she plan to do with money she stole from you—her lover, so to speak?" he asked.

"To be honest, Michael, Jackie may just be trying to blackmail me to be back with her. I believe eventually she'll give it back—at some point. She's only holding the money and jewelry as leverage. That's all," ReeRee replied.

"Oh, I hope so. Because that's a lot of money and some valuable material I bought for you. It ain't no way we gonna let her get away with what belongs to us, sweetie."

"There's something else I've got to tell you too, Michael," ReeRee placed him on notice.

"Damn. There's more?" he responded—not too happily either.

"Yeah, unfortunately. She took that journal of yours too. The one I made those copies from," ReeRee revealed.

"Now see... she doing too fuckin' much, sweetie! She's gone too far. That journal don't have anything to do with you. Why she bothering that? That's my personal business and a breakdown of what me, my family, and business partners got going on. That crazy bitch did mention something about turning the journal over to the Feds if I didn't back off from fucking with you, along with spending all the money. Now that I remember better. At first, I didn't know what the fuck she was talking about. But now I do. I just need for you to say whatever and do whatever to get our shit back from that stupid bitch, okay?" Nightmare stated.

"Don't worry too much about that, sweetie. I'll be sure to get our belongings back one way or the other. I know Jackie very well and know what she wants. Just let me handle it. I got it. I promise," ReeRee said, trying to keep Nightmare calm.

"Good. Because I don't need no more issues on my plate to deal with right now. I already got to figure out who put a hit on me. And, I've gotta get my visitation rights restored. You not even allowed to come see me as my lawyer at this time. My mom, dad—nobody can't," he let her know.

"Oh wow! Why is that?" ReeRee asked.

"Because, after the fight with them niggaz, they searched my room and found my phone, two weapons I had, and a small quantity of contraband. I was planning to smoke that little bit of weed," Nightmare lied. He then continued, "Apparently, somebody had made a call and reported to the warden a few lies on me, and they had me under investigation. But now, I clearly know who that was. Why is this chick so psycho and impulsive about you, ReeRee?" he wanted to understand Jackie's train of thought.

"Your guess is just as good as mine, baby. But I told you—I got it. I'll handle it, okay?" she assured him.

SOULLESS GOON | PRINCE

"Well, you say you got it, so I'mma let you deal with it how you see fit. Just take care of it, because she doing too much," Nightmare responded. *You better handle that shit long before I figure out a way to get at this bitch. Don't nobody take shit from me and think it's all good,* he thought over.

"I've got to look into a few other things Jackie has going on too," ReeRee said to Nightmare.

"Look into a few other things like what?" he asked, clearly letting her know that since she brought it up, he wanted to be in the loop.

"Well, Jackie and I had a legal service together, and I've been getting emails from the court about her representing two new guys on their cases. One is out on bond, and the other guy is already in Federal prison. This is so not like Jackie. But my point is, the fee that was charged by her to represent these fellas was far too low to represent those two guys with the type of offenses faced. And the other was already convicted of high crimes," ReeRee said.

"So what you trying to tell me, baby?" he asked in a matter-of-fact type of way.

"What I'm trying to tell you is that I don't want to jump to conclusions on anything. And I intend to get the facts straight before I make any remarks about your situation with being stabbed. I know, without a doubt, Jackie reported to the warden everything she found out about you and me. But the part about her choosing to represent those two clients for the low retainer fee that she had—it makes me question a lot of things. That's what I'm gonna look into," ReeRee said in response to Nightmare's inquiry.

Certain points went over Nightmare's head. He missed them.

<label>204</label>

Chapter 25

ReeRee began to loathe and burned with fury at all the low-down, dirty, and conniving activities that Jackie had done. But still, she couldn't bring herself to see that something drastic and physically horrific be perpetrated against her lesbian love. To her, they were 'strawberry and chocolate,' a flavorful ice-cream treat to each other and a tasty delight in the eyes of all who had ever observed the professionally astute female sensations out and about socially enjoying themselves.

Prior to Nightmare coming into the picture, the duo had it going on and had begun to hit a high note in their relationship. But due to someone else capturing the attention of ReeRee and having her imagination running wild with lore, things changed. Whether she admitted it or not, she was turned on by the wickedly provocative and insanely hypnotic mystique that the power player, Nightmare, possessed. He held the edge over Jackie and tapped into the natural part of ReeRee that had once been thought to have dissipated—the intriguing feelings of lust that a woman develops for a man once aroused. How else did Nightmare become so successful in the influence he had on her and able to convince her to do the things she had for him? And the best was yet to come.

Nightmare had great works and bona fide hustling schemes in the making. He was a mastermind and a criminally sophisticated version of the people he idolized and styled himself after in his own way—Barack Obama and

Minister Louis Farrakhan—both high-powered and politically ingenious individuals.

Opposite of what ReeRee had in mind in repaying Jackie for the ill she'd caused and the riches she'd stolen, there was absolutely no question as to what Nightmare had in mind to do. All that was left was to set it up and let the killing be carried out. By ReeRee letting him know that it was out of the norm for Jackie to accept the two cases and to represent her newly added clients for the low fee which she had, he felt something odd about that. Albeit, he was poised to avenge himself on both situations.

He didn't rule out the fact that, just maybe, the attempt on his life had been orchestrated and financially cobbled together by Jackie. He'd put two and two together and drew the conclusion as to exactly who the root of his problems was. Indeed, it was Jackie.

The phone call ended between Nightmare and ReeRee, leaving him to think to himself: *This bitch got to pay.* There was no way he was going to allow that bitch to go unpunished, or remain alive for that matter—not after all that she'd taken and done. There was no way on earth he was going to simply chalk it up as a loss, or even a failed hit by a rival. There was too much at stake to let it go. He never revealed his intent, nor did he indicate that retribution would soon befall her once longtime lover. He had to see to it that ReeRee would be good and out of the way once the angel of death paid Jackie a visit, and he had to ensure she'd have an airtight alibi at the time Jackie's days of living had expired.

On another note, in relation to Nightmare being able to get some get-back, he was a deep thinker and a wise fella. He knew enough about the law to know ReeRee was an officer of the court and also had close ties and relations to prosecutors. He also knew good and well that had she been in any possession of any information of a potential crime that would be committed—especially a murder or any crime that had been going on—it was her oath and constitutional duty to report those crimes or intents to the appropriate authorities at first instance, without fail. So he simply played it low and behaved very nonchalantly in ReeRee's presence at the mention of Jackie's name over the phone, by the video call.

Nightmare, of course, had people to get in touch with, to take care of the type of work he needed done. He also had connections to dudes who would knock off an entire family for a $100k price tag. And there you had that bitch Jackie, who had thieved over $500k in cash and jewels from him and his beloved ReeRee. You know she's got to get it.

What was that bitch Jackie thinking about, taking something from me? he thought. But truthfully, it wasn't the money nor the jewels that caused him the great concern he began to experience. It was the journal she'd taken, which really infuriated him the most. That could cause him to get life on top of life and have the majority of his money and assets taken away from him. It could also be damaging to other people who still ran operations and conducted business for him in the streets.

The journal held information about the location of trap houses, safes, property deeds, and other possessions of Nightmare and his partner, Ricky. The journal also had a governmental breakdown of the structure of the crews and the areas, along with other cities and states they'd branched into. There was coded information and non-coded material. Nightmare had phone numbers of people from top to bottom within that journal, also hit-men he could call upon. Again, coded materials.

Although he had an additional copy of every page from the journal—opposite of what was taken in the shakedown— he still didn't need Jackie placing that type of material into the wrong hands out of her being angry and seeking to do him harm within her emotional state.

Truth be told, the life-blood of Nightmare's fractured organization was contained in the pages of that journal, as it revealed the activities of both old and young that had anything to do with the crew. It was a vital component to the enterprise and played a critical role in the well-being or the demise of the family—the Vice Lord family, that is.

Nightmare had gotten pissed at ReeRee because he specifically told her to do all necessary to bring the journal inside and place it in his hands. He knew it was a bad idea for her to take it upon herself to make copies of the book and give only the copies to him—not the actual journal, or returning it to Ricky. Jackie was never supposed to have gotten her hands on that book, let alone use it as leverage against him and ReeRee.

Nightmare was an absolute master of concealing his emotions and showed no type of reactions. Deep down, he knew that the loss of the journal could result in being a death deal in and of itself. He had to play it cool on his behalf because he felt that had ReeRee caught wind of even an inkling of how he may have felt or what he wanted to do to her behind such a foolish mistake, she might have run off on him and possibly abandoned the case as his lawyer—never to be located nor heard from again—as his conviction was still ongoing at that point of their affair. He couldn't have that.

Chapter 26

On The Home Front...

Ricky made it a priority to call Puncho and set up a meeting that was to be between those two only. The intent was to try to sift as much information out of Puncho as possible on the many things he had going on outside his knowledge. He was a top trusted street lieutenant of Ricky's, but had gotten very sloppy with a lot of the things he was doing. Ricky wanted to reveal to Puncho some of the information his inside guys, Doug and Scott, provided him—but hadn't spoken any names. He wanted to see what Puncho's response would be to the news he would share with him.

Ricky was also still battling with the grief he'd felt over taking the life of his own daughter. He and Loretta called around to the family, letting them know that Yasmine had run away—possibly with some older guy she'd met online from another state. The entire family had begun to call around and ask others if they had seen or heard from the missing teenager. Loretta was the one to put out the report with the police, and their search had begun as well.

Atop of his own moral conscience to deal with, Ricky also had to begin the process of getting the affairs of his enterprise situated. The ultimatum Ricky faced was either get the group in order or go down for the crimes his people had committed—if not be killed himself by the henchmen of his supplier, Mr. Francesca, or by some ambitious member from amongst his ranks.

He picked up Puncho and they began to stroll about the city and converse as two high-ranking street legends would.

"Puncho. Lord. We got problems that have to be worked out soon," Ricky began.

"Problems as in?" Puncho questioned.

"I had a meeting with two of my guys on the inside. Everything they told me was not good, Lord," Ricky made him aware.

"Oh yeah? What they stressing?" he inquired.

"They gave me some information on a lot of things we need to get in check. For one, that nigga City Blue up in Milwaukee we been serving all this time," Ricky mentioned.

"Yeah. What about him?" Puncho asked.

"He done flipped on us when he got popped."

"Word? I had a feeling something had happened to that nigga after that last purchase he got. He all of a sudden just got ghost," Puncho stated.

"Yeah, the Feds got his ass. And he rolled over, telling them our team is his supplier. And that he worked for us," Ricky related.

"Ain't that a bitch!" Puncho blurted.

"Goddamn sho' is. But here's more. That old fuck, with the bar thing Roscoe ended up with?"

"We did that right. Ain't no way that got out, I wouldn't think," Puncho stated, to assure Ricky that the job wasn't a sloppy one.

"Shitting me," Ricky responded.

"How? I personally took good care of that," Puncho proclaimed.

"Who was it you took along for the ride?" Ricky asked, to see if Puncho would be truthful.

"It was one of my nephews, a nigga who I know could be trusted," Puncho replied.

"Is that right?" Ricky smirked and sarcastically stated.

"Hell muthafuckin' yeah, nigga! You know I don't play when it comes to something like that. Shit, nephew done did plenty of work for unc in the name of VL, Lord," Puncho adamantly stated.

"Yeah, Lord. I hear what you saying. But here's the thing. When was the last time you seen or heard from your nephew, bro?" Ricky asked.

"Shit, about three weeks to a month ago. Maybe longer. I hadn't kept up. I fronted him a couple of joints to go out of town with and set up shop. He say he had a sweet location to put it down at and expand what we trying to do," Puncho said.

"And you ain't heard from him since?" Ricky asked.

"Nah. But I know my people. He'll be getting back in touch soon. Plus, that nigga owe me a grip, so he ain't got no choice but to reach out to me," Puncho replied.

"Listen bro. You and I been down for a minute now, right?" Ricky asked.

"True that. But what you getting at, Lord? Shoot it straight with me," Puncho demanded from his leader.

"Puncho. My boys on the inside related to me that someone—they never gave me a name—came to them to be protected and revealed everything he knew," Ricky said.

Looking confused, Puncho asked, "What that got to do with us?"

"It has a lot to do with us for them to specifically mention you by name," Ricky responded.

"What they say, Lord?"

"Apparently, whoever it was you took with you to handle that old fuck Smitty Nixon, he reported that shit to the Feds. They gave me accurate details. And they also say that the work you fronted this person—it was two bricks of dog food, right?—he turned it in to them, along with recorded conversation between the two of you. They say the nigga had gotten caught up on a case, and in order to free himself from that, he had to get a high-profile guy for them. He told them

211

he worked for you and the material was yours, that you forced him to deal. The nigga told everything, Lord. They say he told them that you and him took care of Nixon on the way to Milwaukee, but didn't say exactly where y'all buried the body," Ricky said.

**

Puncho held his mouth agape and looked astounded at the information Ricky related.

"You got to be bullshitting me, Lord. I'm about to call this nigga right now and see what's really good," Puncho stated and snatched his cellphone off his waistline.

"I know goddamn well my nephew, E, won't do it like that on me!" Puncho ranted, as he awaited the automated operator to reveal that the number had been changed or was no longer in service.

"Who you say, your nephew, E?" Ricky had asked.

"Yeah, Everett. My sister Glenda's son. Your niece Alana's baby daddy," Puncho replied and then dialed his sister's number.

She answered, "Hello."

"Glenda," Puncho stated.

"What's up, bro? How you doing?" she asked.

"Shit. Just trying to get in touch with that son of yours, E."

"Puncho, I ain't heard from that boy in weeks, maybe longer. Is everything alright?" she asked.

"That's what I'm trying to find out now, sis. If he calls you, tell him to be sure he call me ASAP, okay?" Puncho demanded.

"Will do, Lord," she responded, and they ended the call.

"Puncho, I told you, Lord—they got him at one of their safe houses, bro. And he revealing everything he knows," Ricky stated.

"Rick, you ain't got to worry too much on that. I'mma be sure to take care of any problems my nephew done caused. If anything, I'll be the one that they may come for if an indictment come out from anything he's told them," Puncho said. "If I have to do E myself, I'll do it. So don't trouble yourself too much with that. And what do they plan to do with him—lock him up or keep him in hiding until they get all they can out of him, then relocate him?" Puncho asked.

"I was told nothing about the plans they got for him. Apparently, they intend to juice him good enough, then utilize him as a star witness at a trial for you or me," Ricky related what he knew on the process of such a situation.

"So how will I be able to get a hand on him to question that nigga myself about what you brought to my attention?" Puncho wanted to know.

Ricky gave Puncho a stern look, as if to say, *Nigga, are you serious right now?* He then said, "Bro, what is it to possibly question him about? I have my facts already, and they gave me accurate details," Ricky responded.

"But Lord, look, my nigga. That's my nephew, my flesh and blood. I brought that nigga into this shit and raised him under me in it. We done did too much shit together, and he know too much for me to sit back and wait for the Feds to come snatch me up behind whatever he's told them," Puncho stated in an expression of panic.

Ricky began to have the thoughts that Puncho was, in fact, questioning how truthful he was being about everything he let him know of his nephew. Puncho knew that his nephew, E, was in a relationship and had a kid by Ricky's niece, Alana, and the thought passed through Puncho's mind that maybe E and his girl had been going through some serious problems, and she ran to her uncle for help to deal with E. Possibly he pulled a gun on her and threatened to shoot her or something, and Ricky wanted the nephew dealt with. So, he had to come up with something to justify what he wanted to do to his sister's son.

213

Puncho wasn't going to agree or co-sign shit until he had the opportunity to talk with his nephew first, and then he could decide on what to do from that point moving forward. Puncho definitely knew what type of nigga Ricky was and all he was capable of doing. He also felt as though Ricky could have possibly had E kidnapped and held hostage someplace, and lied to him about the Feds having him and making him spill his guts on all he knew.

"Puncho, look," Ricky continued. "The only possible thing we can do at this point is hope that maybe E will recant his words and tell them a gang of lies, or that some unforeseen circumstances would come about to prevent everything from being told. Besides, like I told you, my boys on the inside never said E told them where you two supposedly buried Nixon. So he can't be truly ratting about everything," Ricky mentioned for Puncho again.

"Yeah, you right. You got a point on that. It's just the fact that you say the nigga ratting," Puncho replied, and thought to himself to take a ride up the highway and have a look at the area where they actually did bury their victim.

The two continued to ride and discuss many matters of business, as Ricky felt it necessary to downplay how intense the situation truly was. He didn't want to anger and rattle Puncho too much and create a potential enemy he would have to go to war with. The plan was to eventually get rid of E and Puncho at some point soon, as there were no other alternative to eliminate the news the uncle and the nephew had made. They both had gone too far and had fucked up too bad. Ricky only had to continue in disguising the scheme he had in mind.

Chapter 27

Sorry, Not Sorry...

After the fallout, Jackie definitely made several attempts to right the wrongs and reconcile all of the differences that existed between her and her love, ReeRee. She sent flowers and candy to the law firm where ReeRee worked, and other gifts that she knew were adored, along with other sentimental objects of affection. But all of her efforts were to no avail. She had even taunted ReeRee with the prospect of returning the cash and the jewels once the other attempts had failed, if ReeRee were to forgive her and they get back to being normal as a couple again. Nothing worked, as it hadn't dawned on Jackie nor rested on her heart the type of danger which she'd placed not only herself in, but also the life and the well-being of ReeRee. And to make matters worse, Jackie never hinted at any time about what she'd done with the journal or where it was located. That by itself held more value and significant meaning than did the paper and the bling.

Jackie made it her business to thumb through the journal and had come to learn of all it contained inside. There was a treasure trove of damning information which had the potential to put Nightmare, ReeRee, and other members that had anything to do with the Vice Lord organization away for a very long time, if not forever. There were lawyers, judges, politicians, and high-level business executives implicated through the pages of the journal in one way or another. Jackie possessed the mother-lode of discoveries any prosecutor would love to present to a grand jury and have massive indictments unsealed that would rock the heels of the Federal judicial system in Chicago, with high-profile figures lined up as defendants.

In addition, Jackie had legal and political aspirations on a scale like no other. She held dreams of being a head U.S. Attorney as she intended to realign herself on the prosecuting side of the bar at some point, while at the same time, she was biding her time to turn in that journal—with her name all over it—as being the one to obtain such evidence and enable the government to make historic arrests. She felt as though she would instantly gain fame and success, and would be subject to fly to the top and acquire the necessary votes to hold office. All that was needed was for her to get back into the flow of things once disposed of the cases she'd agreed to work for the GD defendants who took care of such business against Nightmare for her.

Jackie was intent on bringing to light all that she'd stumbled upon in the dark. She felt no pressure nor threat from the newly created foe that had set no limit in his desire to seek payback on that bitch for the problems she'd caused.

The African princess—Jackie—wasted no further time appropriating the money she'd stole by spending it how she saw fit. She went out and bought a brand sparkling new fire-engine red big-body BMW 760 IL luxury vehicle. She also went on a multi-day shopping spree with a hefty portion of the money, and had even went so far as to donate a lump sum to the government of her native French Ivory Coast that sponsored charities and hosted groups in the country to raise awareness to combat abuse of women and the mistreatment thereof.

Jackie sent emails to ReeRee to let her be made known as to exactly how she was spending the money, and in return, ReeRee reported to Nightmare everything she'd gotten directly from the horse's mouth.

ReeRee had been hard-pressed for money, as the theft had knocked a hole in her financial stability and had also placed a severe strain on the relationship and level of trust she had with Nightmare. Also, ReeRee had no plans to return to the relationship once held with Jackie, as she'd been betrayed to a high degree. That, along with the fact of the two of them having been involved in a terrible fight with each other, made it absolutely impossible for her to even contemplate the thought of getting back with Jackie. There was no way in hell they'd be able to co-exist in the same room together, let alone share the same bed again, without another serious altercation taking place—if not one ending up killing the other.

Might it also be mentioned that Jackie was sure to provide the LGBTQ community headquarters with a generous donation, as she prided herself on being one of their most prized and honored delegates and legal advocates.

That bitch had fucked over Nightmare and ReeRee, then began to act as if she'd done no wrong. She didn't realize that in the view of Nightmare, a brutal killing of her was the only solution to the violations that was committed. She must have felt her eventual death impending quickly, because, along with passing off the journal to a trusted family member to turn over to someone she'd met—who worked as an assistant in the U.S. Attorney's Office in Chicago, if something were to happen to her—Jackie had gone so far as to have her sister take a blood oath, that she would allow nothing to happen to the journal and promised to avenge her death if such were to occur, by fully cooperating with authorities to bring justice to the guilty.

***

Moving forward, Jackie visited a national convention in Houston, Texas, that was held to honor prosecuting attorneys on both federal and state levels. She had particularly sought out a female prosecutor from one of the Chicago divisions of the Federal courts or U.S. Attorney's Offices. She found a confidante in one—Hope Steinbeck—a mid-thirties, slightly tall, frail-framed, red-headed Jewish litigator who worked as an assistant to the top U.S. Attorney of Chicago. After asking a person or two to direct her to someone—anyone—from that particular office, she'd been referred to Hope and took the opportunity to introduce herself between the keynote speakers at the convention.

"Excuse me, hello. How are you?" Jackie had greeted upon approaching Hope near the refreshment concessions and extending her hand to shake that of Hope's.

"I'm fine. How are you?" Hope replied, and the two shook hands.

"Yes, I'm Jackie—Jacquelyn Francois-Claudel—and I was directed to you as being someone I may be able to confer with about some information I've received of ongoing high-level activities by a criminal enterprise that's operating in your jurisdiction," Jackie stated.

"Oh really? Okay. What you got?" Hope responded.

"Please allow me opportunity to make you aware, briefly, of my background if you will, and then I'll get into the specifics of all I'd like to bring to your attention," said Jackie.

"Okay, go for it."

"I'm from Los Angeles, and that's also the city and jurisdiction where I practice. For the better part of six years, I've clerked for the U.S. Attorney of the Southern Jurisdiction of California. I briefly stepped away from the prosecuting side of litigation and entered into the private area of practice. Once I am to complete the current cases that I'm on, I definitely intend to return to assisting prosecuting," Jackie had related.

"Sounds like you have a solid plan, Jackie," Hope complimented.

"Thank you. But here is the thing I wanted to talk with you about. I have a female friend who finds herself involved with a high-ranking gang member, who is incarcerated in federal prison," Jackie opened up about ReeRee and Nightmare.

"Oh wow. It sounds like it could get troublesome at some point," responded Hope.

"And that's the reason I'm trying to get a handle on it now. But anyway, she is a friend of mine who I went through law school with. She was retained by the particular inmate I make mention of, to handle a post-conviction petition—a Twenty-Two Fifty-Five Bivens application. Somewhere along the line, her client obviously said all the right things to seduce her, and she fell for him without the slightest thought in the world that such acquaintance could turn out to be detrimental," Jackie said.

"Tell me about it. What was she thinking? Doesn't she know it's not good to mix business and pleasure?" responded Hope.

"At times, we have loved ones that we must do all the thinking for. She was just being a woman and fell for a guy. But, nonetheless, that's not good on any level," Jackie said to an attentive Hope, as she took a drink of her apple juice and perked her ears for more of what Jackie had to share with her.

Jackie continued, "But where she went wrong is here. Her client/new boyfriend had her travelling to and from Chicago and elsewhere, picking up money—most likely illicit funds—and stashing it or laundering it for him. God, I hope this girl don't get caught or get into any trouble before I have the opportunity to get advice and help her," Jackie said.

"I'm telling you. My God. Because it sounds like what she's headed for is trouble," Hope blurted in response.

"Other than moving money around and going to visit with him more than she should on attorney-client visits, I don't believe she's got anything else going on," Jackie stated.

"So, what was it you sought me out for again? I didn't catch it," Hope had urged Jackie on to make her point.

"Oh. Yeah. Um, I had stumbled upon this address book, or journal, or something to the effect of that, my friend had been holding onto for the guy she's involved with. Apparently, she must have had the intent to pass it off to him at some point soon, upon one of their future visits. She was the middle person between him and the guy she picked up money from in Chicago. But what this book contained inside was a detailed breakdown of the criminal organization he is the former leader of."

"Oh okay. I see where we're going with this now," replied Hope.

"Yeah, it's more like an annual report or progress report, if you will, of the enterprise," Jackie noted.

"Is that right? Loaded with evidence to possibly prosecute?" Hope wanted to know.

"You damn right it is. A treasure trove of it, honey. But I can't turn it over just yet. I've got to be sure that my dear is free from any involvement and has nothing to do with a continuance of a criminal enterprise. For all I know, she may possibly be getting extorted and forced to do all that she has by a threat on her life. Once I get down to the bottom of the business between the two, I'll be sure to forward the book to you, if you're interested."

"I'm always interested in being sure America serves justice against the guilty," Hope quickly responded.

"Good. Because I tend to think the same way. That's why I wanted to bring it to the attention of someone."

"Well, you've got the right person for that. And everything in this book had originated in Chicago, correct? In my jurisdiction?" Hope asked to confirm.

"Yes, that's right," replied Jackie.

"Okay. Then here is my card. Whenever you're ready, please contact me," Hope stated and passed Jackie a business card.

"Will do," responded Jackie, and they went about their separate ways.

At the point of Jackie linking up and gaining an acquaintance with Hope, she felt secure that, no matter what, no one from Nightmare's team would be able to do her any harm. If push came to shove, if the pressure began to become too much, or if the possibility truly existed that ReeRee was on the verge of having Nightmare's convictions tossed, she would immediately contact Hope and send her that journal to begin an entirely new line of prosecution to re-bury his ass in prison again.

She was to utilize the damaging evidence contained in the journal as her 'life insurance policy,' so to speak, against Nightmare, and keep him at bay from making any significant and meaningful progress with ReeRee. At least, this was the concept.

Chapter 28

Moving Along...

Thinking wisely, ReeRee was able to utilize her side-guy, Andrew, to help her get back on her feet, money-wise, and get situated in an apartment outside of being in the same residence as Jackie. He had helped ease the stress and the pressure that she faced in going through all the drama and the extra shit her former lover began to put upon her.

Once escorted by the police, per court order, ReeRee had gone to the house she and Jackie previously shared to get the rest of her belongings. The court order mandated Jackie not be present at the hour she was to show and retrieve what was hers. This was so to prevent any further fighting between the two, especially not so in the presence of the police.

In the comfort of her own domain, ReeRee was able to regain focus and concentrate again on litigating the cases she was assigned and retained to do.

When not in the act of litigating matters before the court, or configuring numbers regarding an account of a client for tax purposes—she freelanced as an accountant as well—ReeRee and Nightmare would chat their souls away in phone conversation and make other connections through letters. But Nightmare had loved to hold video calls with her, as he'd bought a phone down at the prison in Miami.

"Sweetheart, I've got some good news to share with you," she said to him in the recent conversation that they had. "Everything seems to be moving along well."

SOULLESS GOON | PRINCE

"And what's that? What seems to be flowing so smoothly?" he asked in response.

"I was told that we could receive a ruling from the court a little sooner than expected on your case."

"Oh yeah. That would be great if we get what we're seeking," he said.

"Sure will. We have fought hard and long enough, and have suffered long enough too. And I feel that some relief should be granted to bring about an end to this ordeal," ReeRee said.

"Baby, I'm so sick and tired of this prison shit. Always being ordcrcd around and told what to do, you know," Nightmare responded.

"I feel where you're coming from on that, sweetie. You know I've been performing and doing all I know to do in seeing to it you get the proper justice, from the courts, you deserve," ReeRee stated.

"I do deserve some form of justice, if not but getting this life sentence off my back, you feel me?"

"Of course you know I feel you, baby. How is your health coming along?" she wanted to know.

"Oh, it's going good. It wasn't as bad as initially thought to be. The doctor told me I may only have to wear this damn bag for about a year longer and no more. The blade had only penetrated about a half inch, and most of the damage was done to the core muscles and not really on my intestines. Thanks to those sit-ups and crunches, I've been saved from many years of agony and physical complications. I only wish that I knew who was responsible for ordering the call on me, and who exactly the dudes were that was stupid enough to answer up to it," Nightmare spat from an angry vein with venom seething.

ReeRee remained silent as he ranted about being mobbed and stabbed. As he continued to speak, she was able to detect the poison that oozed from his tongue and stained each word he expressed on the situation. Nightmare was pissed. The very memory of that dreadful morning would forever be ingrained on his thoughts.

"I've been in contact with my people up in Lew-Burg, and I was sure to tell them to keep me up on any developments or info they get about who got me. And once they know who, waste no time to go in. To make-believe it was 'World War Four.' Bypass the 'third' one," he stated.

"Baby, please be careful how you speak over the phone, okay?" ReeRee reminded.

"Yeah, you got a point there. It's just this shit shouldn't have been allowed to happen. That's the part which gets to me. But it's cool. I've got the power to make the call for all my people at every camp to go ahead and do what they got to do against them niggaz. They touched the wrong guy. It's not the small fry who I want ate. My appetite is on 'super-size.' I want the big fish that has the most flavor," Nightmare stated.

Nightmare fumed with anger and desired to bring pain to the opposition. At any time he got into the mind frame to go in and destroy any enemy, it was a done deal. His intent would not be changed on any level. In an effort to straighten the tone and allow for ReeRee to continue to have a good perception of him—as opposed to what his attitude about being stabbed gave off—he switched the topic and began to speak along the lines of her possibly picking up more money for him.

"Sweetheart, look. As soon as you possibly could, I need for you to clear your schedule and be ready to go meet up with my people again. I've already been in contact with him and he knows what to do and what to pass off to you. It may be a few months away. Nonetheless, I need you again. For that," Nightmare had said.

"Look at me, baby," he asked to fully have her attention as she seemed to drift momentarily.

"I'm here, Michael. I hear you and I'm paying attention," she replied.

"I'm saying it like this because it's important, okay," he mentioned. At any time he discussed business, his demeanor would turn from being that of a docile mixed dude to a serious-minded street commander at the crack of the whip. Nightmare always demanded absoluteness of eye contact, just as Teddy would order in his days of grooming him and Ricky to hold top spots.

***

Standing firm on business, ReeRee was sure to give Nightmare all he'd askcd for in regards to the attention he silently demanded. Business and money was a discussion necessary for her to have with him, since Jackie had wiped her clean out, and she had to rely on Andrew from there more than she wanted to—without tapping into the money stashed in New York and Philly she previously put away. The money her mother was holding had special attachments to it.

As ReeRee and Nightmare talked on video call, she gazed deeply into the screen of the phone and listened to her incarcerated man.

"Say, check this out too, alright," he said, and cracked a smile as if he had something heartwarming to tell her.

"What's that, baby?" she responded.

"When we get this case overturned and I'm freed, you and I gonna go to Macy's, and I'm gonna buy the biggest broom I can find there, and sweep you off your feet and make you fall in love all over again, okay? But this time, it'll be like never before. My promise to you," he said to her charmingly.

ReeRee giggled and relished in the moment, as he flattered her with his poetically laced lines of deceit. He knew she loved compliments, flattery, and affectionate sentiments. And any time he needed her diehard dedication and superior commitment, Nightmare never failed to employ one of these types of tricks and schemes he readily kept up his sleeve. He'd perfected the craft of being a master at mind manipulation and psychological indoctrination.

The two lovebirds blew kisses as they ended the FaceTime session. Prior to terminating their conversation, ReeRee was sure to make him aware it was her intent to make a transition—at some point at least—from the office at the firm she worked for in L.A. to an office space of her own as a private attorney, there as well or possibly in some other similar city.

ReeRee felt as though the demands of the firm were beginning to be a little too much for her and not affording her the pay she could make on her own accord. Also, once she begins to do her own thing, the requirement to be transparent won't be as mandatory as it is in the firm as an employee. She'd be able to do all she pleased and make her money in many ways—how she saw fit, not according to what the firm's assignment called for.

Chapter 29

As the relationship with Andrew played on, ReeRee began to party alongside him, mostly on weekends, at entertainment events he would host. At these such gatherings, there was every vice known to them available to be used or either abused. Andrew held rank and a lot of clout amongst music mogul buddies, as he'd welcomed some of the top people in the industry to his Los Angeles home to get down and party hardy with him. Indeed, he had additional side-pieces in females he dealt with other than ReeRee, but this was fine by her.

Unbeknownst to him though, she'd resorted to some of her old ways and habits—selling a little pussy on the side to top-paying customers, then dressing it up as if she was only accepting gifts from the dudes she'd developed such acquaintances with.

Nonetheless, ReeRee owed no one any explanation for her actions, but rather had to convince herself that this was her situation—something she made a conscious decision to undergo—as opposed to the reality she'd reentered back into: a world of being addicted to the lifestyle and the culture of dealing out sexual pleasure. It was the same way as she had in the beginning—a necessity and a means of survival, to make ends meet and to make it through to a higher level in life. These were the convincing notions she told herself.

There was now an upside to her with selling the sexual services she had to offer. She'd evolved into a far more mature version of herself, as opposed to the ordinary little twenty-something-year-old she was back then, turning in her earnings to a pimp. ReeRee now professionalized her side hustle. Instead of the average and random Joe-Blow tricks, she now had a sophisticated clientele, which consisted of a federal agent, high-profile people in the music business she'd hooked up with at parties and through being tied to Andrew, corporate businessmen, and other prominent attorneys about the City of Angels. By all means, she operated as a high-priced escort—someone who didn't need much use of the internet to find success.

Aside from her own aspirations to be independent, one of the main reasons that ReeRee opted to leave the firm was because one of the guys who worked there, that she dealt with every so often, became too obsessed with her. Lincoln Sanford was an early-fifties veteran attorney, who was second in command at the firm behind their boss. He was a white guy, married, with adult sons and daughters by his wife. He was so cool at first, but then he caught feelings and began to be a pest—an annoying, skinny bastard who got on her nerves. He simply didn't know how to keep himself under control.

Besides the $1,000 or more a session he paid ReeRee to be with him, he'd sought to lavish her with the extras. And that—the extras—had come with a hidden obligation, which ReeRee desperately tried to distance herself from.

I need my own fucking office away from this dude and this place, she used to think to herself.

***

ReeRee was fortunate to connect with another female legal assistant—someone who was herself on the rise. Together, the two were to potentially do the groundwork and lay the foundation for the legal services they had in mind to offer.

ReeRee had always been open and straightforward with Nightmare about her sexuality and parts of her personal business. Prior to him, she hadn't been so relating and honest with a man she had involvement with, as there had been few to none—other than her high school love she experienced a moment with. The thing she had with Nate was something else altogether: an estranged relationship that was totally obscure from a normal love affair.

There was a level of trust established between the two of them—she and Nightmare—that was to be genuine and sincere. The bond they shared showed the potential of extending toward eternity, as they drew closer and closer on a daily basis, through each phone call, visit, and thought. So, at the time when she began to reveal to him the facts of her being intimately involved with another female—a Maria Santos-Rosario—it came as no surprise to him.

With Nightmare being Nightmare, he actually welcomed the thought and the challenge he was to face in having two women at one time. ReeRee broke the news to him in an email. She laid out all the details about she and her new lesbian love, and forwarded it to him through the CORRLINKS system on the same day she was to make a third trip to the Windy City for another court appearance and meeting with Ricky. Nightmare felt the need to utilize the facility communication services to prevent any suspicions of him having a contraband cell phone. He was really content with being housed in the Miami Fed pen and didn't want to be transferred to no other place. So, he needed to be on his best behavior.

Nightmare became illuminated and glowed with excitement at the idea of her being happily situated with someone (especially another female) until he was to get free, if this blessing was to occur. Things were all good on his end of the love triangle, so long as the significant add-on was to be properly informed of what he and ReeRee had going on. ReeRee felt she'd toiled like crazy and worked hard and long enough to be able to enjoy the best of both worlds—which she liked. This, of course, was having a dick and a clit, whensoever she wanted either. Besides, the life she'd envisioned at one point in time while she was with Jackie could now finally be fulfilled. This was one with Maria, but with far less drama, zero aggression, and absolute bliss. This was what she truly wanted and had striven to have.

Nightmare had never been the type of guy who was to get in his feelings and emotions behind a woman. He gave ReeRee the 'okay' of approval to proceed with all that her and Maria wanted to establish. By him entertaining the thought of reciprocating between both the careers he adored—Kingpin/leader/hustler, and player/pimp/ladies' man—really made Nightmare feel mighty in his own way. Calling shots and controlling bitches—the ultimate dream that any street nigga could ever wish himself to be capable of. To stress the point, his title in the Vice Lord organization was indeed 'Almighty Chief.' And so, he had to reassert his image and reputation to reflect that line-up to the outstanding name and title.

Nightmare figured it would be possible to maintain two high-profile women at the same damn time, if not more were to be brought into the mix. It was definitely him who stood the chance to benefit the most from a three-way love thing.

Chapter 30

On To The Next One...

The sensational duo, ReeRee and Maria, became acquainted with one another at an event in New York City, hosted by the American Lawyer's Guild and the Legal Advocates Association. The meeting of the two happened between the time Nightmare was in the hole, healing, and awaiting transfer. ReeRee patiently bided her time to make him aware of this, as her and Maria began to travel back and forth between L.A., Palm Beach, and Miami, Florida—the last being the city Maria was born, raised, and lived in until going off to college.

There were a couple of occasions that Jackie had been out and about herself in L.A. and had spotted the two socialites together at a gala and a dinner party that people of their class and cultivation attended—and my God, did that deranged lunatic bitch flip the fuck out. Jackie couldn't handle the sight of the newly affectionate duo. She went beyond bananas in public. It became unbearable for ReeRee to see Jackie behave in such an unstable and unprofessional way.

Maria had made the statement to her new lover that the "wild one"—Jackie—had absolutely no class as an elite of society and possessed no quality of a lady. Maria silently questioned, *How did ReeRee become involved with such a person that carried on the way she saw Jackie make a shameful mess of herself?*

With those round, beautiful, and dazzling eyes, she only stood and looked at Jackie, then at ReeRee, and finally back toward "the wild one" with a discerning look about her face.

Jackie was subsequently arrested the last time for domestic dispute and public disturbance. At the scene, she had lashed out and attempted to attack ReeRee and Maria. She was enraged. Her intended victims looked on at her in grave concern for Jackie's psychological well-being. They knew she wasn't right in the head any longer.

Jackie virtually rendered herself temporarily unfit to be an attorney and was subject to be penalized by the bar behind the arrest.

ReeRee had had enough. Her move to the Sunshine State for a second time couldn't come fast enough. But eventually, it would come. It was in progress. Once the move was to take place, Nightmare was to make his move and get the payback he burned with madness to have against Jackie. He wanted this bitch wiped out and completely erased from the earth, without a trace. This would be for the old as well as the new. And this would also teach the bitch a lesson—for the bullshit she'd instigated, and for the tyranny that the bitch was subject to do if he didn't act fast.

Epilogue

Facing His Greatest Fear...

Following a seemingly long night out on the town, over in Las Vegas on the main strip, Nightmare was ready and very eager to get inside the comfort of the expensive hotel suite he'd reserved for a two-week stay. He'd lied to ReeRee and Maria about him supposedly traveling to Illinois to visit his parents, and to also wish his son well, as he was in the process of entering college.

His two ladies were hard at work in litigation on a lawsuit being worked out for a client of theirs regarding divorce, and they weren't able to go along with Nightmare for his journey. He had every intention in the world to do right by being faithful to the lovely women he was the man over. But there was something so captivating, so desirous, and so heart-thralling about this one particular female he'd always longed to give the dick and put it on her well, that forced him to pursue.

In the past, before his imprisonment, she had made several advances at him and had literally thrown herself into his command, had he chosen to entertain the moment. She was willing to be all he wanted her to be, or do all that he needed her to do. All that was needed was for him to snap his fingers and say what it was.

Such never happened, because Nightmare feared the negative repercussions that came with fucking the daughter of his "Chief/leader/boss," and the niece of his best friend.

Although several years younger than he, Alana felt herself game enough and attractive enough to finally hook Nightmare one day, and relieve herself of the uncontrollable crush she was overwhelmed with. It was no doubt about it— she was fucked up over Nightmare. And it showed in many ways.

Throughout the time he was away in prison, she'd written him very long love letters expressing how she was gonna do X—Y—and Z to him once he got home. They even enjoyed a visit or two during his stay in federal lockup. Then finally, the day was at hand for her to back up all she'd said and show and prove what she was all about for the man known as Nightmare.

Her friendship with ReeRee and Maria was only a façade to find out all there was to know about Nightmare and the both of them. That way, she could move around more effectively, as she and him drew closer.

It was never suspected by ReeRee that Alana would someday go headfirst after her dude—not even after Alana deliberately acknowledged to her, personally, how strong her lust and crush for Nightmare was, on one of Jettica's trips to Chicago. No attention was paid to those remarks.

At long last, the both of them—Michael and Alana—were together inside a hotel suite and away from everyone. Alana was ass-naked, lustfully teasing and sashaying around the suite for Nightmare as he looked on from atop the bed, sipping on a glass of Dom P. Alana had poured his glass for him. He had on his silk boxers and a wife beater, gripping his dick tightly as he watched her.

All of a sudden, he became very woozy-headed and drowsy like never before. He passed out, totally unconscious, as Alana had added an extra dose of fentanyl to the sleeping agent to get the job done. A packet of Sweet'N Low was also mixed with the powerful tranquilizing drug to prevent the bitterness in taste. He never knew a thing, as she was extremely smooth in how she slipped the substance in his drink.

At the point of Nightmare being out cold, Alana handcuffed him thoroughly to the bed by his wrists and ankles. She then called her uncle Ricky to hurry and come to the room to take charge of the situation. Ricky and another—Zu Lord—arrived. They saw that Alana had done a good job tying Nightmare's ass down and were eager to get the rest of the party going. Ricky slapped him viciously.

Whop!

Then, he dashed ice water in his face. He shot him up with an anti-overdose drug to revive him.

"Ah. What the fuck!" Nightmare uttered.

"Yo-yo-yo. What's good, my guy? If it ain't ol' Nightmare. Look at your ass now, nigga! No more of a threat nor 'Nightmare' than a helpless baby. Wake your bitch-ass up, nigga!" Ricky snarled, then slapped him again—and again—and a third time, successively, for good measure.

Whop-Whop-Whoo!

Ricky ordered his help to gag Nightmare, so as to muffle any screams.

"I knew you were no good, nigga. I shouldn't have never trusted you after your conviction and me getting free with no prison time to serve. You tried to get me, Night. You attempted to swap me out with you. But it didn't work out like that. And now, once I put an end to your ass, I'll reign supreme in the Vice Lord Nation, and you'll be no more. Not even a worthy mention. After all these years, I'd never known you been busy trying to fuck my niece. You know that's against the rules. Had my brother known you were up to this type of shit, we'd been exterminated your ass. Now, here—accept this long-overdue measure of justice and be on your way to meet your maker ... the devil himself," Ricky scalded, then began to stab Nightmare brutally in the heart with a twelve-inch steak knife—twelve being the same number of jurors which convicted him. He plunged the weapon into his chest over and over and over again, maybe forty times, with not the slightest show of remorse.

"Take that, you mixed mutt!" Ricky lastly spat.

Nightmare jumped from his sleep in a cold sweat and crazed way. He was between his prison cot and the wool blanket in the cell where he resided. He was very close to getting those heavy convictions crushed and only had pleasant dreams of how nice life as a free man would be for him once more—until the nightmares began and held him restless. He had experienced a terrible one on this particular night, by all means. One like no other.

He dozed back to sleep yet again. In doing so, another nightmare crept upon him.

"Hello, Michael. How are you? Long time no see, huh? Do you still recognize me? I didn't think so. Especially not with *this* here done to me by you," the voice of the disfigured female reminded, as she pointed to the gunshot wound she'd suffered to the head by Nightmare—and then to the one in her pregnant belly.

The entire left side of her head and a portion of the back of her skull had been blown off by a high-caliber pistol, a .45. Brain splatter and thick blood oozed down onto her neck, shoulder, and back. The two bullet holes in her stomach oozed blood and were still smoking from the hot pieces of lead that burned and sizzled on the insides of her body like sausage in a frying pan. The unborn baby within didn't stand a chance.

Antoinette pointed to her head ... then back to her midsection ... head ... then midsection simultaneously, to indicate with her finger that she wanted Nightmare to take a good look at the damage he'd done.

"Look, Michael. Please take a really good look at what you've done. How could you? Me and our unborn daughter—she was eight months pregnant—was maliciously murdered by you, all because of your jealous nature. You actually had the audacity to accuse me of being pregnant with someone else's seed. All because the guy bought me a 'mother-to-be' gift. Yes, he was an ex-boyfriend of mine, but I was no longer involved. You shall die and go to hell for what you've done! You shall die and go to hell! You shall die and go to hell!" she had the opportunity to express three times before Nightmare awoke.

Then, he jumped to his feet—this time behind the second consecutive bad dream he'd experienced in less than an hour.

"Oh shit! What the fuck ... What the fuck ... What the fuck!" he shouted, while frantically whisking his head from left to right ... then right to left.

The correctional guard banged on the cell door with his flashlight to get his attention. It was the 3 A.M. count.

"Gentry. You okay in there?" the staff member asked.

"Yeah. I'm okay," Nightmare responded. "I was having a bad dream. A *nightmare,* coincidentally," he made known to his overseer.

"Okay. Just checking on you," the C.O. concluded and continued on.

"Damn! I got to get it together," Nightmare stated to himself and stepped over to the sink to wash his face with cold water.

He was tired as ever and really needed to rest properly. Nightmare had been up for nearly four days brainstorming and trying to put things in perspective and figure it all out. His deal with Mr. Rahman had been secured and only needed now to be cemented with the special request asked of him. It was an absolute fact that the job would get done at some point or another. And once accomplished, five additional bricks of heroin would be rewarded. Also, Nightmare's anxiousness ran high in knowing he could be a free man in due time. A lot was going good for him—and if anyone, it was he who needed the progressive energy the most.

His body began shutting down again, and before he knew it, he was asleep once more. Not even three minutes into it, another bad dream was upon him.

It was of the mother and little girl he and his crew had gruesomely murdered by drowning in a bathtub and putting a bullet into the head of the adult female. The grown-up held the hand of the young girl as the both of them just stared at Nightmare continuously, occasionally shifting their heads from one side to the other as they looked on at their killer in utter silence. Finally, the lady spoke up.

"Did the ends justify the means?" he was questioned.

Nightmare didn't know what to say regarding the question.

"Speak to me, sir. I asked—did the ends justify the means?" she repeated.

Reluctant, he answered.

"It wasn't personal, miss. Only business. I did what I had to do," he stated to the murdered victim of his.

"So you mean to tell me that taking the life of a mother and a second grader was 'doing what you had to do,' as you put it?" she countered.

"I had orders," he responded. "Two lives for batches of drugs? Your brother and boyfriend placed the both of you in that predicament by doing what they had," he attempted to justify.

At that point, the adult remained silent, and the little girl stretched out her arm—a stuffed doll clutched in her hand extended—and the face of the doll was looking Nightmare's direction. The doll's face began to construe and grimace at him angrily. The little girl then withdrew an ink pen and placed it in the palm of the doll, then gently sat the doll down on the floor. The doll began fast-stepping toward Nightmare with the pen gripped tightly. And then, the pen appeared to transform into a very sharp, pointed twelve-inch nail.

He was already shell-shocked in a sense of being stabbed again from the incident in Lewisburg, and there it was—the same scenario repeating itself for a second time. Anxiety wreaked havoc upon Nightmare. He began to have a panic attack. He threw up the vegan meal he'd eaten earlier in the day.

The doll finally made it to him, then leaped up onto his tall, lean frame to begin stabbing and biting. He shouted and squirmed as the dark black Voodoo doll with nappy dreadlocks chomped down on him and whacked away.

Nightmare jumped from his sleep yet again and ran toward the door in an attempt to get away, just like the time he had in Lewisburg before passing out from his actual stab wounds and loss of blood. He ran into the cell door and hit his head, knocking him to the floor and making it possible for him to fully become revived.

"Goddamnit! I wonder how many more muthafuckin' nightmares am I gonna have, in one fuckin' night?" he yelled out to nobody in particular but himself.

He was sure to stay up this time to prevent more of the same from happening.

Ain't that a bitch!

The man who was infamously known as "Nightmare" was afraid himself of nightmares. And as the saying goes: "So as you sow, you shall also reap!"

The Beginning...

ABOUT THE AUTHOR

PRINCE is a writer of gritty, raw, dark, and suspenseful contemporary urban/street crime fiction. The works of his embody American society and African-American culture as is, in the way that it is. Nothing less. Nothing more. The characters he creates are realistic in nature, in all of their wiles and ways. The style of writing Prince has developed, speaks for itself. You're drawn in the more and more you read, until you're locked there; with one way in and no way out. In a word to describe his skills within the craft: it's **LETHAL.**

Prince, vehemently declares at every opportunity that, *"WRITING IS HIS ONLY SALVATION!"* He stands firmly on business with this.

The works he's released thus far in addition to this, is the popular **BLOODLINE OF A SAVAGE** series (three installments to date); **THESE VICIOUS STREETS** series (three installments to date); and **RELENTLESS GOON** series; (three installments to date) and **THE DIRTY SIDE OF MONEY** (three installments to date) to name a few. More captivating stories are on the way.

Prince is currently hard at work on his next installment of the story you've just read. Look forward to new releases from him soon. He highly encourages feedback and engaging conversation about his books in general and the writing industry as a whole. You may contact him at the following:

PRINCE A. TAUHID #952058
MACON STATE PRISON
P.O. BOX 426
OGLETHORPE, GEORGIA 31068
iamprinceforever3000@gmail.com

"I write what the streets remember. My pen bleeds ether!" Prince (Thá Author)

The Pen Is Mightier Than The Pistol
EMBRACE WRITING!

ALSO BY PRINCE:

Bloodline of a Savage 1-3
These Vicious Streets 1-3
Relentless Goon 1-3
Savage Family Empire 1-2
The Dirty Side Of Money 1-3

COMING SOON IN
THE SOULLESS GOON SAGA

SOULLESS GOON 2
Ill-Omened

SOULLESS GOON 3
Executioner's Song

SOULLESS GOON 4
Last Rites

SOULLESS GOON 5
Death's Anthem

SOULLESS BASTARD
The Beginning
(Prequel)

SPIN OFFS FROM
THE WORLD OF SOULLESS GOON

SON OF A SOULLESS GOON
(MJ's Story)
(FROM THE WORLD OF SOULLESS GOON)
ASSASSIN'S CREED
(Minister's Story)

(FROM THE WORLD OF SOULLESS GOON)
RED DAHLIA
(Jettica's Story)
(FROM THE WORLD OF SOULLESS GOON)
INFLUENCE
(Ricky's Story)
(FROM THE WORLD OF SOULLESS GOON)
SECRETARY BIRD
(Trinity's Story)
(FROM THE WORLD OF SOULLESS GOON)

Lock Down Publications and Ca$h Presents
Assisted Publishing Packages

Due to an increase in the price of services we have increased our prices. The prices below reflect the price increase as of 11/1/24.

BASIC PACKAGE	UPGRADED PACKAGE
$699	$1000
Editing	Typing
Cover Design	Editing
Formatting	Cover Design
	Formatting
	Upload eBooks to Amazon
	Upload Paperback to Amazon
ADVANCE PACKAGE	**LDP SUPREME PACKAGE**
$1,400	$1,700
Typing	Typing
Editing (line editing/content)	Editing (line editing/content)
Cover Design	Cover Design
Formatting	Formatting
Copyright Registration	Copyright Registration
Proofreading	Proofreading
Upload eBooks to Amazon	Set up Amazon Account
Upload Paperback to Amazon	Upload eBooks to Amazon
	Upload Paperback to Amazon
	Advertise on LDP's Amazon and Facebook Page

***

Other services available upon request.
Additional charges may apply

Lock Down Publications
P.O. Box 944
Stockbridge, GA 30281-9998
Phone: 470 303-9761
Email: lockdownpublications@gmail.com

245

Submission Guideline

Submit the first three chapters of your completed manuscript to ldpsubmissions@gmail.com. In the subject line add **Your Book's Title**. The manuscript must be in a Word Doc file and sent as an attachment. Document should be in Times New Roman, double spaced, and in size 12 font. Also, provide your synopsis and full contact information. If sending multiple submissions, they must each be in a separate email.

Have a story but no way to send it electronically? You can still submit to LDP/Ca$h Presents. Send in the first three chapters, written or typed, of your completed manuscript to:

LDP: Submissions Dept
P.O. Box 944
Stockbridge, GA 30281-9998

DO NOT send original manuscript. Must be a duplicate. Provide your synopsis and a cover letter containing your full contact information.

Thanks for considering LDP and Ca$h Presents.

NEW RELEASES

BLOODLINE OF A SAVAGE 1-3
THESE VICIOUS STREETS 1-3
RELENTLESS GOON 1-3
BY PRINCE A. TAUHID

THE BUTTERFLY MAFIA 1-3
BY FUMIYA PAYNE

A THUG'S STREET PRINCESS 1&2
BY MEESHA

CITY OF SMOKE 3
BY MOLOTTI

GET IT IN SLUGS 1 &2
BY B. STALL

STANDING ON HER BUSINESS 1&2
BY DG SANTANA

STEPPERS 1,2&3
THE REAL BADDIES OF CHI-RAQ
BY KING RIO

THE LANE 1&2
BY KEN-KEN SPENCE

THUG OF SPADES 1&2
LOVE IN THE TRENCHES 2
CORNER BOYS
BY COREY ROBINSON

TIL DEATH 3
BY ARYANNA

SOULLESS GOON | PRINCE

THE BIRTH OF A GANGSTER 4
BY DELMONT PLAYER

PRODUCT OF THE STREETS 1-3
BY DEMOND "MONEY" ANDERSON

NO TIME FOR ERROR
BY KEESE

MONEY HUNGRY DEMONS 1-2
BY TRANAY ADAMS

HUB CITY MENACE 1-3
BY J. WHITE

A THUGGISH PASSION 1&2
LAND OF DA HOOLIGANZ 1-4
KILLAZ ON STANDBY 1&2
BY IRA B.

FO'EVA ROLLIN 1&2
BY ASSA RAYMOND BAKER

THE LEVEL UP 1&3
BY LUXURY KING

Coming Soon from Lock Down Publications/Ca$h Presents

IF YOU CROSS ME ONCE 6
ANGEL V
By Anthony Fields

A THUGS STREET PRINCESS 3
By Meesha

CORNER BOYS 2
By Corey Robinson

THA TAKEOVER
By Keith Chandler

BETRAYAL OF A G 2
By Ray Vinci

SAVAGE FAMILY EMPIRE 1&2
SOULLESS GOON 1,2&3
THE DIRTY SIDE OF MONEY 1,2&3
By Prince

FOR MY ENEMY'S SAKE
AMBITIONS OF A SLIDER
FRESH OFF DA PORCH
By IRA B.

THE TRUCKLOAD 1-4
TIPPIN' THE SCALES 1-3
BAD BITCHES WIT GUNZ 3
PROBLEM SOLVED 2
By Christopher "Diesel" Hornezes

Available Now

RESTRAINING ORDER 1 & 2
By **CA$H & Coffee**

LOVE KNOWS NO BOUNDARIES 1-3
By **Coffee**

RAISED AS A GOON I, II, III & IV
BRED BY THE SLUMS I, II, III
BLAST FOR ME I & II
ROTTEN TO THE CORE I II III
A BRONX TALE I, II, III
DUFFLE BAG CARTEL I II III IV V VI
HEARTLESS GOON I II III IV V
A SAVAGE DOPEBOY I II
DRUG LORDS I II III
CUTTHROAT MAFIA I II
KING OF THE TRENCHES
By **Ghost**

LAY IT DOWN I & II
LAST OF A DYING BREED I II
BLOOD STAINS OF A SHOTTA I & II III
By **Jamaica**

LOYAL TO THE GAME I II III
LIFE OF SIN I, II III
By **TJ & Jelissa**

IF LOVING HIM IS WRONG…I & II
LOVE ME EVEN WHEN IT HURTS I II III
By **Jelissa**

PUSH IT TO THE LIMIT
By **Bre' Hayes**

SOULLESS GOON | PRINCE

BLOODY COMMAS I & II
SKI MASK CARTEL I, II & III
KING OF NEW YORK I II, III IV V
RISE TO POWER I II III
COKE KINGS I II III IV V
BORN HEARTLESS I II III IV
KING OF THE TRAP I II
By **T.J. Edwards**

WHEN THE STREETS CLAP BACK I & II III
THE HEART OF A SAVAGE I II III IV
MONEY MAFIA I II
LOYAL TO THE SOIL I II III
By **Jibril Williams**

A DISTINGUISHED THUG STOLE MY HEART I II & III
LOVE SHOULDN'T HURT I II III IV
RENEGADE BOYS 1-4
PAID IN KARMA 1-3
SAVAGE STORMS 1-3
AN UNFORESEEN LOVE 1-3
BABY, I'M WINTERTIME COLD 1-3
A THUG'S STREET PRINCESS 1&2
By **Meesha**

A GANGSTER'S CODE 1-3
A GANGSTER'S SYN 1-3
THE SAVAGE LIFE 1-3
CHAINED TO THE STREETS 1-3
BLOOD ON THE MONEY 1-3
A GANGSTA'S PAIN 1-3
BEAUTIFUL LIES AND UGLY TRUTHS
CHURCH IN THESE STREETS
By **J-Blunt**

CUM FOR ME 1-8
An LDP Erotica Collaboration

SOULLESS GOON | PRINCE

BLOOD OF A BOSS 1-5
SHADOWS OF THE GAME
TRAP BASTARD
By **Askari**

THE STREETS BLEED MURDER 1-3
THE HEART OF A GANGSTA 1-3
By **Jerry Jackson**

WHEN A GOOD GIRL GOES BAD
By **Adrienne**

THE COST OF LOYALTY 1-3
By **Kweli**

BRIDE OF A HUSTLA 1-3
THE FETTI GIRLS 1-3
CORRUPTED BY A GANGSTA 1-4
BLINDED BY HIS LOVE
THE PRICE YOU PAY FOR LOVE 1-3
DOPE GIRL MAGIC 1-3
By **Destiny Skai**

A KINGPIN'S AMBITION
A KINGPIN'S AMBITION II
I MURDER FOR THE DOUGH
By **Ambitious**

TRUE SAVAGE 1-7
DOPE BOY MAGIC 1-3
MIDNIGHT CARTEL 1-3
CITY OF KINGZ 1&2
NIGHTMARE ON SILENT AVE
THE PLUG OF LIL MEXICO 1&2
CLASSIC CITY
By **Chris Green**

SOULLESS GOON | PRINCE

A GANGSTER'S REVENGE 1-4
THE BOSS MAN'S DAUGHTERS 1-5
A SAVAGE LOVE 1&2
BAE BELONGS TO ME 1&2
A HUSTLER'S DECEIT 1-3
WHAT BAD BITCHES DO 1-3
SOUL OF A MONSTER 1-3
KILL ZONE
A DOPE BOY'S QUEEN 1-3
TIL DEATH 1-3
IMMA DIE BOUT MINE 1-6
DYING FOR LIKES
By **Aryanna**

A DOPEBOY'S PRAYER
By **Eddie "Wolf" Lee**

THE KING CARTEL 1-3
By **Frank Gresham**

THESE NIGGAS AIN'T LOYAL 1-3
By **Nikki Tee**

GANGSTA SHYT 1-3
By **CATO**

THE ULTIMATE BETRAYAL
By **Phoenix**

BOSS'N UP 1-3
By **Royal Nicole**

I LOVE YOU TO DEATH
By **Destiny J**

I RIDE FOR MY HITTA
I STILL RIDE FOR MY HITTA
By **Misty Holt**

SOULLESS GOON | PRINCE

LOVE & CHASIN' PAPER
By **Qay Crockett**

TO DIE IN VAIN
SINS OF A HUSTLA
By **ASAD**

BROOKLYN HUSTLAZ
By **Boogsy Morina**

BROOKLYN ON LOCK 1 & 2
By **Sonovia**

GANGSTA CITY
By **Teddy Duke**

A DRUG KING AND HIS DIAMOND 1-3
A DOPEMAN'S RICHES
HER MAN, MINE'S TOO 1&2
CASH MONEY HO'S
THE WIFEY I USED TO BE 1&2
PRETTY GIRLS DO NASTY THINGS
By **Nicole Goosby**

LIPSTICK KILLAH 1-3
CRIME OF PASSION 1-3
FRIEND OR FOE 1-3
By **Mimi**

TRAPHOUSE KING 1-3
KINGPIN KILLAZ 1-3
STREET KINGS 1&2
PAID IN BLOOD 1&2
CARTEL KILLAZ 1-3
DOPE GODS 1&2
By **Hood Rich**

THE STREETS ARE CALLING
By **Duquie Wilson**

SOULLESS GOON | PRINCE

STEADY MOBBN' 1-3
THE STREETS STAINED MY SOUL 1-3
By **Marcellus Allen**

WHO SHOT YA 1-3
SON OF A DOPE FIEND 1-4
HEAVEN GOT A GHETTO 1&2
SKI MASK MONEY 1&2
By **Renta**

GORILLAZ IN THE BAY 1-4
TEARS OF A GANGSTA 1/&2
3X KRAZY 1&2
STRAIGHT BEAST MODE 1&2
By **DE'KARI**

TRIGGADALE 1-3
MURDA WAS THE CASE 1-3
By **Elijah R. Freeman**

SLAUGHTER GANG 1-3
RUTHLESS HEART 1-3
By **Willie Slaughter**

GOD BLESS THE TRAPPERS 1-3
THESE SCANDALOUS STREETS 1-3
FEAR MY GANGSTA 1-5
THESE STREETS DON'T LOVE NOBODY 1-2
BURY ME A G 1-5
A GANGSTA'S EMPIRE 1-4
THE DOPEMAN'S BODYGAURD 1&2
THE REALEST KILLAZ 1-3
THE LAST OF THE OGS 1-3
By **Tranay Adams**

MARRIED TO A BOSS 1-3
By **Destiny Skai & Chris Green**

255

SOULLESS GOON | PRINCE

KINGZ OF THE GAME 1-7
CRIME BOSS 1-4
By **Playa Ray**

FUK SHYT
By **Blakk Diamond**

DON'T F#CK WITH MY HEART 1&2
By **Linnea**

ADDICTED TO THE DRAMA 1-3
IN THE ARM OF HIS BOSS
By **Jamila**

LOYALTY AIN'T PROMISED 1&2
By **Keith Williams**

YAYO 1-4
A SHOOTER'S AMBITION 1&2
BRED IN THE GAME
By **S. Allen**

TRAP GOD 1-3
RICH $AVAGE 1-3
MONEY IN THE GRAVE 1-3
CARTEL MONEY 1&2
By **Martell Troublesome Bolden**

FOREVER GANGSTA 1&2
GLOCKS ON SATIN SHEETS 1&2
By **Adrian Dulan**

TOE TAGZ 1-4
LEVELS TO THIS SHYT 1&2
IT'S JUST ME AND YOU
By **Ah'Million**

SOULLESS GOON | PRINCE

KINGPIN DREAMS 1-3
RAN OFF ON DA PLUG
By **Paper Boi Rari**

THE STREETS MADE ME 1-3
By **Larry D. Wright**

CONFESSIONS OF A GANGSTA 1-4
CONFESSIONS OF A JACKBOY 1-3
CONFESSIONS OF A HITMAN
CONFESSIONS OF A DOPE BOY
By **Nicholas Lock**

I'M NOTHING WITHOUT HIS LOVE
SINS OF A THUG
TO THE THUG I LOVED BEFORE
A GANGSTA SAVED XMAS
IN A HUSTLER I TRUST
By **Monet Dragun**

QUIET MONEY 1-3
THUG LIFE 1-3
EXTENDED CLIP 1&2
A GANGSTA'S PARADISE
By **Trai'Quan**

CAUGHT UP IN THE LIFE 1-3
THE STREETS NEVER LET GO 1-3
By **Robert Baptiste**

NEW TO THE GAME 1-3
MONEY, MURDER & MEMORIES 1-3
By **Malik D. Rice**

CREAM 2-3
THE STREETS WILL TALK
By **Yolanda Moore**

SOULLESS GOON | PRINCE

THE STREETS WILL NEVER CLOSE 1-3
By **K'ajji**

LIFE OF A SAVAGE 1-4
A GANGSTA'S QUR'AN 1-4
MURDA SEASON 1-3
GANGLAND CARTEL 1-3
CHI'RAQ GANGSTAS 1-4
KILLERS ON ELM STREET 1-3
JACK BOYZ N DA BRONX 1-3
A DOPEBOY'S DREAM 1-3
JACK BOYS VS DOPE BOYS 1-3
COKE GIRLZ
COKE BOYS
SOSA GANG 1&2
BRONX SAVAGES
BODYMORE KINGPINS
BLOOD OF A GOON
By **Romell Tukes**

CONCRETE KILLA 1-3
VICIOUS LOYALTY 1-3
BLOODY MONEY BAGS
By **Kingpen**

THE ULTIMATE SACRIFICE 1-6
KHADIFI
IF YOU CROSS ME ONCE 1-3
ANGEL 1-4
IN THE BLINK OF AN EYE
By **Anthony Fields**

THE LIFE OF A HOOD STAR
By **Ca$h & Rashia Wilson**

NIGHTMARES OF A HUSTLA 1-3
BLOOD AND GAMES 1&2
By **King Dream**

GHOST MOB
By **Stilloan Robinson**

HARD AND RUTHLESS 1&2
MOB TOWN 251
THE BILLIONAIRE BENTLEYS 1-3
REAL G'S MOVE IN SILENCE
By **Von Diesel**

MOB TIES 1-7
SOUL OF A HUSTLER, HEART OF A KILLER 1-3
GORILLAZ IN THE TRENCHES
OOPS CRY TOO 1&2
THE DAUGHTER OF A CARTEL BOSS
By **SayNoMore**

BODYMORE MURDERLAND 1-3
THE BIRTH OF A GANGSTER 1-4
By **Delmont Player**

FOR THE LOVE OF A BOSS 1&2
By **C. D. Blue**

KILLA KOUNTY 1-5
TENDER
By **Khufu**

MOBBED UP 1-4
THE BRICK MAN 1-5
THE COCAINE PRINCESS 1-10
STEPPERS 1-3
SUPER GREMLIN 1-4
A GANGSTA'S SON
By **King Rio**

MONEY GAME 1&2
By **Smoove Dolla**

SOULLESS GOON | PRINCE

A GANGSTA'S KARMA 1-5
By **FLAME**

KING OF THE TRENCHES 1-3
By **GHOST & TRANAY ADAMS**

BAD BITCHES WIT GUNZ 1&2
PROBLEM SOLVED
By **"Christopher Diesel" Hornezes**

QUEEN OF THE ZOO 1&2
By **Black Migo**

GRIMEY WAYS 1-3
BETRAYAL OF A G
By **Ray Vinci**

XMAS WITH AN ATL SHOOTER
By **Ca$h & Destiny Skai**

KING KILLA 1&2
By **Vincent "Vitto" Holloway**

BETRAYAL OF A THUG 1&2
By **Fre$h**

COUNTDOWN OF A KILLA 1&2
SEX, MURDER AND GOD 1&2
GUNS DOWN, BOTTOMS UP 1&2
By Lo-Life

THE MURDER QUEENS 1-7
By **Michael Gallon**

FOR THE LOVE OF BLOOD 1-4
By **Jamel Mitchell**

SOULLESS GOON | PRINCE

HOOD CONSIGLIERE 1&2
NO TIME FOR ERROR
By **Keese**

PROTÉGÉ OF A LEGEND 1,2&3
LOVE IN THE TRENCHES 1&2
By **Corey Robinson**

THE PLUG'S RUTHLESS DAUGHTER 1&2
By **Tony Daniels**

BORN IN THE GRAVE 1-3
CRIME PAYS
By **Self Made Tay**

MOAN IN MY MOUTH
By **XTASY**

TORN BETWEEN A GANGSTER AND A GENTLEMAN
By **J-BLUNT & Miss Kim**

LOYALTY IS EVERYTHING 1-3
CITY OF SMOKE 1-3
By **Molotti**

HERE TODAY GONE TOMORROW 1&2
By **Fly Rock**

WOMEN LIE MEN LIE 1-4
FIFTY SHADES OF SNOW 1-3
STACK BEFORE YOU SPLURGE
GIRLS FALL LIKE DOMINOES
NAÏVE TO THE STREETS
By **ROY MILLIGAN**

PILLOW PRINCESS
By **S. Hawkins**

SOULLESS GOON | PRINCE

THE BUTTERFLY MAFIA 1-3
SALUTE MY SAVAGERY 1&2
By **Fumiya Payne**

THE LANE 1&2
By Ken-Ken Spence

THE PUSSY TRAP 1-5
By **Nene Capri**

DIRTY DNA
By **Blaque**

SANCTIFIED AND HORNY
by **XTASY**

BOOKS BY LDP'S CEO, CA$H

TRUST IN NO MAN
TRUST IN NO MAN 2
TRUST IN NO MAN 3
BONDED BY BLOOD
SHORTY GOT A THUG
THUGS CRY
THUGS CRY 2
THUGS CRY 3
TRUST NO BITCH
TRUST NO BITCH 2
TRUST NO BITCH 3
TIL MY CASKET DROPS
RESTRAINING ORDER
RESTRAINING ORDER 2
IN LOVE WITH A CONVICT
LIFE OF A HOOD STAR
XMAS WITH AN ATL SHOOTER

www.ingramcontent.com/pod-product-compliance
Lightning Source LLC
Chambersburg PA
CBHW071135260626
47162CB00003B/794

* 9 7 8 1 9 6 5 4 4 8 7 1 7 *